Treading Water

by Allison Agius

PublishAmerica
Baltimore

First printing

ISBN: 1-4137-7542-X
PUBLISHED BY PUBLISHAMERICA, LLLP
www.publishamerica.com
Baltimore

Printed in the United States of America

For Ian, who always believed in me.

Chapter 1

Jackie Lawson gazed out of the bedroom window. The leaves on the trees were beginning to turn and soon they would litter the street below, becoming tangled in the hedgerows. The roses in the garden opposite had passed their best, their petals showering the soil.

Jackie lay her forehead against the cool pane. Her head thrummed, as it did every morning, but she was used to it now. It was a way of life.

She stood up straight and wiped her breath off the window. *I'm past my best*, she thought, gazing at the roses, tears of self-pity rolling down her face. She knew, being only thirty-six, that she was being melodramatic, but felt powerless to do anything about it. There was a deep satisfaction in feeling so desperate.

Yesterday morning they'd had another of their tight conversations over breakfast.

"How are things at work?" she asked.

"Okay, you know," he said, focusing on spreading butter over his toast as if the secret of the universe were in there somewhere. He never looked at her anymore and she hated it.

"No, I don't know, that's why I'm asking," the snap of her words hung in the air.

Philip sighed into the silence. A huge heavy sigh that swept up and settled over her like a thick cloud of dust.

"Jackie, do we need to do this now?"

She knew she shouldn't but she couldn't help herself. "Do what?"

Finally he looked up and glared at her. His eyes cold and grey, his mouth tight and ugly, twisting with his words. "The big histrionics. I merely want to eat my breakfast and read my paper in peace before I go to work."

Impotent rage filled every space of her body, forcing water into her eyes.

"Oh god," he said, throwing his toast viciously onto the plate so it bounced across the table and landed in her lap, butter side down. He stood up sharp, knocking his chair over, "I'm going to work," he said and strode out of the room.

It was typical of their exchanges, she thought as she gazed unseeing into the street. At least Emma hadn't been there to see it. At least she was upstairs, doing whatever it takes eleven-year-olds to do all morning.

Her chest tightened. What could she do, really? Leave? Ask Philip to leave? The enormity of what she was contemplating left her drained. The harsh words, the back biting, the carving up of the life they had shared, the complex details that would have to be worked through. It would be like swimming across a weed-infested lake. A swamp, full of entanglements and hidden secrets.

If she didn't have to go through all that, if she could just arrive on the other side, single, free of him, well, that was a different matter. But she didn't feel she could go through all the swimming it took to get to the other side. She would drown in the process, be pulled into the murky depths and lost forever.

She cast her mind back through her life with Philip, trying to catch a memory of good times. All couples had them, surely they couldn't be any different? But she knew they were. With rising dread she knew. She had always known, it bobbed under the surface, threatening. She pushed it down, and kept it down, trying to drown out the truth. Still it was there. And that was just the start of it. Other things lurked deep within her. Unknown things, long forgotten. Bubbles bubbled.

The clattering of Emma in the kitchen pulled her back. Emma. Of course they had Emma to consider. Next week she would be going back to school, the last year in Juniors, though they didn't call it that anymore, now it was called year six. She was growing up so quickly. Next year she would be in secondary school. Emma—her child, their child—who had some how been reduced to nothing more than a mere factor of consideration.

Jackie shook her head, forcing the thoughts aside as she adjusted the curtains and straightened the coordinated tie back. Over the years, weary of her increasing internal battles, she had found solace in her surroundings. She still could sometimes.

She looked round the familiar room. Her eyes traced the dark green trellis she has stencilled up the corners and along the cornice, the small meadow

6

flowers she had hand painted whilst balanced precariously on stepladders. Her shoulders ached for days when she had finished.

This was the first room she tackled, and over the last twelve years she had worked through the rest of the house, and with her eye for colour, and her attention to detail, she had transformed it.

It was dated now and needed redoing. Now she was looking at it with a critical eye the room looked amateurish compared to the rest of the house. *At least I've got good at something.* She sighed and turned back to the window. When had interior decorating become so important to her? How had her viewpoint reduced from studying a law degree to thoughts of soft furnishings? She was so much less than she used to be.

The ache for numbness roared up inside her again and she felt herself drawn to the familiar relief of alcohol. She pushed it aside. It was too early, not before lunch, never before lunch.

A hook of fear caught in her throat but she refused to swallow it. No. She did not have a drink problem. Drunks drank when they woke up in the morning. Whiskey on their Weetabix, that sort of thing. Drunks couldn't function in the everyday world. Drunks didn't function at all in fact. They didn't wash, couldn't take care of themselves or others. Didn't eat or cook or shop or do anything normal. She did. She was normal. Just because she overindulged now and then didn't mean she had a drink problem. Besides, it was the weekend. Saturday.

She bent over and smoothed out the duvet on the bed until her breathing slowed. Philip was rarely home on Saturdays. In fact, he was rarely here at all anymore.

A bubble. If only.

Ivy-root regrets spread through her body. Pushing deep, forcing through, squeezing tight. She tasted the bitterness in her mouth and tears of pity crowded her eyes. If only. How many "if onlys" can one body hold? How many regrets could one body contain before it gave up, gave in, expired?

Emma's voice pulled for her attention, calling up to her.

"Yes?"

"I've made you some tea, mum."

Her daughter's kindness made Jackie feel weak. "I'm coming," she called back.

"Don't forget you're dropping me off at Lottie's later," Emma added, a false lightness in her voice.

As Jackie made her way downstairs her heart tightened at her daughter's underlying message: *Don't drink – you're driving.*

Chapter 2

As Elizabeth Walker pulled into Bromwich Street any trepidation she felt about the move was replaced by a quickening of her pulse. *A home of my own, at last*, she thought.

The house, her house, ranged over three stories. A tall terraced building in a wide road generous with trees, quiet too, for somewhere so near town.

Liz got out of the car and glanced up at the steely grey sky, hoping it wouldn't rain. She noticed the trees blushed with colour where the leaves were beginning to turn. In a few weeks they would be beautiful browns, reds and golds fluttering down into the street. Her street.

She paused in front of One Hundred and Thirteen. Black railings framed a concrete front, decorated with two large fern trees in pots, standing sentry-like on either side of the large bay window. The front door was original, made from heavy oak and had a feeling of security and permanence. The interior doors had a similar feel to them and it was this that had attracted Liz. All that heavy wood and heredity smacked of a solidity she had yearned for since her mother's death a year ago.

"Of course, it's completely impractical," her father said when they first viewed it. "It's ridiculously large for one person for a start."

Liz had stood in the "first reception room" gazing at the high ceilings, cast iron fireplace and polished china doorknobs, the estate agent's details clasped in her fist. She couldn't disagree with him. He was absolutely right. What did she need with two reception rooms, a dining room, three bedrooms, converted attic, cellar and a kitchen large enough to feed a family of eight and still have room to swing the cat!

"The upkeep will be tremendous," he continued.

Liz nodded. It didn't make sense. It *was* ridiculous. Yet she found herself mapping out what to do with each room. In this room her grand piano would look perfect in the bay window. The second reception room could be her office. She'd convert the smallest bedroom into a dark room which would leave a spare room for guests. Who knows, maybe even her father would stay over. She hadn't said this to him of course.

Her divorce three years ago caused a further fracture in their already fragile relationship. She was a disappointment to him, she saw it in his eyes every time her looked at her.

When her mother was alive she acted as a cast, holding them together so the fracture wouldn't weaken and break completely. But now, now she was gone, and no matter what they did nothing helped. It was as if they'd mended in this skewed way that could never be fixed now. Still, he tried. They both did

Now, as Liz stood in front of the house, her house, she gave herself a hug. A hint of roses came to her on the breeze and she thought of her mother's kind eyes and gentle hands. Her laughter caught in Liz's heart and she ached with longing.

Neil came and stood beside her.

"A handsome place for a handsome woman."

"I wish Mum could have seen it. She'd have loved this place."

Neil put an arm round her and gave her a squeeze. "Who knows," he said. "Maybe she can."

The scent of roses came back, stronger this time and Liz thought of her mother in the garden, the sunlight making her hair look like spun gold. A basket over one gloved arm, sacaturs in the other, cutting roses for the house.

"When she was alive the house always smelt of roses. They were her passion."

Neil said nothing and they stood side by side in the comfortable silence of old friends.

"It's big," Liz said eventually.

"I thought that's what you liked about it?"

"It was. It is. It's just…" she paused. "I'm not sure I have enough furniture to fill it."

"Maybe not now, but you'll grow into it."

Nobody tells you how suddenly grown up and old you feel when you lose a parent, she thought. She was on the cusp of some new and exciting

ALLISON AGIUS

adventure. A period in her life when she was going to grow up and fill this woman's body, be who she really was without the loving support of her mother in the background, with only a father's disapproval for comfort. The trepidation she had felt earlier returned.

"What if I can't?" she asked Neil quietly.

Neil misunderstood her question. "Well in that case, you can take in a lodger or two, maybe a few orphans and a couple of strays, before you know it you'll be bursting at the seams."

She hit him playfully across the arm but her tension eased.

⬧

"So do you think Alan Metcalf will ask you out then?"

"Lottie!"

Lottie landed heavily on the bed besides Emma. "Well?"

"No, but even if he does I won't go out with him."

"Why not? He's scrummy."

Emma scrunched up her face. She wasn't sure why. She was nearly twelve and the only girl in her class who hadn't had a boyfriend last year. Lottie had had several boyfriends and had even let one of them kiss her. Lottie was brave, thought Emma, not like me. Lottie climbed trees, beat up on boys and let them kiss her. She tried things none of the other girls did. Emma wished she could be less frightened. When she told her mum, her mother said, "Being brave is about being afraid and doing it anyway," then she looked really sad, as if she didn't think she was very brave either.

Emma shrugged.

"Aw come on, spill the beans."

"I don't know," she paused for a moment and then changed tact. "Lot, do your parents fight?"

"Sometimes."

Emma's parents fought every time they saw each other. Recently coming round to Lottie's had made her realise how different her family was.

"Do your parents ever go out together?"

"Not very often. I think they'll go out a bit more now Matt's thirteen."

"Why?"

"He can legally babysit us now." Lottie pulled a face and they giggled.

"I wonder what year six will be like?" Lottie said when they fell quiet.

Emma's stomach tightened. She only had one more year at Crawford
Street School and then they went to secondary school. Lottie was excited
about it, she got excited about everything. She was always talking about the
new school, the teachers, the boys, the work, their periods starting and going
out on their own. Emma just wanted things to stay the same. Why did
everything have to change? It seemed she just got used to things and then they
changed again. And next year she'd have to get used to a whole new school
with everything different? She didn't want to change schools, kiss boys, and
bleed from her body. Already her chest felt sore sometimes. Lottie said it was
where her breasts were growing.

Lottie had been her friend since day one. Just strolled up to Emma and
introduced her self. She did that with everyone, that's why she had so many
friends. Loads of them. She made it look so easy, talking to people she didn't
know. "Turning strangers into friends," she said. It was another thing about her
that Emma envied.

"D'you think we'll have Mr Johnson this year?"

"Dunno," said Emma.

"Oh I hope so. He's gorgeous."

"Well, we'll find out on Wednesday, won't we?" Emma felt miserable at
the thought. She didn't want Mr Johnson, she wanted her old teacher, Mrs
Henderson. It all felt so…scary. She knew it was silly but it was how she felt.
Sometimes she wondered if other girls felt like that. Not Lottie of course, but
did any of the others? Angela West was quiet, maybe she felt the same, or
Teresa Fawson, perhaps. But she didn't know how to ask them.

Did others feel the same as her? Deep down? Even Lottie. She looked at
Lottie raking through the CDs, her curly hair looking exciting and abandoned.
Her own hair was dead straight. *No*, she thought, *not Lottie.*

Her friend turned round and waved a CD in the air.

"Want to listen to my new Popstars CD?" she asked.

Emma shrugged. "Sure, why not."

Jackie saw the removal van when she returned from dropping Emma off
at her friend Lottie's, its back wide like a whale's mouth. She went up to her
bedroom window to take a closer look and watched a couple jostle each other
playfully as they carried boxes and small pieces of furniture into the house.

They didn't seem to have much. Maybe it was their first home. Two removal men, one skinny and one fat, huffed and puffed, red faced and sweaty as they struggled with a black shinny grand piano. The fat one had the cleavage of his bum hanging out of his jeans, making Jackie smile.

The couple looked very happy together. The young man was casually dressed in faded jeans and a granddad shirt, he had dark floppy hair and, from what she could see, a tanned toned body. *He'd be considered classically handsome*, Jackie thought, *if you like that sort of thing. She obviously did*, Jackie thought as she turned her attention to the woman.

Her dress sense struck Jackie as odd at first. She wore a cheap floppy hat over red curly hair, designer jeans and a large baggy cardigan that came way past her knees and looked like it came from a flea market. A strange combination but it looked stylish somehow. *If I wore something like that I'd probably look like a bag lady*, she decided.

Jackie pulled her cardigan around her and ran her hands over her navy M&S skirt as if it were an amulet, some way of protecting her from the outside world. The waistband gaped but it didn't register with her, she was too absorbed in them. In the pieces of their lives they were removing from the van.

He looked a lot younger than the woman and she tried to gauge their ages. The woman was probably around her own age, late thirties, although she dressed much younger. Jackie sighed, that is what comes of having a younger man. She would be surprised if he had even reached thirty.

Jackie shrugged. If it worked for them why not? But watching them pulled at something inside her; snagged her and she turned away, worried if she continued to watch she might unravel.

She wandered aimlessly round the house. Moving from room to room, straightening the Barbie duvet on Emma's cabin bed, picking up a pen top from the stairs, plumping the fat green cushions in the lounge. And then she started again, like a prison warden on her rounds. As she strolled through the house a second time she straightened pictures. The pictures she had bought on the many holidays she and Emma had shared. Each view transported her to another time and place, far away from her reality. She felt the sun cleansing her, purifying her blood. She heard Spanish guitars and smelt the fresh salt sea air in the dawn. She heard the whispers of the wind on the hills and the clink of the Chianti bottles in the cool evenings in a restaurant by the sea. A mingle of languages, smells, sights and sounds enveloped her.

In every country they visited, Jackie took a small piece and lodged it inside herself. She carried it with her like a talisman, and on cool days like today, when the afternoon stretched before her in silence, she melded these pieces together to create her own unique picture, transporting her to another time and place.

The return was as sharp as lemon juice in a paper cut and Jackie caught the unmistakable desire in the back of her throat for something to blunt the pain. She bit her lip hard. It was too early. Even for her. And besides, she'd promised herself.

She glanced at the clock. It was only two. Still she reasoned, it was after lunch, and in the place she desired to be, Saturday afternoons were spent sitting in the late afternoon sun with an open bottle of wine. If she couldn't be there, at least she could adopt some of the lifestyle as a compensation.

Would it make any difference? One or two glasses on a Saturday afternoon? Perhaps if she drank them at the dining table with the weekend papers, maybe had radio 4 on in the background? That seemed quite civilised and she didn't have to pick up Emma that afternoon, Abbey was dropping her off.

As she headed for the kitchen a little whoop of joy went off in her chest. If it made her happy, if she made sure Emma was okay, if no one needed her, what was the harm?

Chapter 3

Philip woke wrapped up like a tortilla in the sheets. He rolled onto his back, pulled his fingers through his hair, placed his arms behind his head and smiled. His body was sore from the previous night's activities and he could smell the stale sweat from his armpits.

The bed was empty but he could hear Nikki moving round the apartment. She always rose earlier than him. Philip took a deep breath and sighed, his body loose and relaxed as he glanced round the familiar room, admiring his lover's good taste.

Women, thought Philip, *decorate their bedroom with flowers and pastels but not Nikki.* She was a minimalist. White walls, cream carpets and a few well-chosen pieces of art. At home they had insipid pictures of quaint Mediterranean homes and irritating landscapes. Flowers everywhere.

In this room Nikki had two small abstract pictures, slashes of colour against an otherwise colourless room. The effect was startling, like blood spilt on white sheets. There was a bronze statue of two lovers in an intimate embrace and a nude of herself when she was sixteen painted by her lover.

No bottles, perfumes, creams or potions. None of that shit that usually cluttered up the bedroom furniture. Not that she didn't take care of herself. Nikki always looked fantastic. No, she took care of herself, she just didn't make a mess doing it.

Jackie always seemed surrounded by clutter. In fact, the whole house was cluttered. Every surface decorated, every wall stencilled or crammed with pictures, every window crowded with fabric, every cushion tasselled. It was endless. He was crowded at home, hemmed in. Here he had the luxury of an uncluttered life, clear tops and no strings. He could breath, more importantly, he could think.

Reluctantly his thoughts moved to the Douglas case. Douglas Property Development had entered into an agreement with Murphy and Taylor building contractors on a huge twenty-five million pound development and regeneration scheme along the Tees river between Stockton and Middlesborough. The plan was to provide homes, restaurants, shops, water sports and a whole host of leisure facilities based on the water. In short, a lifestyle.

Everything had gone smoothly until it came down to payment. There was a discrepancy between what was originally agreed and Murphy and Taylor's final account. A big discrepancy. Murphy and Taylor claims Douglas property had given them the okay whilst the latter denied all knowledge of such an agreement.

Through a series of errors by both parties, silly errors, errors their lawyers should have picked up, it was now virtually a case of one MD's word against the other. *God knows how some lawyers pass their exams,* thought Philip. Incompetence in his field never failed to amaze and irritate him.

Philip had been rash taking on the case, he knew that now. Peter Douglas, the Managing Director of the company, was a friend, although acquaintance would be a better description. Nikki was his PA and it was Peter who had introduced them. Perhaps that's why he'd agreed to take on the case.

He shook his head. Still, taking on the case was one thing, agreeing to a no win no fee had been ludicrous, *and* without the partners knowledge or agreement. As the case progressed the knot in his solar plexus got tighter and tighter. It reminded him of a game he and his brother had played when they were kids. They'd get two lolly sticks and an elastic band, wind them up until they couldn't be wound any further, then let them go and watch them whiz across the room. *If it got much tighter in there,* he thought, *I'll find myself doing just the same.*

The case was getting expensive. Philip had done a little jiggling at work so his time and expenses weren't being put through, well, not on this account anyway, but Janet Higgs, his lanky, buck-teethed, over-keen junior, had penned through her time. There hadn't been anything he could do about that, not without bringing her into his confidence, and the fewer who knew about this the better. With her hours going through it was only a matter of time before one of the managers or senior partners picked up the unpaid account and started asking questions.

And he had such a shit case. A really shit case. What on earth had possessed him? The first rule of thumb is always, always look through the case *before* you agree anything. But he knew why. It had been the juxtaposition of Peter Douglas asking him what Nikki was like in the sack followed immediately by talk of his commercial dispute. Fazed and desperate to change the subject Phil had agreed to take on the case. Had Peter known what he was doing? Phil shook his head, it didn't matter. The fact remained that now, not only was he going to arbitration in a few months time with a poor case, he was also in the shit at work. Unless he did something about it. And quick.

Two weeks ago, in a desperate pitch, Philip had set Jack Woods on the case. Jack was a private investigator Philip called in from time to time to help him get evidence to discredit witnesses or disprove testimony, especially in insurance cases. Although he disliked the man he was good at his job and Philip was prepared to put personal tastes aside, when he didn't have a choice.

"Hey big fella, awake so soon? I thought you'd need much more recovery time."

Philip's mouth widened into a grin. He had been good last night. Surprised even himself.

Nikki strolled towards him, her head lowered, her eyes trained on him, her body tight and firm. He could feel a stirring in his body. She lent forward and he inhaled her perfume, a heady mixture of jasmine and rose. God but she was a horny bitch.

But was it worth the doleful looks from Jackie and the pangs of guilt that hit him from time to time? He shrugged the question away. He needed Nikki. She excited him in a way Jackie never could. He reached out to grab her but she pulled away.

"Ah ah ah," she said, shaking her head and standing upright. "You know the rule. Shower first, I don't want you when you're smelling of seconds."

"Arh come on Nik, just this once."

Nikki laughed and shook out her long blonde hair, shifting her weight from one leg to the other so her silk nightie slid seductively across her hips. Did she know what she was doing to him?

"No way big fella, shower first. It'll be worth it."

Philip groaned. "But I'll have lost the impetus by the time I've showered."

"And you think I can't to anything about that?"

Of course she could, he knew she could. God could she. He pulled himself up and stumbled along the hall to the shower room, leaving Nikki to sort out the bed.

She picked up the bed sheet Philip had dropped on the floor and waved it open, allowing it to float down parachute like to embrace the bed. She smoothed out the sheets admiring her well-manicured hands. *I have a problem*, she thought.

After years of watching her mother live an ordinary life Nikki decided at thirteen she would not. She wanted a life of ease and excitement. She wanted silk underwear and crisp cotton sheets, manicured nails and champagne breakfasts, not hotpot and supermarkets, bingo and soaps. Her mother had worked hard and loved Nikki but she was a stupid woman. Very stupid. Nikki watched as one man after another came, took everything her mother could give, then left. When Nikki had asked her why she put up with it, her mother told her it was difficult to explain but that one day she would fall in love and understand. Nikki doubted that very much.

At sixteen she became aware of her physical attributes and had used them to attract men of money. Generous men. Now she had a comfortable lifestyle, an interesting job and money in the bank. She had it all...almost.

She'd been seeing Philip just over a year now. He was an attractive man, a high flyer with a sexual appetite to match her own. But, now there was a problem.

This time things were different. This time she had feelings. Her emotions, normally so controlled and regulated, now resembled a pinball. She had never experienced this lurch when she heard his key in the door, this tightness in her chest when he looked at her, or the desire to smell the gift of an occasional worn shirt he left behind.

She was lost in unfamiliar territory, a wilderness of emotion without a map, an address nor the vocabulary to ask for directions. Love, she decided, if that was what this was, was an exquisite pain, like a sorbet, sweet but with a sharp edge.

She wanted him. He was a rising star in the firm and had the potential to earn big money. That wasn't all of it, but she was honest enough to know she wouldn't have fallen for him if he'd been her dustman.

She was approaching forty and her looks were beginning to tire. She reckoned she had another five good years in her before the wear and tear really started to show. After that it was saggy city or operations. Philip was her last hope.

Nikki wasn't stupid. She knew she looked like a Barbie doll, with her blonde hair, perfect make-up and trim figure, hell, enough people had said it. But it didn't do her any harm. It meant people underestimated her and you could get away with a lot when people underestimated you. No, she wasn't stupid. She was well aware that Phil's main attraction to her was her elusiveness, her no–strings policy. If he knew she wanted him he'd be off like a shot. She would have to be careful.

His wife wasn't anything to worry about; Nikki had met her at a charity function the previous year and dismissed her as competition. The wife was a flabby, wrung-out little lady with no guile, wit or intelligence in evidence. She spoke in a quiet squeaky voice that grated. No, there was no real competition there.

Her danger was the *idea* Jackie represented rather than the woman herself. The stability, family, the woman at home keeping body and soul together. Whilst Nikki fulfilled Philip's sexual appetite, Jackie represented security and approval for him.

For now.

And that is my target, she thought, dragging her nails over the top sheet creating deep lines in the fabric. She wasn't doing battle against Jackie—that would be easy. And besides, she had no personal grudge against the woman. No, she was doing battle with what Jackie, her daughter and the house represented. That was the enemy.

She had to formulate a plan that would lure him, hook him and reel him away from that ideal, and replace it with her self, without losing any of her magic.

And there was her dilemma. There was her problem.

How could she remain elusive and catch him at the same time? She plumped up the pillows, reshaping them into the rectangles they should be. She would have to tread carefully. Phil wasn't stupid either. In fact, in many ways she thought they were very similar. She heard the shower go off.

She would formulate a plan and in the meantime, she would keep papering over her cracks and fucking his brains out so he couldn't think straight. At least it would buy her some time.

Chapter 4

Sunday, a day of rest, Liz reminded herself ruefully as she stood up to straighten her aching back. She was in the back room, her office that would be, unpacking her books. Neil had gone to get fish and chips from the local chippy, a rare treat. She looked thin to everyone else but there had been times in her life when she hadn't been, and she was determined never to go there again. Still, fish and chips once in awhile were okay.

It was strange to be alone in such a big house. Not unpleasant, she decided after a few moments, just strange. Although she had lived on her own at the flat she had heard other people, below and above her. They had met on the stairs and passed the time chatting. Even the cat from the flat below had visited her once in a while. Here there was no other living thing, coming, going or staying. It was just her.

Her mother's untimely death had left a hole. Liz had shared everything with her mother who had then explained things to her father, like an interpreter for people from two different planets. It was Mum she clung to through the loss of the baby, the divorce and the confusion over her sexuality. Her father would pat her occasionally during the whole ordeal, red faced and stuttering, and yet, ironically, it had been his advice that had brought her here now.

It had been the day of the funeral. It was late and they sat alone in the kitchen. Liz was drained by the events of the day, the service, the churchyard, the hand shaking and condolences. Faces of sympathy swam in front of her now, morphing into one. If anyone had asked her who had been there she wouldn't have been able to name anyone individually. And yet, at the same time, her mind seemed crisp and bright, like a winter's sun. Un-blinding in its understanding of the priest's message. Everlasting life. God of everything seen and unseen. She was with them, her mother, unseen. Liz could sense it, she could smell roses everywhere she went. It was her mother, she was there, and whilst she was there Liz could not shed the tears expected of her by the onlookers.

They sat in silence, Donald and her. The kitchen clock filled the room with its sound, echoing off the walls, its tock the boom of Big Ben instead of the comforting tick it had once been.

And then he spoke. Seemingly plucking something from the silent space between the tocks.

"Elizabeth," he always called her that. Never Liz, nor Lizzy as her mother had, always Elizabeth. "Don't wait for the future," he said, "on what might be. Live for today. Otherwise you wake up one morning and life has passed you by."

She had shrugged the words off at the time, shed them like a wet coat when you come in from the rain, but now, now his words broke across her body like a wave, soaking into the very heart of her.

Had he been talking about himself? It hadn't occurred to her at the time but in the midst of her grief had she missed his outstretched hand? Her chest tightened at the thought. All their lives her parents had worked and saved hard, planning to travel together in their retirement.

"We're going to such places, Lizzy," her mother said, her voice hushed and breathless when she spoke of it. "India and Africa. I'm going to climb the Himalayas and watch the sun rise over Machu Pichu." She talked as if it would all take place at the same time.

Liz felt a stab of pain and the room closed in. She hurried through the house out into the bright sunny afternoon. After taking a few deep breaths the pain began to subside and she looked around her.

The garden needed some work but basically it was good. There was a large tree in the corner and she could put a bench under it for hot summer days in the shade. The grass needed reseeding and the borders were unkempt but it wouldn't take much. She would ask her father for one of her mother's rose bushes. They'd do well along the wall to her right. By next year she would have a garden her mother would be proud of.

She stood and took it all in. *I'm standing in the garden of my own house. All these months searching and then all the excitement waiting to move and now I'm here.* But she didn't feel like she thought she'd feel. Instead it seemed like an anticlimax. Like boxing day when everything was unwrapped and there was that hollow, what-was-all-the-fuss-about feeling.

Now what? Where do I go from here? She couldn't keep on the way she was, writing stuff she hated, with no direction, no focus, and no friends other than Neil. Sweet as he was she needed a more substantial relationship in her life now. She'd had a couple of relationships since the divorce but nothing serious. She was ready now. Ready to start her new life. The thought restricted her breathing until she remembered she'd promised Neil she would find the teapot before he returned. She walked back to the kitchen, relieved to be busy.

"Mum. Mum"

The words filtered into Jackie's fogged brain waking her. She opened and closed her mouth, licking dry lips and tasting the foulness of her breath.

"Mmmmm," she said, her eyes closed.

"Mum it's eleven, you asked me to wake you at eleven," Emma's strained voice pulled at Jackie's heart and a wave of anger rose inside her. "Thanks sweetie," she said through gritted teeth.

"D'you want tea?"

"That would be great."

Jackie held her body taut, listening to her eleven-year-old daughter pad out of the room. When the door closed she relaxed and became aware of the pain.

Her brain thundered in her skull, crashing against the bone. *I've done it again*, she thought, *I've bloody done it again. I promised myself I wouldn't do this and I have.* Her heart sank and tears threatened but she swallowed hard and opened her eyes a fraction. The brightness of the room told her it was a beautiful day and her heart sank still further. Why couldn't it be raining? Somehow it wouldn't be so bad to be in bed this late if it was raining.

Jackie unwound herself and stretched out in the five-foot bed. When Emma was little she would come and snuggle with her in the mornings. She had loved that. It filled some gap inside her, helped her feel content for a while. But Emma was older now, had lost the sweet fragility she once had and didn't need Jackie that way anymore. The thought saddened her.

Slowly Jackie sat up. Pain from her head blinded her, sending a wave of nausea to her throat. She waited until it passed then moved again, propping herself onto the pillows.

Why do I do this? And the question sent her slipping into the abyss of defeat. Every time she woke up like this she promised herself she would stop drinking. It was so easy to make the promise when she felt like this. Until the next time she was alone with the night stretching out in front of her, like a staggering climb up Everest.

I miss the warmth of another body in the bed, the sound of another person's breathing, Jackie thought. Not just in bed either, now she came to think of it, but in her life. It wasn't Phil she missed, it was just the body. It could be anyone. She was never keen on sex anyway.

Had sex been tainted for her by the…she couldn't finish the sentence and consoled herself with the thought that it had never been that wonderful anyway. She never told Phil. Never explained how she lost some vital part herself in that clinic. She couldn't even define what it was but she knew it was gone. Was it that place or had it happened earlier in those lonely dark nights when she was small? Was it already gone and that place was merely a reminder?

Memories trickled down from her childhood. The place she called home as a child was only on the other side of Newcastle, but it might as well have been on the other side of the planet.

Winston Street was a long steep hill of terraced houses. The wind always blew icy cold down that street, even in the summer. Strong gusts pushing against her, making her feel unsafe. Each house had a small concrete back yard and the front door opened direct into the living room. Theirs was number ninety-seven.

Memories tumbled over her, bringing with them the familiar smells of her childhood. Soap suds and cooking smells and firelighters; the television that was always on in the corner with her father nodding off in his chair. He smelt of stale tobacco and his chin made a rasping noise when he ran his hand over it. The same routine; the same chair; everything was the same. Stifling.

She remembered huge slabs of meat pie and soggy cabbage, beans and eggs swimming in grease. And her father, sitting on the opposite side of the table, smiling at Jan and winking. *His special girl.* She pushed the dangerous memory away but it ebbed back.

She laid there, a prisoner of her foul-feeling body, memories lapping at her as she watched dust motes dance in the needle of bright sunshine peeping through a chink in the heavy curtains. When she was a child she believed they were fairies, hundreds of them. It would fascinate her for hours. Once she'd confided this to her mother who, to her shame, shared it with the whole family.

Shuddering, Jackie roused herself creaking from the bed, needing to move, to escape her whirling mind. She slipped into her towelling flip flop slippers and as she left the bedroom caught sight of herself in the cheval mirror.

I look old and haggard, she thought. Her huge white t-shirt reached passed her knees and billowed out, the skin beneath her eyes appeared dark and baggy, her thin lips were pale and cracked, the brown wavy hair hung lank and unkempt about her face. She pushed back her fringe, shrugged and smiled to see if it helped. It didn't. She was looking older than she should. The disgust rose again.

Emma was sitting in the dining room eating toast and glued to the TV. Jackie went into the kitchen and switched on the kettle and saw Philip's post in a neat pile waiting for his return. She was loathed to admit it but she didn't like her husband. She used to, but not anymore. He was pompous and arrogant now and she feared it was would rub off on her, like leprosy. He hadn't always been like that. Once he had been young and fiery and funny.

The kettle came to the boil and Jackie made herself a cup of coffee and put bread in the shinny toaster. Needlessly she straightened up the post pile. It was disloyal thinking of him like that. He, like her, was trying to make the best of the bad situation they found themselves in. And he was making a better job of it.

The guilt lay, another layer, along with all the rest, like a thick winter blanket. She was unaware of it. Had become used to the weight, even found it reassuring, like a toddler with its cumbersome piece of rag. Her comfort blanket.

She leant against the kitchen cabinets sipping her bitter coffee, relishing her own space. Waking up. The sound of the TV from the dining room next door filtered through but it was so faint she was able to ignore it.

Thinking it might help her to wake up, she kicked off one of her slippers and placed her bare foot against the cool stone tiles. It sent goose pimples across her body, making the pale hairs on her arms stand on end, but it didn't do the trick. It didn't shift the hangover she had.

She looked over to the side door in the kitchen. There stood three empty wine bottles waiting to go out. Three! She hadn't realised she'd drunk that much yesterday, and it was becoming a habit. She carried her coffee back up to the bedroom and sat on the bed, breathing deeply.

A wave of panic flooded over her again. *Was* she becoming an alcoholic? It was only a few bottles of wine. No, the thought wouldn't have occurred to her if she really was an alcoholic. They were always the last to know. And, she didn't drink during the day, well, not much anyway. Not often. It wasn't a regular thing. Everyone had the odd glass with their lunch. People went to the pub at lunchtimes from work. And she always brushed her teeth before Emma got back so she wouldn't know.

She was just being ridiculous.

Jackie heard the clatter of crockery and the banging of kitchen unit doors as Emma bumped round the kitchen. Seconds later all other sounds were drowned out by blasting pop music. In her mind's eye she could see Emma dancing round the kitchen, miming the song into a yellow handled teaspoon. It brought a smile to her face, thawing the intensity of her emotions and giving her space to breathe.

This time, this time I'm going to stop, she promised herself, *if not for me, then for Emma, perhaps even for Philip, but definitely for Emma. I can do this, I'm bigger than this. Today I quit.*

A slow smile spread across her face and a small feeling of triumph began to burn deep inside her. This time she would do it, this time was different.

Chapter 5

It was Wednesday, the first day of the new school term, and Jackie returned from school with Emma on her mind. She knew her daughter didn't react well to change but she had seemed chirpy over breakfast and Jackie decided she'd be alright. She'd settle after a few days, she always did.

As she entered the house the silence descended on her. Every day from now until half term she would come back to this. The silence, with the day stretching out in front of her. As she walked through the hall and kitchen to get to the dining room, her breath sounded as if it was coming from outside herself. This was the worst part of the day, this beginning on her own.

Once I've cleaned up the dining room I'll feel better, she thought. But for those first few minutes, the walls closed in. She treaded water whilst everyone else, everyone out there, had a life. They were living while she was just exchanging one day for the next. Getting nowhere, going nowhere.

Treading.

In the dining room breadcrumbs were strewn across the table and floor, cornflakes sat congealed in blue breakfast bowls, and she turned away, switching on the TV in the corner to stave off the silence.

Silence. The ultimate reminder that her house, like her life, was empty.

She collected the bowls, throwing them together. Teeth clenched. Half her mind on the TV, the remainder aware of the scratch for something to blur her reality. If she could concentrate on the TV it would soothe her. The scratch deepened so she turned up the volume. It would draw her in, like sleep, like alcohol.

It was a talk show, this morning the topic was sexuality and as she listened her body tightened.

"He's my son. It's his life. I can't dictate to him who he loves." The woman's hair was blonde, short and coiffure. She was dressed in a cream silk blouse and fawn cardigan.

The audience applauded but Jackie didn't believe her. She looked too beaten down, lines of worry marked on her face, pain and humiliation showed in her eyes, but, most of all, Jackie recognised a lack of conviction in the woman's voice.

"It's different for my husband," she continued softly. "I think..." she hesitated, twisting the string of pearls round her neck. "Well, I think he sees it as a threat, a reflection on his masculinity."

The host, a tall thin man in his late forties, pushed the microphone into the woman's face. He softened his voice so it had the consistency of treacle. "When did you last see your son?" he asked.

"Five years ago."

The audience gasped. She was a phoney. Jackie nodded at the TV, pleased with herself. She knew it!

"And why is that?" the host continued.

"My husband won't have him near the house since he...came out." The woman looked as if she'd just said "cunt" in front of a million people.

"And is it true that he's banned you from visiting your son?" the host persisted, despite the woman's obvious discomfort.

The woman bowed her head, the audience waited, Jackie stood in the doorway to the kitchen, waiting, breath held, the breakfast bowls still in her hand.

"Yes, he has," she said finally.

More gasps. One woman, young, with a shaved head and a ring through her nose stood up, waved her fist and shouted something incomprehensible. Her face was distorted with hatred. *She's gay*, Jackie said to herself, *no mistake. All crew cuts and dungarees.*

As the camera passed over the audience Jackie observed the women. Some didn't look like lesbians, they were normal, like herself. Those, she'd decided, were women who'd got confused. It happened to everyone when they were growing up. They weren't really gay. Gay women walked funny, like gorillas. Horrid creatures. Her mind whispered *Clare wasn't*, but she ignored it.

Jackie turned away and filled the bowl in the sink with hot soapy water.

What would I do if Emma was gay? The thought terrified her. She wanted Emma to be normal, life was so difficult already without added complications. *How would my parents react if I were gay? Equally horrified,* she decided. And the thought made her skin crawl with fear. A dark shadow prodded her body. *I must ring them.*

Other fears pushed against her. Memories. She shook her head. She would not, could not even contemplate them. A brief vision of Clare came to her mind. Soft, gentle Clare. And the dark shadow veered up again, shrinking her heart.

She moved her thoughts, frantic to replace this haunting. This haunting that brought up fear and disgust. She was an evil, evil woman. She bolted to the TV and turned it off. The silence pulsed.

Returning to the sink she plunged her hands into the hot water. It was too hot and she enjoyed the brief pain while they became accustomed. She tamed her lion mind, bringing it to thoughts of her marriage, a more acceptable set of circumstances. A whisper, or was it?

God she could do with a drink. No! She had promised herself. For Philip, for Emma. She had promised for herself. Fuck it! Family! Fuck them.

She lifted a bowl and crashed it into the stone sink. It shattered, little pieces rose up and showered her. The sound echoed around the empty house. Breathing hard she clung to the sink for support, feeling the cold stone numbing her shaking hands, anger and rising panic rampaged through her,.

Her body shuddered, a steam express of emotions thundering through her veins. She wanted to run. To hide. But she had nowhere to go. No where. The panic rose higher. No where. No one to talk to. Nothing. No one. It was unbearable, this pain, this fear and then, through the haze she heard a small thin voice, echoing from the past.

"You know where I am if you want me…"

Clare. Clare. There was always Clare. And with that thought Jackie bent over the sink and wept with shame.

Liz sat at the kitchen table cradling a mug of decaf between her hands and, as she contemplated her day ahead, she ran her fingers through her wet curly hair to prevent it frizzing.

This was it. Here she was. Home. This was her castle with a bolted door between her and the world. She recognised a mixture of joy and trepidation inside. She hadn't pinpointed the reason for this yet but knew it would come to her in time, and probably quicker if she didn't interrogate herself.

Not one to linger on self-examination, she moved her thoughts to her work, itemising where she was as she did every morning before starting.

There were several pieces on gardens commissioned by an upmarket national magazine *Jardinière*. She had submitted work to them before and they'd been pleased with it, so she wasn't surprised to receive the commissions. She had no training in this area but she had always helped her mother so she'd had to do little research. She'd also pitched a few feature ideas on similar lines to Peter Marsh, editor of the local newspaper and her former boss. She made a note on the pad in front of her to chase him for a response and then let the pen fall.

She had a series of articles on the single woman in London on the go. These were for a London magazine, *Underground*, Liz had written for previously. Her latest piece was on the hot spots to eat alone. The irony of the article was not lost on her but she pushed it to one side. The deadline was the end of this week but it was nearly ready to go and only needed tightening up.

Of course, she thought, *it's all trite. Mindless trite.* She wondered if anyone would read her articles and even if they did, what did it matter? They didn't make people think. They didn't make the world a better place, unless you thought clearing green fly off roses made it better. She smiled; her mother would have.

She sighed, bringing her mind to the house. Little had been done yet. She wanted to set up her dark room in the small back bedroom but over the weekend she had spent the time sorting out her study and the main bedroom, a place to sleep and a place to work were essential. Besides, with the house move and the work piling up she'd had little time recently to get out with her camera.

Work. There was still the Internet line and fax machine to set up and they had to be her priority today. As the thought crossed her mind her body became too heavy to move. She tightened her grip around her coffee mug and took a deep breath. Thoughts of the boxes of her mother's writing sitting on her office floor disquieted her. She had come across them a few days ago. Her father had sent them along with her grand piano and some other bits and pieces, obviously mistaking them for hers. When Liz was seven she had told her mother she wanted to be a pianist when she grew up. Her mother had hugged her and said that all she had wanted when she was a girl was a large house filled with children and to spend her days writing. When Liz had asked her why she didn't, her mother had laughed. "Things aren't always that simple, Lizzy," she said in her soft, gentle voice.

It was never mentioned again and over the years Liz had forgotten the conversation. With the arrival of the boxes it came flooding back and left an uncomfortable feeling in the pit of her stomach. Her mother's voice came flooding back, a soft voice, easily talked over—was she also easily walked over?

How had she ended up in a small cottage as a doctor's receptionist to Liz's father with only one child? Anger began to burn in Liz's stomach. She'd never read any of her mother's work until the other day. Some of it was excellent. It heightened the fact that all Liz was writing was crap. Unimportant.

Had her father known of her mother's dreams? Had he dismissed them? It would be just like him to think it was a lot of nonsense. A man of science who had no time for the arts.

The moment the thought crossed her mind she knew it was untrue. He had always encouraged her in whatever she wanted to do. They had all taken theatre trips together, her father read a great deal, enjoyed the arts as much as she and her mother had.

So what happened? What had stopped them filling the house with children? What had stopped her mother following her dreams?

She ran her fingers through her hair again, trying to push the thoughts aside. It was nearly dry. She pulled the notepad in front of her closer. Picking up her pen she began doodling, it helped her to change tack, she did it when moving from one article to another. She needed a new routine, to go with her new life.

She wrote the word "Running" and circled it. It was possible to shift her run to mid-morning instead of first thing, that way she could start work earlier and the run later would break up her morning. Then she crossed it out. If she didn't run first thing she wouldn't run at all.

Yesterday she had gone for a walk to check out the lay of the land. The town centre was only ten minutes walk away and she had discovered a gem of a bistro where she had taken lunch.

She wrote "Bistro" amongst the circles she had scrawled on the paper. The bistro could be her saving grace. This could be her mid-morning coffee break. It was only five minutes walk and perhaps not even that. She could walk down, take coffee, watch the world go by and be back at her desk in less than forty minutes.

Satisfied with her decision, she looked at the clock propped on one of the kitchen units and leaning against the wall. *I'll put that up on the wall later today*, she promised.

It was ten already and time she was at her desk. She had to be strict, she knew her tendency to while away hours achieving nothing. She stood up to galvanise herself to start work. Thoughts of her parents, especially her mother, still hovering.

It didn't occur to her to call on her neighbours.

◈

By mid-morning Phil had cleared the messages his secretary handed him when he walked into the office, and he sat back in his chair feeling pleased with himself. Here he was in control. He lent forward and pressed the intercom.

"Janet, get me some coffee?"

"Yes, Mr Lawson."

He leaned back into his chair and put his hands behind his head. If only everything in his life was this simple.

Something was happening between him and Jackie but he couldn't figure out what. Life was becoming more uncomfortable at home. They couldn't go on the way they were, either of them, yet a divorce was out of the question.

Thoughts of Nikki came up. Sweet, elusive, undemanding Nikki. They had met at a charity dinner. It was the first time he'd had an affair and he couldn't believe it when she came onto him. He had considered her out of his league, which was probably what enticed him into the liaison in the first place. He imagined Nikki would discard him within a few months. Yet here he was, a year later and still with her. Did he have feelings for her?

He imagined a life with Nikki, uncluttered, uncomplicated Nikki, with her sweet smells and her attentive ways. Not to mention the mouth of a goddess around his cock. The thought brought a stirring in his groin and he jumped when Janet knocked on his office door and entered with his coffee.

He picked up the china cup and sipped the hot liquid in an attempt to swallow the discomfort Janet's intrusion had caused.

What did Jackie want? The guilt choked him like a room full of smoke. He spent a lot of time away from home and now there was this affair, but wasn't he doing Jackie a favour? She was unresponsive to his sexual demands, always had been. Even on their wedding night. His mother had warned him they were too young, it was too quick, was she pregnant? There was the irony.

Pregnant, married, not pregnant.

The miscarriage had hit them both hard at first, but then there was Emma two years later. He smiled at the awe of watching his daughter emerge into the world. So tiny. Holding her had made him feel Herculean and humble all at the same time. His parents had been delighted, especially his mother after having sons herself. He had basked in his parents' approval, his daughter making up for his previous misdemeanours.

And now there was nothing. His daughter was drifting even further away from him to some distant island called womanhood and his wife was empty and devoid of affection for him. Somewhere along the line all his good intentions had crumbled to dust, dry arid dust, and he wanted to get out, escape, breathe. But there were his parents to consider.

He hadn't seen them in a couple of months and he hadn't instigated a call to his mother for several weeks. When he considered them, he knew ending his marriage was not an option. Besides, he already spent more time with Nikki than he did at home. What would he gain by rocking the boat? Upsetting everyone? Assuming Nikki wanted that.

He picked up the phone and dialled his parents number, holding his breath as he listened to the ring tone, hoping he would get the answer machine. His heart sank as his mother answered.

"Philip, how lovely to hear from you. How are Jackie and Emma?"

"They're good, thanks. How are you?"

"Great! Daddy's out playing golf. He's golf mad, you know. I say to him I'm not going to miss him when he's dead, I'm a widow already."

Philip winced. Didn't his mother listen to what came out of her mouth?

"I just called to touch base, you know, can't talk long because I'm at work."

"Must you start off every conversation with 'I can't talk long'? You're always busy."

"But it's true." He heard the little boy wail in his voice and hated it.

"I know, but I do wish you wouldn't labour the point. After all, we're not going to be around forever, you know?"

Philip had never known a more robust couple in their sixties. "Mum I hardly see Jackie and Emma as it is," he whined.

"That's as may be, but they're a little younger than we are and as a consequence are likely to be around for longer, don't you think?"

It wasn't so much a question as a statement of fact and one Philip could hardly argue with. He felt the discomfort of once again being wedged into a corner and heard himself say.

"How about we come and visit?"

"Are you sure?" she asked and before he could answer she added, "that would be lovely. Oh, your father will be pleased. How about Sunday week? For lunch?"

"Can we make it the following weekend?"

"Good, that's settled. We'll see you around one."

As Philip replaced the receiver any power he felt drained from him.

Chapter 6

Friday morning and the weekend looms again, Jackie thought as she walked down the path carrying three large carrier bags stuffed with newspapers to put by on the pavement to be collected for recycling. She paused after putting the bags down and observed the mounting leaves on the street. It had rained a couple of days before and some of the leaves had become mashed under foot. She looked back at the path and regretted not sweeping them up earlier. Now it would be a dirty job and take her twice as long. The thought made her feel tired and her body sagged. With an imminent visit to Philip's parents, everything made her feel tired.

There was again that sharp nip to the air she had become aware of earlier in the week. Winter was drawing closer and there might only be a few more warm days before the long cold season began. She shuddered at the thought and pulled her arms around her.

"Hello," said a voice behind her and made Jackie jump, eyes wide, her heart thumping.

"Gosh I'm sorry, I didn't mean to startle you. I was out running and I saw you so I thought I'd stop and introduce myself."

Jackie looked at the woman in front of her and recognised her as her new neighbour. *She's taller than me, and slimmer*, she thought. The woman had a long lean face circled with tiny tendrils of curly hair and sprinkled with freckles. Her green eyes sparkled and her mouth was large and generous. She was flushed with a light sheen of sweat and she was out of breath.

What struck Jackie most was how comfortable she looked with herself.

There was no tension. Her face looked open and enquiring and Jackie shrank beside her.

"I'm Liz," the woman said, holding out her hand. "The new next door neighbour?"

Jackie automatically shook the hand, still reeling from her sudden smallness.

"I would have knocked or something, but to be honest I've been at sixes and sevens," she laughed. "Still am."

Jackie nodded, warming to the woman. "It takes time, doesn't it?"

"You bet. And I work from home, which gives it another added complication."

Jackie nodded. "I don't work," she said wanting the ground to come up and swallow her, wondering why she had said it anyway.

"Right, lady of leisure then."

"Not really," Jackie said. "I'm starting at the local school next week, helping out, and I've got a little girl. Then there's the house, they're big houses these."

"You can say that again. I'm beginning to wonder if I took leave of my senses. Why did I think I needed something so big?" She laughed again.

Jackie waited, she'd been wondering the same herself and let the silence hang, hoping her new neighbour would enlighten her.

"How old's your daughter?"

"Eleven. I don't suppose I can call her little anymore," Jackie shrugged, sad at the statement.

"They grow up so fast."

"Do you have children?"

"Me? No. Single woman. No dependants."

"It's a big house just for you," Jackie said, fishing again.

Liz nodded and the women looked at one another for a few moments.

"What do you do? From home I mean. Your job?"

"I'm a writer."

"Really!" Jackie became excited. "Oh then you must meet Em, she wants to be a writer. She'll be so excited to know we have a real live one living next door to us."

"Well, I wouldn't get too excited," Liz said. "I'm not a novelist. I worked as a journalist at the local paper. Now I free lance, still do some pieces for the paper, but I write articles for magazines."

"Oh I see. Well, I'm not sure what kind of writing Emma wants to go into. I still think she'll be excited. She's always scribbling stories and making up magazines in her bedroom, writing songs and poems. To be honest, I think writing is writing to her."

Liz nodded and smiled. "It's nice she has such a passion at an early age. I had no idea what I wanted to be at that age. Did you?"

No one had asked her what she wanted to do for such a long time the question caught her off balance. Yes she had known. She had known where she was going and what she wanted to achieve but she shook her head in agreement.

"I'd better get in the shower before I cool down too much. It was really nice to meet you."

"Yes, it was lovely to meet you too." Jackie was heading to her door, her thoughts moving to the path that needed clearing when she stopped and turned round. "Liz," she called.

The woman turned back. "Yes?"

"I was wondering, well, I know you're really busy with work and such but, well, if you're ever in the need of a break and fancy a coffee…?"

"Oh yes, I'd love that. How about Monday afternoon?"

Jackie shook her head. "My afternoon at the school, but I could do Tuesday."

Liz raised her head to the steel grey sky as if looking for inspiration. She looked back at Jackie. "I think that's okay. Tell you what, if I have any problems I'll come and give you a knock, is that okay?"

"Great! Make it about three and then you can meet Emma. I know she'd kill me if I had a real writer in the house and let them leave without meeting her."

Liz laughed. "I'll see you, and Emma of course, Tuesday."

"I'll look forward to it," said Jackie and turned back to the house with a lighter heart to get the broom.

Nikki had left work early to make her monthly visit to the beauticians. The rigmarole of waxing, tinting and dying took up more and more time. It frightened her sometimes. The previous week when she removed her bra she would swear her tits dropped an inch. Still, four hours and then it was over for another month.

And, she reminded herself, there was a special reason today. Philip was taking her out to dinner, not to just any place, but to "John Doe," the place of the moment in town, and the most expensive. Traditional English food was making a comeback and John Doe specialised in it. Connoisseur sausages with mustard or cheddar mash; ale and meat pies with a crust you could stop a door with; roasts and vegetables laced with gravy. She could feel her hips groan and her dress stretch just reading the menu, but everyone who was anyone went there. The table had been booked for three weeks and they'd have had to wait much longer, only a friend of a friend owed Philip a favour. Nikki hated the food but it was the place to be. She would just have to choose a fish dish and ask them to hold the batter.

Sandra, her regular beautician, came in and smiled her saccharine smile. "How are we today, Ms Hatton?"

"Well, thank you, Sandra."

"Lovely," said Sandra, though clearly not listening. Nikki wondered what she would say if she told her the truth.

"Well actually, Sandra, I'm approaching forty and my looks are fading fast, which is a problem because I trade on them a great deal. I've been involved with a married man for the last twelve months and I have to figure out a way of getting him to leave his wife without him realising I even want him."

"Ms Hatton?"

Nikki jumped. "Sorry I wasn't listening."

"Will it be your usual today?"

"Yes."

"If I can just check your booking with you before I begin." Sandra picked up her clipboard. "You're booked in for full leg wax, bikini wax and underarm wax. An eyebrow shape and eyelash tint and finally, a manicure and pedicure. Was that all?"

Nikki nodded—wasn't it enough? Listed like that she felt the fear creep up through her toes.

Sandra leaned in closer and peered into her face.

"What?" asked Nikki loudly.

"Ms Hatton I think you might want to start thinking about some electrolysis on that top lip."

Nikki's hand flew to cover her mouth. "What!" she muttered from behind her hand.

"It's nothing to worry about I can assure you, and it's perfectly natural for a woman of your age."

Had Nikki imagined it or had the wretched girl emphasised "woman of your age."

"Do whatever you think needs doing," she said sharply.

"Yes, Ms Hatton," said the saccharine Sandra and turned her back to prepare her trolley.

Nikki felt herself close to tears and blinked hard to hold them back. *At least with the waxing*, she thought, *I can let the odd tear fall without suspicion.*

"So have you got anything?"

Jack Woods shook his head, the flesh on his face wobbling. "Nothing so far," he said.

Philip leaned over the dim café table and squinted his eyes at the man opposite him. "Look, I don't have much time and you're paid to do a job, so do it!"

Jack took the large cigar out of the corner of his mouth. Philip watched the soggy end with fascinated disgust as Jack waved it round. "I've dug into the background of the case. I've tailed Murphy for the last three weeks, checked into his business dealings and his credit ratings. I even broke into his home. He's clean. He's got some friends you wouldn't want to mess with, but other than that he's clean."

Philip sat back and stirred the grey liquid in the ceramic mug that was supposed to pass for tea.

"We're in arbitration in less than four months. Four months, and if I can't discredit his testimony I'll lose the case."

Jack emptied his cup and smacked his lips, then he replaced the cigar in his mouth pushing to one corner with his tongue so he could talk.

"I dunno what to say? If he's clean, he's clean. What can we do?"

"Jack, I need this. I am close to losing my job. I need to bag a win. Especially this one. Douglas is a big firm, a lot's riding on it."

He didn't mention the unclaimed hours and risks he'd taken so far. If he lost they'd be liable not only for the costs run up on the case so far, but Murphy and Bradford's costs too. If he was caught he could wave any possibility of a partnership goodbye. Assuming he still had a job when the partners found out what he'd been up to. He set aside the risk of disbarment. He had to win. He had to.

"Why aren't they using their usual firm?"

"They'd heard how good we are." Philip laughed to cover his lie. He hadn't told Woods the no-win no-fee terms. Why should he? What the hell had it got to do with him anyway?

"Seriously, how come you got it?"

"They wanted to try us out."

"Boy, are they trying you out," Jack paused. "Look Philip, I'm not trying to tell you your job but I've been in this business a long while. This case, it's cut and dried from what I see. You'd be better telling them to settle rather than trying to take this to court."

Philip smiled, this is another thing he didn't like about Jack, his logic. He watched Jack chew on his cigar.

"Don't you ever light that thing?" Philip's voice was full of irritation.

"Nar, it's bad for your health."

"Well it's bad for my digestion watching you play around with it like that."

"Stop being such a pain in the arse, what's the matter with you?"

Philip took a swig of his tea and spat it back into the cup. "God! How can you drink this shit?"

"I think you need to get laid."

"Piss off, arse hole."

Jack stood up, his huge girth hung over the table in Philip's eye line. "Want another drink?"

"You must be joking!"

As Jack idled his way over to the counter, Philip's mind worked furiously trying to come up with a plan. Jack was right. He didn't really have a case and he couldn't afford not to have one. He'd waited years for an opportunity like this. It was his way to the top. The only way to bring money in for the firm in a big way, and the only way to bring in money was to win. Here was his big chance to prove he was more than just a good lawyer. If he could win this case he'd be promoted, no doubt about it. If he lost he'd be lucky to stay employed. A tight band was pulling round his head. He was nearly forty. When he'd started out he'd expected to be going for junior partner now, not floundering like this, scrabbling to keep his job. How had he got in this position in the first place? Shit, shit, shit, shit, shit, shit, shit!

If his boss Jeremy Walford found out he'd be strung up. The prick was always hanging round, watching him. Walford may be a senior partner, but he was jealous of Philip. He could tell. It was just the way he spoke to him, always trying to belittle him, making sure Philip knew his place in the great scheme of things. It wouldn't surprise him if Walford wasn't the reason he hadn't been offered a partnership already.

He had been working for this all his life and he was so close. So close now. He couldn't let it slip away because of a bad decision and an uptight prick of a boss. He couldn't. He wouldn't.

Jack grunted his approach and slowly lowered himself down opposite Philip. "I need to lose some weight," he said.

"You're always saying that," Philip reminded him.

Jack sighed. "Look, there is one thing."

"What?"

The large man paused. "There is one thing you might wanna look at. A few years back there was a complaint made against Murphy."

"And?"

Jack scrunched up his face as if he were forcing out the words. "Could be nothing, but looks like Murphy handled things a bit of rough on that one."

"Name?"

"It's all in there," he indicated the manila wallet he had handed to Philip when he first came in. "Guy called Ash Patel. A small business man who got Murphy's firm to do some refurbishment for him back in the eighties."

"Good work, my man."

"I gotta warn you, it's a long shot. Probably nothing."

"There's no such thing," said Philip, rubbing his hands together.

Jack took a slurp of his tea. "Good luck," he said.

Chapter 7

When Emma arrived home that evening her mother was in an unusually buoyant mood.

"I met our neighbour today, Em," she said.

Emma dropped her school bag on the kitchen floor, shed her coat in the same place and headed for the bread bin. She was always hungry when she got home and a lemon curd sandwich was her favourite. When she felt the soft creamy sweet mixture in her mouth she began to relax and feel safe.

"She had just finished her run."

Emma listened as she lifted the lid on the terracotta pot marked with large black letters "Bread."

"Are you listening?" her mother sounded short.

"Yes, I'm just making a snack at the same time. I'm a woman, I can do two things at once."

She glanced over her shoulder to see her mother smile at their favourite saying. Satisfied, she returned to her task.

"Her name's Liz. She's a writer."

Emma turned to her mum, knife suspended in her hand. "Really?"

Jackie nodded, a pleased expression on her face. "I knew you'd be impressed."

"What does she write?"

Emma watched as her mother shifted from one foot to the other. "Well, that's just it. She's not a novelist so..." she shrugged.

"So what?"

"Well, I'm wasn't sure you'd still be interested."

"Are you kidding?"

"Liz seemed to think it was important."

"What kind of writer is she?"

"She's a journalist, free lance."

"Oh wow, excellent Mum. A real live writer next door."

She turned back to the bread and smeared a large glob of yellow curd across the bread.

"She's coming over for coffee next week."

"When? I bet I'm at school." Emma's heart sank.

"No. I asked her to come late afternoon so you could meet her."

Emma slammed the top slice of white bread onto her sandwich, picked it up in one hand and turned to hug Jackie. "Mum, you're the best," she said as she skipped out of the room.

In her bedroom she put Boyzone Greatest hits on the CD player, and then sat back on her bed to eat her sandwich. It had been a good day, all in all.

In English they'd had to write a piece of poetry that had a rhythm appropriate to the content. She had decided to write a poem about a train and was trying to match the rhythm but had been unable to concentrate. She was sure Alan Metcalf was watching her and her face got redder and redder during the course of the lesson. At lunchtime she'd asked Lu about it and she had agreed.

Emma decided she quite liked Alan after all. He made her heart do strange things in her chest and she felt her muscles become tight when he was close to her, but she felt weird about it too.

She wasn't sure what to do or what to say to him and she couldn't talk to her mother. Emma smelt the stale alcohol on her mother's breath in the mornings and noticed a faint aroma under the toothpaste smell most afternoons when she got home.

Her parents relationship was odd and over the last year or so Emma had picked up on little things her mother said that suggested she wasn't happy with her choice. Emma felt miserable when she compared her home with Lottie's.

Lottie complained about having older brothers and a noisy home and thought Emma's home was nicer because it was so quiet, but Emma would have loved to have had company, brothers or sisters to tease and confide in. A couple of years ago she'd asked her mum if she would ever have another child and her mother had laughed and said one of Emma was enough for anyone. Was that why they hadn't had any more? Was it her? It had to be her, didn't it? Other people had more than one child, most people in fact. Was it why her father stayed away from home too?

The bread and curd turned to mush and grew in her mouth. Her throat tightened as she tried to swallow. Tears came up in her eyes. If Alan Metcalf liked her now, it was only because he didn't really know her. She would, she decided, keep him at arm's length.

At seven-thirty the doorbell on Nikki's apartment rang. *That would be Philip, always punctual.* She took one last look at herself in the full length mirror in the bedroom.

She had on a Dolce original she had bought in Paris three years ago. It was a little out of date in London and Paris, but way ahead of its time here in the Northeast. Philip hadn't seen this dress, she had been saving it for just such an occasion. Tonight was the beginning of her campaign.

The skirt was made of a pale grey chiffon and flowed away from her, accentuating her long thin legs. The bodice was encrusted with pearlised sequins so it clung to her. Her breasts were pushed up and her waist was pulled in. She had never looked so good. She turned this way and that, watching the folds of the dress swish and sway. Her body was silky and hair free, dusted with a light spray of CK One.

She gave herself a little squeeze, pleased with how she looked. *Let battle commence,* she thought as she picked up her grey pashmina.

Philip was waiting in the car when Nikki emerged. Although it was dark he could see her clearly under the street light and she took his breath away. She was a vision of beauty, a goddess and the contrast with this before him and Jackie was painful. Why did life get so complicated?

She glided over to the car, stood at the passenger side and leaned down. He pushed the button to lower the window.

"Are you going to open the door for a lady?" she asked.

He jumped out of the car and ran round the other side, opening her door.

She stood and smiled at him, displaying perfect white teeth, her perfume rising between them.

"Are you hungry?" he asked, his appetite rising in another area.

Nikki tossed back her head and laughed, pushing her finger into his chest. "Oh no you don't, big boy. I've been waiting three weeks for this, and besides, we need to talk."

The words sounded ominous. "What about?"

Nikki stepped neatly into the car. "Later," she said and winked. He looked at her small perfectly manicured hands nestled in her lap and as he closed the door his excitement turned to stomach-churning apprehension.

Chapter 8

"How are things at home?" Abby asked Jackie as she picked up the stapler.

Abby and Jackie had struck up a hesitant friendship waiting in the playground for the girls. Over the years they had been thrown together more as their daughters became best friends and finally their rather tentative friendship had been cemented when they both volunteered at the school.

It was Monday afternoon and they had been assigned the task of mounting the children's work from a year two class. The pictures showed the story of the willow pattern on the Chinese pottery. Jackie thought some of them were really quite good. The best ones would be displayed in the hall whilst the others would go up on the walls of the classroom. Abby and herself were mounting the pictures onto large pieces of coloured paper to act as a sort of make-shift frame.

Jackie paused, scissors in hand, to consider how she should reply.

"They're probably about the same," she said and smiled.

Abby pulled a face and tucked her heavy brown hair behind one ear. "That bad, huh?"

Jackie continued cutting a piece of coloured paper to size and shrugged. "What can I say? I never see him, most of the time it's just Emma and me. We're going to his parents at the weekend."

"What's that like?"

"Dreadful."

Abby laughed. "Sounds like you need a little excitement in your life."

"You can say that again. Pass me the stapler."

44

Abby leaned over.

"Thanks," said Jackie. "We've got a new neighbour."

Abby stood up straight. "Have you met them yet?"

"It's not them, it's a her."

"In a house the size of yours?"

"That's what I thought. Strange, isn't it?"

"Very. So, have you met *her* yet?"

Jackie nodded as she aligned the picture on the paper back. She glanced up. "Met her last week. She's coming for coffee tomorrow."

Abby raised an eyebrow. "And?"

Jackie stapled one corner and moved the paper round. "She's a free lance writer and lives on her own. That's all I know."

"She sounds intriguing."

"I'm looking forward to it to be honest, make a change, a new face."

"Shall I take Emma tomorrow then? Lottie'll be delighted."

"No. I promised Emma she could meet her, real live writer and all that."

"Okay. Well, you can fill me in on the gossip next week."

Jackie smiled at her friend. "Promise."

Philip sat in his office brooding over the pile of paperwork before him. It never ended. His whole office seemed swamped in piles of paper. Files of clients everywhere and post that needed a response to it yesterday. Usually he rose to the challenge, but the last few weeks it had got harder and harder to find the enthusiasm.

The Douglas case seemed to drain him of energy. The realisation of the position he'd put himself in weighed heavy and try as he may, his mind would not stay focused on the task in hand. And now, instead of shedding light on the tangle of client's cases awaiting his attention, something Nikki had said last week was going through his mind over and over again. Effervescent in its implications and pulling him into he knew not what.

They had sat in her apartment after the meal. It had been a wonderful evening, worth every penny of the huge bill that arrived at the end of the night.

Philip loosened his tie and opened the top button of his shirt. His stocking feet propped on the oak coffee table, his body sunk into the brown leather sofa. He hadn't wanted her to buy it. He'd told her it would be cold and hard but she insisted and she'd been right.

But that was Nikki all over. He watched her now, stood at the drinks cabinet mixing him a whiskey and soda. Her blonde hair, expensively cut, hung in layers down her back. She had changed out of the fabulous dress she was wearing earlier into cream linen trousers and a white silk vest that clung to her bra-less breasts. She stood in bare feet, a light tan to her skin and the room filled with the scent of her freshly applied perfume.

She rested her pale blue eyes on him, make-up was smudged under her eyes, giving her a sultry sexy look.

As she swayed across the floor, the ice clinking in the glass he felt a stirring. *Maybe I am falling in love*, he thought. He looked at her and she raised a neatly plucked eyebrow. She knew, and he hated that she knew and he loved it that she knew. He was powerless in her presence.

He reached for his drink and took a sip. The warm liquid moved through his throat, down his chest and into his stomach. He sighed, lay his head back and closed his eyes.

"I've been doing some thinking," her warm husky voice caressed his ears. Oh it was so much different here from home, this was his port in a storm.

He didn't move, didn't respond but they both knew he was listening. He always listened when she spoke.

"I think it's time you understood that I'm not exclusive."

His head wrenched itself up, his eyes fixed hers, trying to understand this new game of hers. She had always insisted on independence and if he was honest, it was probably what made her so alluring. She was unattainable. Always just out of his grasp, he never knew what she would say or do next. Even in bed. Still, she had never been explicit about it before and he didn't like the idea of some others man's hands moving over her body, of another man's lips touching her mouth, her breasts, her… he stopped himself. *Maybe I do love her.*

She smiled slowly. "You've always known it, besides, it would be unreasonable of you to expect me to be waiting for you and not have a life of my own. I know it's what you want, but still, I felt we needed to clear the air a little, you know, be fully open about what's going on here."

"What is going on here?" he asked, his voice came out husky, not as clear as he would have liked.

Nikki titled her head back and laughed gently. Her throat looked so long and alluring. In fact, he thought, she had never looked so goddamn sexy as she did right at that moment.

"We're having fun, Philip. Isn't that what you said? I grant you the fun has gone on a lot longer than I expected, but still, it's just fun."

"So why the big speech?" There was an edge to his voice.

"I'm not sure. I've been thinking and I suppose I felt it needed to be reiterated, just in case either of us had forgotten."

He nodded, saying nothing but it had been in the back of his mind all weekend. And now, in the cold light of Monday morning it was in front, pushing everything away. Haunting him. Of course, he'd tried to talk to her about it but she'd refused.

"There's nothing to talk about," she said, as if he was just a small corner of her life. She was so infuriating.

So unlike Jackie. Jackie he could manipulate, cajole and if all else failed, scare into submission. He hated it that she let him but he knew he could. With Nikki he was the prey.

And she was slipping away from him. Had she already found another beau and was preparing the ground to give him the slip? It was an uncomfortable thought.

"So, how you settling in?"

"Great thanks," Liz was walking Benjy by the river with her father.

"Good neighbours, Elizabeth?"

Liz thought about Jackie and smiled. Beneath the sad eyes and tired face, Liz had caught a glimpse of her real beauty. She wondered what was going on in the woman's life to cause such unhappiness and looked forward to getting to know her better.

"Yes," she said. "Very good."

They walked on, the air fresh from rain, watching the full river flow by. It was a calm day disturbed only by the sounds of the gurgling river, Benjy's ferreting and from a distance, the low rumble of traffic from the by-pass.

Liz watched as a yellowed leaf floated by. For now summer still hung in the air but the trees were turning and autumn would come soon. Autumn. She loved the rawness of autumn mornings. When she was jogging the cold nip on her arms made her feel alive. She had come running by this river often. Further flattening the muddy groove worn into the grass. It made her feel as if she were making her mark, adding her feet to the hundreds who had gone before to carve this path in nature.

She missed the countryside. Funny how she had never considered that when she was looking for a permanent place to live. Still, as she was living alone it probably wasn't a good idea to live in the middle of nowhere as well.

"How are you?" she asked.

"Good. Very good."

"See anything of Ruth Buchas?"

Ruth Buchas was one of a plethora of women in the village who had set their sights on Donald. She was a widower of sixty-eight whose strange hats quivered when she spoke. Every Wednesday she brought Donald something "home baked."

Donald scowled at his daughter. "Very amusing, Elizabeth. You know how irritating I find the woman."

"Her heart's in the right place."

"Maybe so. I just wish she'd point it in another direction."

Liz laughed. "What did she bring you this week?"

"Tart," he said shortly. Liz raised her eyebrows. "Bakewell," he added with a wry smile, stroking his beard.

They fell back into silence as they walked. Liz considered how she really felt about Ruth Buchas. The woman's flirtatious attentions hadn't bothered her before, she would even say she'd encouraged them, but now, since finding her mother's writings, she felt different. Something was amiss. She needed answers.

"I expect it's nice to finally have a place big enough for your piano," Donald said, breaking into her thoughts.

"Yes," she said.

"Feels funny, that front room, without it."

Liz knew she had to ask. This was the moment. "You know you sent some boxes over with it?"

"Mmmm," he sucked on his empty pipe, emitting the familiar hissing sound. He had stopped filling it several years ago on the advice of his replacement in the village, Dr. Mike Green.

"Did you know there were a couple of boxes of Mum's writings in there?"

As she said this Benjy returned with something bloody hanging from his mouth. It turned out to be nothing more than a missed kill from the mornings shoot, but the moment passed. Liz wasn't sure if her father had not heard her question or chosen to ignore it.

Chapter 9

At three on the dot the doorbell rang out through the empty house. Jackie was pleased—she liked people to be on time. She led Liz through the hallway into the kitchen, trying to see the house with fresh eyes. Was it okay, she wondered?

As if reading her mind, Liz said, "Your house is lovely. You have a wonderful eye for colour and I love the way you put things together."

"Thanks," said Jackie puffing up. "Coffee?"

"D'you have decaff?"

"Sure."

"Mind if I have a poke around?"

Jackie was taken aback by the question but could see no reason to refuse. "Okay."

Liz, much to Jackie's relief, hadn't meant the whole house and kept her inspection to the kitchen and the dining room.

"Your layout is a little different to mine."

"Oh?"

"I've got a door here," she said, indicating with her two arms outstretched as if she were a policeman directing traffic, to a space next to the large kitchen window. "Of course, it's on the opposite side."

Jackie nodded.

"And here," she walked through to the dining room and pointed to their French doors. Jackie watched the stranger move, envious of her graceful movements. Liz turned round, a distracted look on her face. "That's it," she cried suddenly, "the rooms are the other way round." She sounded as if she'd solved an enigmatic problem. She attempted to explain the layout of her own house and then stopped. "You'll just have to come round and see for yourself," she said, allowing her arms to float to the sides of her body, or so it seemed to Jackie.

She smiled and placed the mugs of coffee on the table.

"Mugs okay?" she asked, although what she would have done if the other woman had said no she couldn't imagine, not having anything else in the house.

"Perfect. You'll have to excuse my enthusiasm," she said as she pulled out a chair and sat down at the table. "I've just bought my own house and I'm slightly obsessed with it. A bit like a woman with a new baby."

"Is this your first place then?"

"Yes and no," she picked up the mug and took a sip. "I was married and had a place of my own, with my husband of course, but it wasn't really mine." She put the mug back on the table. "Before that I shared a house with a bunch of students. Again, not really my place. Since the divorce I've lived in a flat but it was rented. It's not the same. So I guess this is really the first place I've had that's just mine."

"Where's your husband?" Jackie asked, bringing the man to mind she had seen helping Liz move in a few weeks ago.

"Don't know and don't care."

"I see, like that, was it?"

Liz paused, her mug half way to her mouth. "No, it wasn't like that really," she put the mug back on the table. "Let's just say we weren't compatible."

Jackie laughed. "I wonder if there is such a thing sometimes."

"What about you?"

Jackie shrugged. "What's to tell? I'm a stay-at-home mum, not very fashionable these days."

"Is it fulfilling?"

The directness of the question startled Jackie but she answered it truthfully. "Not really."

"What were you doing before?"

"Before what?"

"Before all this," Liz gestured with her arms.

"Nothing. I met Philip at college, so it's always been all this."

"What did you study at college?"

"Law."

"And?"

"And what?"

"How come you didn't follow it through?"

Jackie's face reddened. "I failed my finals."

"So why not retake?"

Liz made it sound so easy, but it hadn't been, not then. It had all been so hard.

Jackie lowered her eyes and noticed small brown toast crumbs on the table from breakfast. Her slovenliness shamed her.

"It was," she paused, looking for the right words to sum up the events without telling the whole story. "Complicated," she said at last.

Liz traced the rim of her mug with her fingers and Jackie watched, mesmerised. They were beautiful fingers, long and elegant.

"I'm sorry, I didn't mean to pry. I guess it's the journalist in me. Old habits die hard."

"You didn't pry it's just…it's a long story."

"Maybe another time."

"Maybe."

To Jackie's relief the doorbell rang.

"That'll be Emma," she said, standing up. "She's dying to meet you."

As Jackie introduced them Emma looked confident, but Jackie could see the two tell-tale spots of pink on her cheeks and her smile was crooked and shy.

"I hear you want to be a writer," Liz said as Emma joined her at the table still in her coat, her bag dumped on the floor.

Emma nodded. "I write all the time."

"That's a good start. Practice makes perfect."

"What do you write?" Emma asked, picking up the juice Jackie set before her.

"All sorts. Mainly articles for magazines and features for newspapers."

As Emma listened she gulped the orange juice down, leaving an orange moustache along her top lip.

"I want to do that."

Jackie knew this wasn't true and smiled. It was typical of her daughter to say what would please. Emma wanted to be a novelist. Later, if Jackie mentioned it Emma would insist Jackie had got it all wrong.

"Is it fun?"

"It's alright, but it's not what I dreamed of doing as a youngster."

The word "youngster" struck Jackie as a strange word for Liz to use.

"What did you want to do?" Emma asked.

"I wanted to be a concert pianist."

"Really?" This delighted Emma and she wriggled with glee. "Why didn't you?"

Liz smiled sadly. "Not good enough…or not brave enough."

"I've heard you play, through the wall. I thought you were terrific," said Jackie.

Liz threw back her head and laughed with delight. Jackie noticed the white vulnerable throat, a small pulse beat under the skin.

Jackie warmed to the woman as she watched her daughter chatting happily to her, any earlier discomfort forgotten.

Liz was animated, emphasising her conversation with long sweeping gestures of her arms and fingers. Her movements lilting, it was like watching a willow dance in the wind. Her lithe body under control and yet relaxed. Watching Liz made her more relaxed and she noticed Emma seemed unusually animated and confident.

I want to be her friend, she found herself thinking as she continued to watch her. *I want her in my life.*

Philip replaced the receiver, made a note to ask Janet to send a confirmation letter to his client detailing the position, and swiped the pen over the bar code to ensure his time and hers was added to his client's bill.

He turned his attention to the Douglas case and flicked through the notes in the hope he'd missed something. Philip hated to admit it but the detective was right. There was nothing to help his case. He hadn't looked at the Ash Patel stuff, but from what Jack had said in the café there wouldn't be much in there to help him either.

He went over the case again in his mind, trying to get the facts straight, making brief notes to simplify things first.

Colin Murphy, the Managing Director at Murphy and Bradford, claimed Peter Douglas agreed to the additional costs over an informal lunch and Murphy then had a letter sent to that effect two days later. Douglas refuted this and claims the letter was an opening offer only and that negotiations were still under way. No doubt a copy of the letter would be among the evidence the other side would present.

Douglas insists he sent a counter offer a week later which Murphy and Bradford claim they did not receive. Unfortunately, Peter Douglas was still searching for a copy of the letter.

How the lawyers allowed the work to continue without clarification was beyond Philip, but then, it wasn't unusual for these wrangles to occur and he couldn't complain, it was how he made his living.

He lay his pen down on the desk and leaned back in his chair to think. His mind began to wander as it did so often these days. He hadn't hinted to Jackie of the problem he had with his promotion. She just thought everything was fine. But he knew if he told her she'd fret and he couldn't cope with reassuring her as well as himself. It was another reason to spend time away from her.

Women had a way of wheedling these things out of you. He'd learnt that from his mother. Except Nikki, she was different. She never drilled him. Never. Good job too. He'd lied to her, inflated his importance. Not too much, but she thought he was a definite for promotion to junior partner. How could he have known then that they'd have more than a brief fling? Fat fucking chance now! He was waiting for dead man's shoes unless...unless he did something outstanding.

His mind came back to the case. He pulled open the manila file Jack had given him. It might be worth going through the notes on the Ash Patel contract, maybe Jack had missed something. As he read through it his heart leapt. He stopped and read again, just to make sure he hadn't made a mistake. On second reading it was even clearer. The bastard Jack had been winding him up. Philip read Jack's report with the appetite of a starving man. Ash Patel owned a chain of corner shops across the region. In 1989 he approached Murphy and Bradford to do a revamp job on all of them so they would all have the same image.

Mr Patel was quoted thirty grand for the job but the final bill came out at nearly fifty. Mr Patel had refused to pay and lodged a complaint with the Association of Master Builders. Mysteriously, a few weeks later Mr Patel withdrew his complaint and paid in full.

Philip shook his head in awe of Jack. He didn't know how he got his information but he was bloody good at his job. Thank God.

He clapped his hands together. "You beauty, Jack," he said aloud, rubbing them together furiously. Patel could be the key to winning the case.

Philip pulled out his mobile. He needed Jack to find this man and if he made the right noises he could save Philip's neck.

Chapter 10

The following week, as Jackie collected the milk from the doorstep she caught a glimpse of her new neighbour's curly head bouncing down the road. She was jogging and Jackie's insides shrivelled in shame, her self-loathing driven deeper. She stood shivering in her cotton robe, her brain drumming against her temples with a raging thirst and a breath foetid with last night's alcohol.

She watched as the woman disappeared round the corner, intrigued. Who was the man who had helped her move in? What did a single woman want with such a large house?

If it were me, she thought as she closed the front door against the chill morning, *if I was free, I wouldn't buy a house here*. She began to daydream of the small whitewashed cottage built on the side of a mountain in a warm Mediterranean country with gentile weather and isolation. When Jackie shared this dream with Abbey she asked why Jackie wanted to trap herself away from life when she was so young. But it couldn't be any lonelier, there was nothing more isolating than being in a relationship with someone who didn't want you. Her days were filled with nothing, but the nights were worse.

When she returned to the kitchen Philip was tucked behind the morning paper. *Couldn't he get the milk when he picked up the paper?* she thought. He looked so calm and relaxed, so contented. Bitter acid flooded her veins.

"I just saw our new neighbour jogging down the road," she said.

"What's she like?" he asked from behind his paper.

"She's nice. Really nice."

54

Philip didn't respond.

"Do you want eggs?"

"No thank you."

"Is Em up?"

"She's in the bathroom."

Jackie wanted to draw him from behind his paper. He turned the page.

"Should I make eggs for her?" She winced at the whine in her voice.

"How should I know. Ask her," he said with thinly disguised irritation.

Jackie took a breath and despite her better judgement waded in again.

"I just thought she might have said something to you."

Philip lowered his arms, crumpling his paper into his lap as he did so.

"What is she going to say? 'Morning Dad, I want eggs'!"

Jackie flinched. Why did she try? It was so obvious he didn't want to talk to her so why did she do this? When would she learn? Why did she stretch herself out like this and make herself so vulnerable? She had an image of Christ on the cross, that was her. She was not a religious person but enjoyed the image of the martyrdom it provided for her. And then, quite unexpectedly, tears sprang to her eyes. She despised herself these indulgences and yet, couldn't help herself. She was weak, weak, weak. Philip's voice cut into her like a dull knife, hacking and tugging at her.

"What now?"

She shifted her head towards him and the movement spilt the tears from her eyes. They ran down her cheeks and made her heart ache.

"Nothing," she said, her voice a whisper. Her body tightened. She didn't want another scene. She didn't want him to spill his vitriolic anger over her before the day had begun.

"Don't say nothing for Christ sake. I can see something's wrong. I'm not an idiot."

"Yes. No. I mean…" What did she mean? What could she say? If she tried to explain she knew he would twist her words and yet, if she said "nothing" again his anger would flare. Her mind worked furiously under the pressure of his eyes. "I…I just," her head hurt, the band tightening. "It's nothing. I don't feel well this morning, that's all." She often resorted to this.

He sneered. "I'm not surprised, the amount you packed away last night."

Was it true? No. She only had three glasses last night, four maximum. Anger swept through her like a forest fire and despite her earlier attempts to keep the peace she shot out at him, over exaggerating her innocence. "I didn't drink last night!"

"Oh didn't you? What about dinner?"

"Philip I had two, maybe three glasses of wine at dinner. No more than you, if I remember correctly."

"Well you don't remember correctly."

Jackie felt muddled and afraid. What did he mean? Was her drinking so bad she was beginning to forget just how much she drank? After all her promises to herself now she couldn't even remember how much she was drinking. Or was he exaggerating?

He leaned back with the expression of a cat tormenting a mouse. Jackie watched, mesmerised and helpless, feeling caught. She could taste his triumph and her insides weakened, her muscles gave way as the anger left her.

"What about the bottle you polished off when I went into the study to work?"

"I just had a few glasses to relax while watching TV." It wasn't fair, what did he expect if he left her alone every night?

"Jackie," he said. "You have a drink problem," he took a breath. "You drink too much."

Every syllable cut into her. "Rubbish," she spat. "We're not in a court room now."

He laughed. "Good job too. You'd have no defence. If you were my client I would have to advise you to plead guilty in the hope of a lighter sentence."

"Stop it, Philip!"

"I work long hours. I'm aware I leave you on your own and I'm sorry for that." His tone was angry now. "But it's not like I'm out having fun. I'm working. Working, for fuck's sake!"

"I know, I know." Jackie could feel the tears again. She didn't want this. Poke. Prod. Cut. Slice. Poke. Prod. Cut. Slice. Every word cutting deeper. Jackie was no match for him. It hadn't always been like this, she reflected sadly. *At Uni I could run circles around you*, she thought with contempt. *Not now.*

"I work night and day and for what?" he spat. "For us. For the family. So you and Emma can have holidays, new clothes, fancy stuff." Philip lunged again. She didn't parry and he took another slice of her.

"You complain that I don't come home. Why would I want to?"

Lunge and slice.

"You're a drunk, Jackie, and you're ruining any chance I have at promotion."

Lunge and slice.

56

"In fact, I think it's safe to say you're a frigging liability!"

Each time he took another piece of her. Gone. Cut away, sliced down. She didn't even have the strength to dodge anymore.

She was nothing. No use. She was destroying his career. She slumped, her body wracked with sobs.

"Now if you don't mind," he said, folding up his paper. "I have work to do. Don't be surprised if I don't make it back tonight. I have a lot of work on and I think I'll use the company flat so I can think." Philip stood up to leave. "Oh, and by the way, don't forget we're going to my parents for lunch this Sunday. Don't make a fool of yourself."

Jackie didn't look up as he left but followed his departure with her ears, listening as he strode out of the kitchen, paused in the hall. She heard the rustle as he pulled on his coat, the tinkle as he collected his keys from the hook and imagined him picking up his briefcase. The door slammed shut and moments later the car engine started and diminished as he drove away.

She took a deep breath, realising she had barely been breathing. As the breath filled her body she found herself surprising relieved at his absence. Small tears continued to find their way down her face.

If she didn't have Emma, would she leave? Would she have the courage that failed her now? And if so, was it really so much harder to walk away now, today, or did she use Emma as a reason not to?

Could she blame Phil for the way he behaved?

She couldn't remember anymore whether his abuse came after her drinking or whether she started drinking because of the abuse. She wasn't clear about anything anymore, even how she felt. Did she still love him? Had she ever loved him? They'd married, yes, but it had nothing to do with love. She wiped it from her mind as she pulled the sleeve of her dressing gown across her face. She heaped everything on him. Blamed him for all her problems and unhappiness, but in the end was it really his fault?

His parting comment loomed up and filled her with dread. His parents. She was clumsy and untidy amongst the chintz and china. They had impeccable manners, yet were incredibly rude to her all at the same time.

She washed her face in the kitchen sink and filled the kettle. By the time Emma emerged Jackie had hidden all traces of the earlier skirmish except for a slight shake to her hands. Emma pretended not to notice, but something bad was going to happen, she just knew it.

It was early afternoon and Nikki tapped the pencil against her perfect white teeth as she worked over the press release. Her boss, Peter Douglas, was away and so the task had been left up to her. The firm, Douglas Property Development, had recently acquired another large amount of land by the dockside and were planning to build more properties of the type Nikki lived in. The press release was almost ready but there was something not reading right, something wasn't working and the more she read it the worse it got.

Jenny, the office junior, came back from the coffee machine and put the plastic cup full of grey coffee on her desk.

"Thanks."

"You'll never believe what's happened?" she said, her usual bulging eyes bulging further than Nikki thought possible. When she looked closer she thought Jenny looked pale and ill.

"What's wrong?"

"There's been an attack. On America."

"What sort of an attack?"

"Planes have been driven into buildings."

Nikki resisted the urge to correct Jenny's grammar.

"It's madness, it's all over the news, thousands have died and they say they're after the president."

Nikki was unable to decipher any of Jenny's ramblings and frustration scratched at her. She really was a stupid woman.

"Slow down, Jenny, and start at the beginning."

"Three planes have been driven into…"

Nikki couldn't resist it this time. "Flown, Jenny, planes are flown."

Jenny took a breath before continuing. "Three planes have been *flown* into buildings. Two into the World Trade Centres and one into the Pentagon. At least, I think it was the Pentagon."

Nikki wasn't sure how much she could rely on Jenny for accurate information, but as she was her only source at the moment she plied her with questions until she pulled out the whole story. It wasn't easy and by the time Nikki had finished her patience had been stretched.

The hum of conversation began to rise around her as the news spread and people left their desks to talk with one another. There was a need to talk with other human beings, confirm that what had happened, had happened. Allow it to sink in instead of it laying on the surface like a slick of fat on cold water.

She picked up the phone to call Philip at work. They had agreed she wouldn't call him there unless it was an emergency. This, she decided, was an emergency. She needed to hear his voice. People everywhere would be calling their families. Philip was the closest she had.

"Philip? Have you heard?"

"It's dreadful."

She imagined him running his hands over his face the way he did when he was tired or worried. "Are you okay?" she asked as if he had been involved in some way.

"I'm fine. You?"

"I'm gob smacked. Has the world gone mad?"

"Quite possibly," he said.

A comforting silence hung between them.

"We've been listening to the radio here in the offices," Philip said at last. "I doubt any work will get done today, some people are already going home. It's too shocking for words."

"Can you come over?" She heard his hesitation. He was thinking of his wife and child and it bit hard at her. She took a breath. "Please Phil?"

"Okay."

"What time?"

"I don't know yet, but I've got my key," his voice sounded warm and soft.

"Great. Philip?"

"Yes?"

She wanted to tell him she loved him. "I'm scared," she said instead. It was also true.

"Me too. I'll see you tonight."

Philip replaced the receiver and took a deep breath. He thought of Jackie and his vicious attack on her that morning. Why did he do that? Why did she let him? It was so easy. Why did he tear strips off her and reduce her to nothing? Some primeval impulse seemed to rise up in him when he saw her so...so...vulnerable.

To ease the tightness he dialled home but there was no answer so he left a message. When she found out she'd ring him, want him to go home but not say. He hated that quiet manipulation. It reminded him of his mother. Of how she would blackmail him into doing things he'd probably be happy to do if only she'd just come right out and ask him. At least he was free of that now. His mother didn't have that power over him anymore.

What would I have done if I were on one of those planes, he wondered. He tried to imagine and his body filed with impotent rage. What else could he feel if he were sat next to his daughter, her eyes wide with fear and looking at him to protect her? And all the time he could do nothing. He ran a few scenarios through his head but each one came to a blank. If he lunged and was killed in front of her how would that help? Did they know they were all going to die? Had they been told what was going to happen or had it come as a sudden realisation as the building sped up to them?

"Beer, Philip?"

He looked up to find Darren Bland standing in his doorway. Bland was young, eager and full of confidence in himself. He needed a slap in Philip's opinion. Too full of himself.

"What?" Philip heard the word come out muffled as if he wasn't sure where he was.

"A few of us are heading to the pub for a beer, nothing we can do here today. Besides, day's almost over now. Fancy one?"

Did he want to sit with this bundle of energy that was snapping at his heels and listen to him and a bunch of others spouting off about the hijacking?

"Best not," he said and turned back to pen the bar code of his last call into one of his client's accounts.

As Jackie rounded the corner of the smaller of the two shopping centres in town she saw ahead of her a large crowd gathering outside the Box Clever window. As she approached someone obliged by shuffling to one side to afford her a view. There were dozens of TV screens showing a plane tunnelling into the side of one of the World Trade Buildings and the buildings collapsing.

Jackie watched, stunned, unable to believe it wasn't a camera trick or some stunt for a Hollywood movie.

"What's happened?"

"Terrorist attack," a man from the crowd said. "One has gone in to the

Pentagon too."

A news reader came onto the screen looking grave in his blue shirt and navy tie. There were no words to accompany him, not out here on the pavement. A few people trickled into the shop to listen, others stood rooted outside, watching, having no need of words. *What could possibly be said?* thought Jackie.

Stunned, she pulled herself away and began to walk home. She decided to take the long way round and walk through the park. It was a beautiful September day and she wanted to put off the quiet house as long as possible. If she timed it right Emma would be home only a few minutes after her and then they could sit down together and take it all in.

The park was deserted and it's desolation only enhanced the feelings of disbelief in Jackie. She turned back and quickened her pace. She needed to talk to someone.

At home she phoned Philip.

"You heard then," he said.

"Yes."

"Dreadful goings on."

"Yes."

There was a pause and then Jackie said. "Will you be coming home early tonight?" Jackie felt herself become small in the silence.

Finally Philip said, "Not especially, love, the world of law still keeps grinding, I'm afraid." There was another pause, then Philip said, "Tell you what, I'll be home by nine—how's that?"

It wasn't what she wanted. She wanted him to come home now, have dinner with her and Emma or maybe go out together, all three of them. Acid tears of disappointment stung the back of her throat.

She swallowed. "Okay, I'll see you then. Will you need dinner?"

"No thanks, I'll grab something myself."

"Right then, see you later."

"Yeah see you around nine," he hung up and left a purring in her ear.

She dialled Abbey's number.

"Jackie, isn't it awful? Can you imagine those people on the planes. I kept thinking about the families. Can you imagine how you must feel sitting there with your child and the planes been hijacked? Trying to stop your children from getting upset when you know you're all going to die? Oh I don't know why I torture myself with these thoughts but I can't help it."

"I know. I've just spoken to Philip and I'm longing for Emma to get home."

"I'm the same. Lottie is due back any minute, the boys about fifteen minutes later. Steve phoned me from work, he's on his way home now."

The news pushed deep into Jackie's heart, twisting, and then she was crying down the phone.

"Jackie? Are you okay? Gosh, I'm sorry I didn't mean to…"

"It's okay. I'm sorry," she said through sobs. "I'm being silly, I'm fine really, just a little, well, I don't know."

"I could kick myself. I guess Phil isn't coming home?"

Jackie sniffed the last of her tears away, determined to push them down. "He is," she feeling foolish. "I'm not sure why I started crying."

"It's probably just the shock of it all. Go and get yourself a cup of tea. Emma will be home soon and you'll feel better then."

Jackie swigged a couple of glasses of wine and by the time Emma got home she was fortified.

The heavy smell of toothpaste and mouthwash on her mother told Emma something had happened to tilt her mother off her finely walked tightrope. She was relieved to find out what it was. Thousands of mothers would smell of toothpaste tonight. It was okay. *I knew something bad would happen today*, she thought and it made her feel wobbly inside.

"Dad?"

"Oh Elizabeth, my lovely. It's good to hear your voice."

"Are you okay?"

"I think I'm just a bit too old for days like this."

Fear gripped her. "Don't say that, Dad."

"It's days like this when I feel lost without your mum. She knew what to say to make me feel better. She knew what to say to make everyone feel better. She'd have rallied round," he chortled. "Held a jumble sale, raised money, made us all feel useful."

His words brought tears to her eyes. For herself but also for her father.

"Shall I come over at the weekend?"

"If you want to."

"You alright there on your own?"

"Fine. A little strange, but it's fine."

"Go and see Ruth," Liz said quickly, before she changed her mind. Silence followed. "Dad?"

"I heard you." He sounded angry.

Liz decided to pursue it. "Well?"

"She's gone to stay at her sister's in Cornwall."

"How do you know?"

He mumbled something.

"I didn't hear you, Dad."

"She sent me a postcard," he said louder.

There was a pause between them, neither knowing what to say.

"Anyway," said Douglas eventually. "Me and Benjy are going for a walk. It's a beautiful day and that's all I can focus on, right?"

"Right."

Chapter 11

The rain pattered on the windscreen. There wasn't enough for the wipers and each shriek strummed across Jackie's nerves like a bow on violin strings until Philip switched them off. She took a deep breath as they passed the angel of the North, trying to find some space in her chest. The outstretched arms seemed oddly reminiscent of a crucifixion today. The forty minute drive to Philip's parents' house seemed to be taking forever. Emma sat in the back singing the same Boyzone lyrics over and over again.

Phil broke the silence. "Shut up, Emma!"

Jackie was appalled by his tone but relieved by the instant silence that followed. Normally she would make some comment in Emma's defence but she didn't have the strength today. It was always the same when they went to his parents, the closer they got, the less of herself she had. Besides, Philip had been in a strange mood all morning. She reeled her mind back. He had been acting oddly since he had come back last Saturday. She glanced at him. He looked tired and pinched. It was probably a work problem he hadn't been able to shake off.

As the car ate up the motorway she turned to watch her surroundings slip by, hazy through the steamed window. There was still a lot of green around but it was muted by the grey skies, even the reddening trees of autumn looked subdued.

Brian and May Lawson lived on the other side of Richmond in Yorkshire, famous for its castle and cobbles. As the car shushed through the wet streets Jackie admired the pretty townhouses built in higgledy piggledy style along the steep cobbled streets. There was something so rich and authentic, so stable and ancient about the town.

They took a left at a mini roundabout and slowed to a stop behind a line of waiting cars at the bottom of steep incline. As they inched forward round the corner a group of runners came into view. Ahead a policeman was stopping cars to give the runners right of way.

It was obvious the runners were nearing the end of a long haul. Their hair stuck to their head, the cotton t-shirts clung to their body, mud splattered up the back of their ruddy legs and their faces expressed different levels of stress according to their states of fitness. Clouds of breath escaped open mouths. An official dressed in a bright yellow jacket stood on the other side of the road, halfway up a hill, cheering and clapping loudly, egging them on up the last hill to the end of the race.

Finally there was a gap and the policeman motioned them through and they moved over the large stone bridge that crossed the river.

"Shame I didn't bring my swimsuit," Emma said from behind as they passed the swimming baths.

Jackie didn't rise to the game, she was too distracted. They were only minutes away from Priory Villas and her mouth went dry.

Philip broke the silence. "Be nice to see Gramps, eh Emma?"

"Lovely," she said. Jackie turned in her seat to look at her and Emma smiled. Jackie's heart leapt and she wanted to hug her daughter.

"Here dear, do you take sugar?"

Jackie shook her head, stung by the question. After all these years she would have thought May Lawson could manage to keep some small piece of Jackie's preferences in her memory.

She took the tea, and felt her hand quiver. The cup seemed precarious, balanced on the saucer. Jackie always used mugs at home, here it was these delicate pieces of china she was sure she would break.

"My mother's," May said misunderstanding Jackie's preoccupation with the crockery. "Wedding gift."

Jackie nodded, said nothing and took hold of the saucer with two hands.

May then turned to her granddaughter. Whatever Jackie felt about the woman she could never fault the attentiveness she paid to Emma.

"I have your favourite sweetheart," she heard May say, "Coca cola!"

Jackie tuned out to listen to the conversation between the men.

"Terrible business, the attacks on the World Trade Centre. Do you think the Americans will attack, Dad?" Philip said.

Brian sat back in the large burgundy armchair by the fireplace, rested his cup and saucer comfortably in his lap and considered the question.

The fire was lit today but usually it was filled with dried flowers arranged by May. She did the flowers for the local church too.

"Yes," he said after some thought. "The Americans obviously have the evidence against Bin Laden and if the Taliban don't hand him over they'll have little choice."

Jackie didn't agree. She had read in the paper that a war would cost fifty-six billion dollars whilst one billion would turn Afghanistan into a democracy inside a year. The people were starving under a regime that took away their civil liberties. Jackie couldn't understand how America could justify bombing a country with so little.

Brian interrupted her thoughts. "If America resorts to bombing it serves them right. What else are we supposed to do? It isn't as if the president is rushing into it. In fact, in my opinion he's being remarkably restrained."

Philip nodded in agreement. "There's little doubt we'll be involved in any conflict too."

"There are armed guards at the base," May said, handing Philip his tea.

"There always are, Mum," he said as he took the cup.

"Yes but we've never seen the guns before."

"What do you expect? We'll be at war in a matter of weeks, perhaps days," Brian added.

"I know, but it doesn't feel like it. Or rather, it didn't. Until I saw those guns."

Jackie took in the surroundings and had to agree. In this large, spacious and warm home in the middle of the English countryside it was difficult to imagine that people would be dying on the other side of the world, and the fact that their country could be a part of it made her shudder.

"It's the protest marches that I can't stand," Brian said with some vehemence. "Our boys will be out there, risking their lives, and some fools are organising marches to protest about it."

"Brian, don't get so uptight about it. It was the same when you were serving and it always will be. Anyway, let's not have all this talk of war." May nodded towards Emma with her head and the two men nodded. She didn't look at

Jackie for agreement.

"Sorry," said Philip and Jackie cringed at his good little boy act.

Jackie hated Emma shut out of adult conversations. She thought Emma should be encouraged to take part, to have her say, to think about the events around them. But maybe they were right, maybe it was inappropriate for Emma, perhaps she did need protecting more than Jackie thought. She felt the keen in the back of her throat. The metallic desire for a glass of alcohol, just to knock off the sharp edge of reality.

Over lunch Jackie listened as May, Brian and Philip put the world to rights. Jackie knew May or Brian glanced at her from time to time but she kept her head down to avoid meeting their eyes. She listened to Philip's syrupy voice, hesitant, careful, making sure he said and did the right things. Occasionally being argumentative just to prove they had no real influence over him, but she could see right through it all.

When Brian had offered her a glass of wine Philip jumped in. "No thanks, Dad, Jackie's offered to drive so I can have her share to."

"She can manage one glass."

"We'd rather not," he insisted. "With Emma in the car and all that."

"Very wise, dear," May cut in. "Can't be too careful these days."

Jackie clenched her teeth.

"When we were first married I always drove, didn't I, Brian?" Without waiting for his response she continued. "I didn't drink very much after you were born, Philip, and then after I had James I just quit altogether, didn't I, Brian? It was easier that way. Felt I could attend to my duties as a wife and mother better."

The deep heat of panic rose up in Jackie. Had Philip said something to his parents? No, he wouldn't. He couldn't bear it if they didn't believe this silly charade he put on for them every time they came. No, he wouldn't.

"Brian was always off on manevoures. I was left alone for weeks on end, wasn't I, Brian?"

"I know how you feel," said Jackie, trying to lighten her paranoia and perhaps engender some female solidarity. "It's the same when Philip has a big case. I don't see him for days and even when I do he's distracted."

"It's good to know he works so hard for his family," May smiled indulgently at her son. "James is doing well," she added. James was Philip's brother.

"How's the market doing?" asked Phil.

Brian leaned forward and took a sip of wine. Jackie watched, mesmerised. "When he phoned last week," he said, replacing his glass. Jackie watched the rainbow patterns of alcohol slip down the sides of the glass. "He told us the market was bearish but he's managing to get most of his customers to hold their nerve, as he's pretty confident it'll settle in the next few weeks."

"How's Rachael?"

Rachael was James' wife. A thin woman who wore too much make-up and had far to many edges for Jackie. She was like a stage show all by herself.

"No baby yet," May said.

Jackie was relieved. It was just as well James and Rachael hadn't had offspring. She suspected her daughter would be shoved to one side when it happened and she wanted Emma to be older and more resilient. It was always Rachael this and Rachael that. She shuddered as memories of her childhood loomed up in front of her. Then it was her older sister, Jan. It was Jan this and Jan that. *Always second best*, she thought. And the dark shadow loomed, breathing hard, threatening to engulf her, suffocate her.

She had strived to be like Jan until the day she overheard her mother talking with a neighbour.

"Yer must have been disappointed, Bev," the neighbour said. "At the time like."

"We were, but what can you do?" she heard her mother say. "If yer sent daughters yer sent daughters."

"Still, Jack'll have her own talents."

Her mother sighed. "I'm not convinced. Our Jack's a sullen cow sometimes. Born a disappointment and doesn't look like she's mad keen to make amends."

The two women laughed as Jackie's heart shrank to the size of a dried pea, small and hard. She insisted the family call her Jackie and not Jack after that, adding to their belief that she was difficult.

The memories pushed at her, gnawing and nagging at her defences till she folded.

Jan. Princess Jan. That's what her sister called herself when they were younger, Princess Jan. Jackie couldn't deny Jan was the prettier one. She took after their mother with her blue eyes and curly yellow hair. Everyone said she was at the front of the queue when God dished out the looks. Jackie had inherited her father's colouring, dark eyes and straight dark hair. It turned out to be a blessing in the end but at the time her only consolation was that she was the brains of the family, the first to go to university, to study Law.

Philip shrugged. "I haven't met her yet. Jackie has though. Haven't you?"

"I'm sorry?"

"Our new neighbour. Dad was just asking what she was like," he said.

"I'm glad that house finally sold then, dear. It's not a great selling technique to have the house next to yours empty."

Jackie clutched her knife and fork hard in her hand. *May talked such rot sometimes,* Jackie thought. Their house wasn't even on the market and even if it was, why would an empty house on one side of them lower the price of their own?

"So, what *is* the new neighbour like then?" asked Brian.

All eyes turned to her and she shifted in her seat, aware of Philip's eyes boring into her fiercely, twitching at his napkin.

"Well?" demanded May.

"She's a writer," Emma piped up. "She writes articles for magazines and newspapers and she works from home."

"Really dear?"

Emma nodded. "And it's what I want to do when I get older so Mum invited her for a cup of tea and I met her. Didn't you, Mum?"

May swivelled her head in Jackie's direction and she nodded, smiling at Emma.

"Well, isn't that nice. Coffee anyone?"

Philip took the wheel of the car. He'd no intention of her driving them back and she seethed silently in the passenger seat. He decided to drive past the army base on the way back to see the armed guards. They weren't used to the route and as they drove through the countryside Jackie looked out for signs back to the A1. In World War Two, all the signs had been removed and she wondered how people had managed to find their way round. Still, they were unlikely to have gone ambling round the countryside for a Sunday drive. The petrol rationing would have put paid to that.

"You could have made more of an effort today," Philip's tone was short and snappy.

Jackie's heart sank. *Here we go,* she thought.

"I did."

"It didn't look like it from where I was sitting."

It is so unfair, she thought, her anger rising. "Your mother is not the easiest of people to get on with."

"I thought you'd blame her. What is it you have against her? I didn't see her being anything but pleasant."

"Well you wouldn't, would you?"

"What's that supposed to mean?"

"You're so far up your mother's backside you can't see shit!"

"Christ Jackie do you have to be so vulgar? Emma, ignore your mother."

"I never come up to scratch, do I?"

"Oh that old chestnut."

"Yes that old chestnut. It's always the same, Philip, why can't you see it?"

"Because there's nothing to see. My mother likes things nice, so what?"

"This is ridiculous I can't take this much more."

"Can't take what exactly, Jackie? What's so bleeding awful about your life, eh?"

"I'm lonely Philip," the answer came out as a wail and caught in her throat, hurting it, making it sore.

"And look what happens when I take some time off to be with you? You don't make any effort, Jackie, it's all me, me, me with you."

Jackie looked out of the window, her eyes smarting. Was it her? Was it really always her? It made no sense, none of it. Jackie had even lost track of what they were arguing about. She wanted to understand, she wanted to cry, she wanted to hit Philip, make him drive off the road and kill them all. But most of all she wanted some connection between them, some point of contact, she wanted to end this lonely life she was living. She was about to reach out for his hand but she caught a glimpse of his face all pinched and hard and changed her mind. She became dimly aware of Emma in the back sniffing and her heart sank. It all seemed so utterly hopeless sometimes.

"The President will come out of this well. His profile's already increased and the States needs something after their last election disaster," Liz said to Neil. They were slumped on the sofa next to each other in the front room digesting the huge meal of chicken risotto Liz had cooked that afternoon.

Neil didn't say anything.

"Only hope he doesn't do anything stupid."

"Who?" he asked.

"The president, dimwit."

"So you think the President conspired to have those terrorist attack his own country because he wasn't very popular?"

"Maybe. Who knows. You've seen the film *Wag the Dog*—anything's possible."

"I don't know Liz, I'm not a subscriber to the conspiracy theory stuff myself, it just doesn't make sense to me."

Liz sighed. "No. Maybe you're right."

"I think air strikes are inevitable though."

"Me too."

"Maybe it's for the best," he said

"Puts all the crap I write into perspective."

They sat in contemplative silence for a few minutes until Liz spoke.

"I've met one of my neighbours."

"Oh, what's she like?"

"Nice. She invited me for coffee."

"And?"

"And nothing. That's the whole thing."

"Come on Liz, spill the beans."

Liz pulled her mouth to one side in an expression Neil recognised as her thinking face.

"She seemed sad."

"Why d'you say that?"

"I don't know…it was her eyes."

"Looking into her eyes, eh?"

Liz picked up a cushion and hit him with it. "Oh Neil, grow up will you."

Neil ducked and laughed. "I'm just looking out for your moral welfare," he shouted as he dodged the blow.

"Moral welfare my arse," she said smiling.

"Language!"

Liz sat back. "She was nice, I liked her." From the corner of her eye she saw Neil grinning out. *"As a friend."*

Neil put his arms up in surrender. "Message received and understood."

Later that evening piano music came floating through the wall from next door. It was strained and poignant. Jackie leaned forward and pressed the remote control to mute the volume on the TV so she could hear better.

Philip had left when they got back from his parents. He told her he had some case notes he needed from the office. She glanced at the clock on the mantelpiece. It was ten-thirty and he hadn't managed to find his way home yet. The haunting melody of the music heightened the truth simmering below the surface.

It rose and glared at her. He wasn't working. He couldn't be.

Neither did he work on Friday evenings, or weekends, or any other night he decided he wouldn't come back. She was an idiot. A stupid fool. She had always known it. Always.

She leaned forward and refilled her glass, spilling a little on the glass topped coffee table. It sat in a little red puddle, like thin blood. *Alcohol was supposed to thin the blood*, she thought.

As she leaned back the room began to spin. She had known this second bottle was a mistake. She'd barely eaten anything at tea time. She watched the pictures on the TV. They filled the dark room with blue and grey light. The news had been extended and she watched without seeing. She didn't really want to know. Not on her own. Not today.

She could barely recall a time when she felt less loved. She picked up her glass and washed down the hard self-pity as if she were taking a pill.

Eventually the music reached its natural conclusion and finished. The muted TV sent blue flickering light around the room. The half empty bottle sat on the coffee table in front of her and a peace was finally beginning to settle inside her.

From the semi darkness shapes emerged and then receded. There was the wooden rocker in the bay window that Philip had brought home two weeks before Emma was born. He'd bought it in a junk shop on impulse. There, on top of the TV, stood the bowl they'd haggled for in Turkey on their honeymoon. They'd gone to Rhodes and just popped over to Turkey for the day. She smiled, what a thrill it had been for her, two countries on one holiday. Those were the days when he tried. When they both tried.

She became aware of the miniature Grandfather clock on the mantle piece. A wedding present from Philip's parents. Tick. Tock. Tick. Tock. Filling the silence. It's relentless measuring out of time. That's my life ticking away up there. Going, going, going, Gone. Just like that. She counted up on her fingers. Fourteen years. They had been married fourteen years. And always a clock, somewhere, measuring it out. Slowly slipping away.

Buggar it, she thought, turning on the volume and opening her third bottle of wine.

Chapter 12

It was three weeks before Jackie saw Liz again. They were leaving for school and Jackie was locking the front door when Liz came running up to them.

"Morning," she said, jogging on the spot.

Jackie smiled. "Bit early, isn't it?"

"Got to get out before I wake up."

"Ah, that's your secret, ambush your body when it's unconscious?"

"Something like that. Listen, I'm sorry I haven't been in contact, I've been swamped with deadlines recently and now I'm a proud house owner I need the money, but the mists are beginning to clear. Do you want to get together for coffee later? My place this time."

Jackie shook her head. "I'm sorry I can't, but I'm free tomorrow."

"Sounds good to me," Liz turned to Emma. "So how's my little budding writer then?"

Emma grinned and babbled about her latest project until finally Jackie had to interrupt. "Come on Em, we don't have time now."

"Would you look at stuff for me?" Emma asked over her shoulder as Jackie hustled her down the street.

"Sure," said Liz, raising her arm, "Anytime."

Jackie threw her an apologetic look and Liz added, "No problem at all. See you about eleven tomorrow?"

Jackie nodded and stopped to watch Liz bound off in the opposite direction. She ran like a gazelle, long legs eating up the pavement. Her ponytail bounced off her back, tendrils escaping everywhere, giving her the appearance of medusa.

"Come on, Mum, we'll be late," Emma said, bringing Jackie back.

Later that day Jackie sat sipping her second glass of wine when the phone rang, scattering the silence of the house into the corners.

"Jack, it's Mum."

Despite Jackie's best efforts her mother still insisted on calling her Jack. It reminded her. It tugged at the buried memories. *'Jack came into this world a disappointment...'*

Jackie took a large gulp of wine from her glass. She hadn't spoken to her mother for months and hadn't seen her in over ten years. They had developed this strange communication of brief telephone conversations and occasional letters.

"Are you there?"

"Yes."

"How are you, love?"

"I'm good. You?"

"Good."

The telephone wire hummed with the unspoken.

"Your dad's alright too, you know him...."

Jackie said nothing.

"I phoned to remind you it's Janice's birthday next week."

"I know."

"You're a good girl."

Jackie said nothing. The wine blurred the edges and she couldn't find anything to say.

"How's our Em?"

"She's fine, Mam."

"She must be shooting up? We see Janice's kids all the time."

Jackie heard the accusation but instead of answering she drained her glass.

"What you been up to?"

"Nothing special. You know how it is, a house this size."

"Janice manages."

Yes, but Janice's house is half the size, Jackie thought smugly.

74

"And she's got a part-time job too," her mother added.

"Since when?"

"She works at the school."

"So do I," Jackie shot back.

"This is a proper job, not voluntary. She's a teacher's assistant, I think that's what it's called."

"Not a proper teacher then," Jackie pointed out.

"Well she's got a lot of responsibility. She's very good at it too."

According to who? Jackie thought. "That's nice," she said. She could just picture Jan swaning round telling everyone how marvellous she was.

"How's Philip?"

"Busy."

"He's always busy."

Yes he is, thought Jackie. Her eyes filled with tears and she swallowed another mouthful of wine. "He's in demand. Thank goodness. We wouldn't be able to afford such a big house if he wasn't," she emphasised the word big.

"You must be proud."

"What d'you mean by that?" Jackie asked sharply.

"Nothing, love."

The silence turned into a high pitched whine.

"Anyway, I must be going. Give our love to Em."

What about me? Jackie thought as she slammed down the receiver. *What about me?* She shouldn't be jealous of her own child, or her sister, but sometimes it felt everyone who should love her was spreading their love so thinly, sending in so many other directions, she was being deprived of what was rightfully hers. She slunk back to the kitchen to fill up her glass, a dark shadow behind her and stale breath on her face.

Miles Davies drifted in from the lounge as Nikki removed her towelling robe, stepped into the bath and sank into the hot suds.

She released a loud sigh as the warm water enveloped her body, cocooning it. It had been a tough day at work and Jenny had been more useless than usual.

Her boss had disappeared for the day, uncontactable, and she had been left to politely deflect various callers desperate to speak with him. One call had disturbed her. The undertone of aggression in the man's voice reminiscent of her father's and the power of her femininity evaporated, leaving her quaking as she replaced the receiver.

She couldn't recall his words now, and it didn't matter. It wasn't what was said, it was the way it was said. She shuddered and turned her attention to the trumpet wavering through the air and allowed the gentle piano notes to play up and down her spine, massaging out the knots of tension

Philip would be here in just over an hour and she wanted to be at her best. She needed to stuff back down this small needy part of herself that had emerged today and focus on her campaign.

Things, she decided, were going well. Since their "talk," a few weeks back Philip had been attentive, charming, and excellent in bed. She allowed a long slow smile to spread across her face and then hugged herself with glee.

Once he was made partner he would be free to divorce Jackie. All she had to do was suggest she had a life outside of him. Subtly. He wasn't stupid. She would have to play this carefully. Very carefully.

He was in the palm of her hand and if he won the Douglas case all she would have to do is clench her fist and she'd have him.

If he didn't win the case, then what? She pushed the thought aside as the music came to an end. Her signal to get ready for Philip. She would cross that bridge, when and if.

Chapter 13

Jackie had tried. Really, really tried. She had promised herself just one, maybe two. She'd meant glasses but it had turned into bottles. Again. Once she had one glass something just seemed to take her over, there was a little click in her head and she knew, just knew she wouldn't be able to stop.

The empty evening in front of the television coupled with the realisation of her husband's infidelity had been too much to bear and she had heard the click last night.

She sat at the kitchen table and hung over the coffee Emma had made her, trying to steady her stomach. The ugly yellow of self-disgust lapped at her throat. Emma crunched through her cereal.

"D'you have to eat like that?" Jackie snapped. "You sound like a pig!" She knew she was exaggerating and hated herself for it.

Emma turned her wide eyes towards her. "Like what?" she asked, her mouth full.

The sight of the chewed-up corn flakes in her daughter's mouth made Jackie want to gip. "Close your mouth when you're eating." She was savage this morning and it made her want to weep.

Emma looked down at the bowl and chewed slowly, quietly.

Jackie cringed, her nerves jangled every cell in her body.

"Your dad's working on a big court case," she said in a softer voice.

Emma nodded but didn't look up. Sprinkles of irritation moved through Jackie.

"Looking forward to half term?" she asked brightly.

Emma nodded again.

Jackie sighed. "Come on, Em. I'm sorry. I don't feel well this morning."

Emma raised her eyes and Jackie saw the tears threatening.

"I'm really sorry, I'm just tired. And I feel a bit sick too."

Emma mumbled something.

"What?"

"Doesn't matter," she said.

"No, come on. I didn't hear you."

Emma looked back into her bowl. "I said you're always sick. And tired."

Sick and tired. It did sum things up. Out of the mouths of babes. Jackie burst out laughing.

"What's funny?"

Jackie, still laughing, lent forward and patted her daughter's arm. "You are, sweetie, you really cheer me up sometimes."

Emma smiled.

Philip lay in bed listening to Nikki in the shower. She'd come back in a few minutes and turf him out to make the bed. He smiled. They'd developed a routine, under all this uncertainty was some domestic order and he liked it. It didn't smother him as he'd expected.

Lying there he realised he was still tired. He hadn't slept well last night. The Douglas case lay heavy on him. Jack had hunted out Mr Patel and taken a statement from him but it wasn't enough. The man was nervous and had merely stated that after reconsidering he had decided the price was a fair one after all. Jack had told Philip that after some cajoling Mr Patel had admitted "bully boy" tactics by Murphy's lads but Patel refused to stand up in court and say that. Without that Philip didn't have a case; even then it was flimsy. It infuriated him, how Murphy could push people round like that. Not Peter Douglas. Douglas and Murphy were as bad as one another. But people like Ash Patel, hard working business men who didn't know any different. The little man in the street.

But to help the little man in the street, to get justice Philip needed more. Not much, just a little. Since he'd read Jack's report he'd been trying to see how they could create more, stretch the truth, embellish it perhaps. Not much, just a little.

Then an idea slowly formed in his mind. The list of people on Murphy's books contained a Sean Hunt. Phil remembered a man called Sean Hunt from way back when he was doing his articles. Could it be the same guy? Had to be. He was a bit of a character from the thin memory Philip had of him.

Hunt had been up for some minor offence and Philip had represented him. He'd been guilty as hell but that was how this business worked sometimes. It had been Philip's first case but he never forgot it. It was then he realised criminal law wasn't for him and opted for commercial law instead, better class of client, well, richer anyway. Sean Hunt had said if he ever needed a favour…well, he needed one now. If it was the same guy then Phil could get a statement from him, ask him to stretch the truth a little and maybe, just maybe add a few non-truths.

Phil stopped. He'd never contemplated anything like this before. Creating evidence. It pulled at his chest. Was he doing the right thing? So many things could go wrong. What if the guy refused or didn't turn up or changed his mind halfway through his statement? Or worse, told them in court what Philip had done?

He flipped the possibilities and consequences through his mind but he had gone too far down the road now to turn back. Next week, it was all set. He couldn't pull out now. Besides, Murphy had got away with this type of thing before. Wasn't Philip being given an opportunity to balance the scales of justice?

He tried to push aside the fact that Sean Hunt had been guilty and sighed. Who was he kidding? It was cheating whatever way he looked at it. How had he come to this? When he'd first qualified he'd been so idealistic. He was going to make a difference to people's lives. Nothing in his life was the way he had dreamed it would be. Not home…not work, nothing. The idealism he had left college with had been eroded by targets, office politics and ambition and now he was considering fabricating evidence to win a case!

He'd bent the rules a few times in the past but had always stayed within the law. This was in a different league. He was taking one hell of a risk. If he pulled it off it meant the case was won and job assured, at least for the time being, but if it went wrong, if he got caught it would mean the end of his career. Then what? He'd be reduced to teaching law in the local college. Was it worth it? He thought of his mother's reaction and shrank at the idea.

He was so absorbed by his thoughts he didn't hear Nikki enter the room.

"You okay?" she said.

He jumped at her voice.

"Guilty conscience?"

"What you doing creeping 'round like that?" he barked.

"Fuck you," she said and turned to sit in front of the mirror.

Philip sighed, sat up and rubbed his face. "I'm sorry, I've got a lot on my mind right now."

Nikki turned round to face him. "The case?"

He nodded. "There's a lot riding on it."

"Peter has every confidence in you. He was telling me today he won't settle in arbitration, says you have it in the bag." He heard the pride in her voice.

She stood up and walked to the end of the bed. "You were restless all night," she told him.

"I'm sorry," he said.

She unpinned her hair and smiled at him.

"D'you want me to take your mind off it?"

He grinned at her. "No seconds till I've showered, remember?"

She dropped her towel. Her skin gleamed with the oil she always applied after a shower.

"There are exceptions to every rule," she told him and crawled across the bed towards him.

Thank God for Nikki, he thought as he buried his head into her breasts, searching for her nipples with his mouth, thoughts of the Douglas case receding.

Chapter 14

"Thanks," Jackie said as Liz set one the mugs in front of her. It had been weeks since she had spoken to her mother and she still hadn't phoned back. It was a constant nag. Another one. It was as if she were hanging over a precipice and holding on by her fingertips.

"It's Redbush," Liz said handing Jackie a mug of what looked like very weak tea. "It's much better for you. Has antioxidants, it's very low in tannin and no caffeine, so it doesn't dehydrate the body."

Jackie didn't think it mattered the amount of alcohol she could put away. She sipped it. It wasn't unpleasant she decided, although it didn't really taste like tea.

"It's an acquired taste," Liz told her.

"All settled in then?" Jackie asked.

"Nowhere near. It's a nightmare, really. I don't want to move again. Ever."

Jackie smiled. "I know what you mean."

"How long have you lived round here?"

Jackie looked up to the ceiling, calculating then looked at Liz. "Twelve years."

"Just before the great event then?"

Jackie looked puzzled.

"Emma," Liz explained.

"Oh yes, Emma. Yes, we moved in a few months before I got pregnant."

"D'you like it?"

"I love the house yes, fell in love with it the moment I walked in the door."

"But?"

Jackie shrugged, unable to voice the years of frustration in a single sentence to a stranger.

"Biscuit?" Liz asked.

Jackie smiled. "I'm sorry I just…"

"You don't have to explain. It seems I should apologise. Again."

They laughed, meeting each other's eyes.

"I have a real knack of putting my foot in it. As I said before, I guess it's the journalist in me, ask the question that goes for the jugular. I'm sorry. I don't mean to pry."

"I know," said Jackie. "Actually, it's not you it's me. I'm not sure how to explain how I feel. I suppose because I'm not sure *how* I feel."

Liz nodded. "I was the same when my mother died."

"Oh gosh, when did she…." Jackie stopped.

"Last year. I'm okay now, but at the time I felt so much emotion I didn't know where to start. I think I got to the point of not wanting to say anything for fear of falling apart, you know what I mean?"

Jackie nodded emphatically. She knew exactly what Liz meant.

"I felt like a woolly jumper with a loose thread. I thought that if I pulled at it I'd come to pieces." Liz laughed and shook her head, her curly hair bouncing around her face. "Oh, I don't know. I'm not making myself very clear."

Jackie placed her hand on the other woman's arm. "No," she said. "Please, I know exactly what you mean."

They exchanged a brief glance and Jackie removed her hand quickly, as if she had touched a hot plate. They sat in silence for a few moments before Liz continued.

"Buying this place was supposed to help me move forward, leave my past behind, start a fresh." Liz thought of the boxes of her mother's writing. She still hadn't talked to her father about them.

"Sounds wonderful." Jackie looked at the woman sitting opposite her as she sipped her coffee. She was so beautiful, so sure of herself, so sorted. "I wish I could be more like you," she said. "You seem to have your life under control."

"Control?" Liz laughed. She stopped and leaned forward, her voice lowered. "Life can be a lot of things…like water," she said. "One moment you're floating on a dreamy lake, the next in danger of drowning in a torrid sea. One day it's fluid and buoyant and the next cold and hard as ice. And in some cases," she paused. "It can be as hot and dangerous as steam." Jackie listened to the woman's lilting voice. "It can trickle in unawares, flood over you rapidly or be something you just whip off your clothes and jump into. Unfortunately, most of us spend our lives waiting, treading water." Liz sipped her drink in the silence. She raised her head and looked at Jackie for a long moment and then said, "But what it most definitely is *not*, is something you can control."

Heat rose through Jackie's body to her face. "I don't believe that," she said in panic. "Everything is controllable." *It has to be*, she thought.

Liz put her mug down, her eyes on Jackie. "Sure," she said. "For a while. We can build dams to hold it back, water wheels to harness it, canals to channel it. We have lots of ways to pretend we're in control, but it's pressing against us all the time. It's exhausting too, keeping up vigilance like that, all alone, for years. Someday something will crack. It's inevitable."

"So," said Jackie overly bright. "Tell me your story?"

Liz smiled. "Nothing to tell really. Had a three year on-off relationship. Got pregnant, got married. Lost baby, lost husband."

"I'm sorry."

Liz laughed. "I'm not. He slept around. We were never right for each other." She stopped. "You're wondering why I married him, eh? Think it was stupid?"

"No. No not really." Clare surfaced and receded.

"Well, you'd be right. It was. It's just," she shrugged. "Baby hormones I guess. No one tells you how vulnerable and afraid you'll feel."

Jackie nodded sadly. "I remember them."

"I suppose I panicked."

It surprised Jackie. Liz seemed so strong, so independent. She couldn't imagine anything causing Liz to panic.

"I just felt so vulnerable, you know, so alone."

Jackie said nothing, memories of her own pregnancies flitted across her mind. Baby hormones made you lose your mind.

"Stupid reason for getting married, eh?"

Jackie looked down at her mug. "There are worse reasons," she said quietly.

Liz leaned forward. "Oh?"

Jackie looked at the woman. Such a lovely face, gentle eyes, soft mouth. Jackie was enveloped in a desire to share, to off load, confide. She wanted to reach out and touch this woman, consume her. As she opened her mouth Liz's eyebrows rose and Jackie, aware of some danger she couldn't name, changed her mind and shook her head.

"It doesn't matter."

Liz sat back in her chair. "Do I need to apologise again?"

Jackie smiled. "No."

"Good," she said. "Otherwise I might not feel I could see you again." She leaned forward. "You know, you're really pretty. Why do you wear these awful baggy clothes? You've got a great figure underneath."

"No!"

"Yes, really you have."

Jackie reddened. She hadn't thought about how she looked for years. Maybe Liz was right, maybe she should think about what she wore once in a while. "I've been dying to ask you something," said Jackie, trying to deflect the sttention.

"Oh?"

"That man... who is he?"

"What man?"

"You know, the one who helped you move. I've seen him a few times since."

Liz paused, thinking and then Jackie saw her face change as realisation dawned.

"Oh, you mean Neil."

"Is he your boyfriend?"

Liz's eyebrows shot to the top of her head. "Good grief, no. He's just a friend."

"I thought perhaps he was your toy boy," Jackie teased.

Liz shook her head, her curls sweeping about her head. "Not my type," she leaned forward conspiratorially. "If you know what I mean."

She didn't but nodded anyway.

"So, this is my fresh start. What about you?"

"What about me?"

"Where would you go if you were going to make a fresh start?"

Jackie launched into her dream home in her dream place. The women chatted easily for the rest of the afternoon creating a warm glow around each other. At the end of the afternoon they had established a firm friendship. As Jackie left, her heart soaring, she resolved to stop drinking, for good this time.

Chapter 15

Jackie woke on Sunday morning feeling proud. The previous afternoon she had set her chair in the late autumn sun shining through the French doors in the dining room, put on a CD of flamenco guitar music on and finally, when everything was ready, she opened a bottle of deep red claret and savoured two glasses. And then she had stopped, at two glasses.

After half an hour she was climbing the walls, desperate to finish the bottle but instead of surrendering to the need she brushed her teeth, picked up her coat and walked the ten minutes into town.

As her drinking had increased her appetite had done the opposite and she had lost weight. Liz was right, many of her clothes were loose and baggy and she decided to buy herself something to celebrate the new Jackie.

It was an unusually warm day so late in October and she sauntered from one shop to another, browsing. It had been a long time since she had treated herself and she had no idea what was in fashion. She always wore dark colours, knee length skirts, cardigans, comfortable trousers and jeans. Today, her head light from the sun, the music and the wine, she wanted to turn over a new leaf. Celebrate her new figure, her new resolve, the new Jackie. She wanted something different. She smiled and whistled, her arms swinging. Thoughts of her new friend Liz filling her mind.

She eventually settled on a pair of three-quarter length rust linen trousers with shells decorating the hem. They showed off her figure and she looked like she never thought she'd look again. Slim, young, trim, attractive. Single.

Then, deciding she didn't have anything to match the trousers she bought a pair of deep rust sandals and a sleeveless cotton knit jumper, perfect for the cool evenings.

She wore them out of the shop, catching glimpses of herself in shop windows as she passed. She even found the occasional head turn. Her heart soared.

When she returned home the answer machine was blinking and her body went heavy. She knew who it was.

'Hi it's me. I'm snowed under with work so won't get home today but I'll be back tomorrow, about one? Sorry, can't be helped.'

He was sorry. She erased the tape and ignored the nagging voice and finished the bottle, only the one.

It was an improvement and this morning she hugged herself as she placed the trousers on the table to wash later, a little of their magic lingered, lifting her despite the mild hang over.

When Philip didn't return at one as promised Jackie decided she and Emma should take a walk. She had turned over a new leaf, things were going to be different from now on. She would take regular exercise, eat better and drink only at weekends.

"Emma," she called upstairs. "Put your shoes on, we're going for a walk."

"A what?"

"A walk."

"Why?"

Jackie sighed. "Just do it."

Emma appeared a few minutes later in the kitchen.

"What we going for a walk for?"

"Because it's a beautiful day and we can," Jackie said briskly. "Now, put your coat on."

"I don't want to."

"Well, you're going to so get on with it."

"Lu lent me her Popstars CD and I want to tape it before tomorrow."

"You'll have plenty of time to do that when we get back."

Emma dragged herself back into the hall to find her coat and Jackie followed, smiling broadly.

"Shame we don't have a dog eh?" she said.

"Mum, are you feeling alright?"

"Em, I'm feeling wonderful."

Emma decided her mother was as mad as a fish but said nothing and followed her out of the house.

Phil returned fifteen minutes later. Upon entering the house the stifling energy of his responsibilities clung to him. He hung up his coat, took a deep breath and ventured into the kitchen. It was empty. He started to walk round the house looking in each room. The house *felt* empty but he found it hard to believe.

Jackie was never out, never. Not without checking with him first. Stupid cow checked her every movement with him. He loosened the top button of his shirt as he experienced the dreadful cloying sensation and took a deep breath. Even when she wasn't here it was still hanging in the air, waiting, wanting something from him.

After a few minutes of wandering round the empty house he found himself in the middle of the kitchen feeling a strange mixture of irritation and exhilaration. Normally he made his excuses and retreated to his study but with the whole house empty it was unnecessary. He wasn't sure how to be in the other rooms. He was a stranger.

On the table he noticed a bundle of washing. The washing machine had come to the end of its cycle and he assumed the pile on the table was to go in next. He pulled out the wet washing and pushed the clumped lot into the dryer. Then loaded the washing machine with the clothes from the table and examined the dial unsure what the numbers meant. Why did there have to be so many choices? Surely a wash was a wash? He selected one of the numbers at random and switched it on. What damage would it do? After all, it wasn't rocket science.

He wasn't entirely sure why he did it, maybe it was to stake a claim on the house, a way of saying "this is mine." Maybe it was the shock of being alone. He felt a strange surge of elation when he'd finished, as if he'd conquered something, followed by a feeling of absurdity and he retreated to his study.

Emma and Jackie arrived about an hour later. He could hear them laughing, being swept in by a gust of wind and leaves that rustled around them. They stood outside his den chatting as they removed their coats.

"I don't think he was honking the horn because I was driving slow," said Jackie laughing. "I think it was because I had such a beautiful passenger with me."

Emma laughed. "Murm." Philip smiled. Their daughter was turning into a beautiful young woman. He'd have to keep an eye on her.

"Did that embarrass you? Good. I'm finally getting my own back on all those sleepless nights."

They both laughed. Philip remembered those midnight feeds. Sometimes he'd get up to make Jackie tea while she fed Emma. He was fascinated that his wife could provide everything their baby needed. Fascinated and inept. Making tea was all he could do. Jackie refused to express milk so he never fed Emma was she was small. Instead he made tea and then watched from the doorway until Jackie got cross and told him to stop staring and go back to bed.

"Phew that wind really got up didn't it?"

Emma laughed. "You've got leaves trapped up in your hair."

"You of course," Jackie said with irony in her voice. "Look wonderful."

As he listened, Philip got a pang of how it could have been. Family life. Children. Pets. Complications and entanglements that didn't pull you under but instead made the soul soar. He tasted it, sitting there listening to them. Here he was on the periphery, as he had been when Jackie was feeding her. How had he been excluded? What happened that had pushed him into the edge of family life? Had he always spent long hours away and lost his place here, or had he lost his place and then sought solace in his work? He remembered the washing and leapt to his feet, pleased. He heard them walking down the hall into the kitchen and he followed.

"Hi," he said as he entered.

They both stopped and turned round. It was like walking into a strange bar where everyone stops talking. "I put the washing in," he said, playing his card quickly.

"You did?" asked Jackie, the surprise obvious on her face.

He nodded.

"Well, thank you, that was, well, it was really nice of you. What time did you get home?"

"Not long ago, just after one."

"How's the case going?"

"It's okay."

"Good," she said, still rooted to the spot.

Emma watched this exchange between her parents, glancing first one way and then another, waiting. Nothing happened. The silence between the three of them grew, a hard rock pushing them away from each other. Jackie looked at Emma and back at Philip trying to think of something to say. Emma looked at her father, a man who shared the same house as her. He looked different.

"I'm going to finish my homework," she said and left the two of them together.

Philip was disappointed but didn't know how to make her stay. He turned to Jackie. "How was your weekend?"

"It was good. I went shopping yesterday. I don't know if you'd noticed but I've lost a bit of weight recently. Needed some new clothes."

"Right."

"I'd better empty the washing machine, looks like the cycles finished."

Jackie expected him to turn round and leave but instead he just stood there, watching. She was aware of every movement her body made as she crossed the kitchen, his eyes tracing her every step. What did he want? She stopped by the washing machine and glanced at him, searching his face for some clue. He didn't seem angry or smug, in fact if anything he seemed sad.

"I was surprised you were out when I got home," he said.

Was that it? Was he going to have a go about her not being here for him when he got home from work?

"I'm sorry. It was a spur of the moment thing. It was such a lovely day and I wasn't sure when you'd be coming home and, well...."

He nodded.

She pointed. "The washing."

"Yes," he said and still he stood there.

Jackie bent down and opened the door, still aware of him.

Her heart sank as she removed the clothes from the washing machine and an involuntary cry escaped her lips as she pulled out her new trousers. Her beautiful new trousers. Last night for the first time in months she had not opened a second bottle of wine and she was convinced it had been because of these trousers. These trousers had given her back the lost years. They had been her new beginning. Her new leaf.

"I haven't ruined them, have I?" he asked, stepping forward.

She bit back her anger, the despair, the grief, the loss. He couldn't possibly understand.

"I'm not sure," she said but she made sure the emotion was readable on her face. She wanted him to feel bad without her having to say anything. She wanted to pretend she was protecting him.

"I'm not going to do the washing again if I have."

Stop it! Stop doing the washing! I do the washing. Don't ever do the washing again! she wanted to scream.

She had blindly scrambled forward, feeble steps they were, but she was making them. Alone. These trousers were a sign. And he had stopped her.

She hated him and she hated herself because she couldn't explain. He'd think she was overreacting. He always thought she was overreacting if she cried, or got angry, or showed emotion. He couldn't understand that he'd taken something of the new her away and she had neither the words nor the strength to explain. It was like scrambling out of a dark hole and just as she was nearing the top he had pushed her back down again.

She knew he hadn't done it on purpose, but still, still he had done it and she had a rage inside that frightened her. She felt her mouth pull tight, drawn like a string bag as she said, "It's okay."

But they both knew it wasn't. And in the silence they heard the final binding thread between them snap.

Emma lay in her bedroom listening to music and wondering if this meant her father would be coming on holiday with them next year. A little river of electricity shot through her at the thought and a smile broke on her face.

Chapter 16

Philip was meeting Sean Hunt in North Lodge Park, about ten minutes walk from his office in town. He had arranged to meet him at lunchtime so his absence from the office would not arouse suspicion. He wasn't supposed to be working on this case and he didn't want any questions from anyone. Not now.

Noting he had a few minutes to spare he nipped into Marks and Spencer's to pick up a sandwich for his lunch. He considered buying Nikki a gift but he didn't have time to look round.

As he walked through the subway that linked the town centre with the park he noticed a young man crumbled in a heap begging for change. Philip had heard about these scams and hurried by with his eyes staring directly ahead, conscious with every step of the man's gaze.

The sky was steel grey as a bitter wind hissed through autumn trees. Leaves rose and whirled through the air, piling up against the railings and batting Philip's legs as he dodged the dog shit on the path and sat on the first bench by the gates to wait. Within a few minutes a tall broad man with a large mop of dark hair ambled through the gates and made his way over to the bench.

Philip stood up. "Mr Hunt?" he asked. The boy he had represented years ago when he was an assistant had changed a lot over the years. He was bigger, broader, harder somehow and Philip felt shrunken and small next to him.

The other man nodded and sat down.

Hunt had a blue dot tattoo beneath his left eye and the backs of his hands were tattooed with images of little devils. It was a home job, the indigo lines seeping into one another so they looked smudged. Philip swallowed hard and looked away, wondering again what he was doing.

"Sign of a misspent youth," the man said.

"Sorry?"

"My hands. I saw you looking at them. Sign of a misspent youth. Boredom. We'd get a needle and a bottle of ink and just draw stuff on each other."

"I see." Philip didn't remember these details but then, it had been a short case and a long time ago. Hunt again reminded him why he'd decided against criminal law.

"Funny place to meet a lawyer."

"I like to get some fresh air at lunchtimes."

The man rubbed his big rough hands together.

"Yer must like it fresh," he said.

"I have a few questions to ask you," Philip ventured.

"Shoot."

The response made Philip flinch. He cleared his throat. "Do you have a erm, criminal record?"

"What's that got to do with it?" Hunt's tone was sharp, like the crack of a whip and it made Philip jump.

"I'm sorry," he said quickly. "But if you have a criminal record the prosecution could claim you're an unreliable witness."

"Eh?"

Philip took a breath and tried again. "If you have been in trouble with the police the other side could say you weren't honest, that you were making things up."

The man looked puzzled. "But we are, aren't we?"

Philip was relieved Jack had briefed the man. "Even so, we don't want to give them a reason to believe you are lying." Philip could feel himself break out into a sweat despite the chill in the air.

"Oh right."

"So have you?" Philip circled his neck and shrugged his shoulders as he waited for the reply, trying to release tension.

"Got into trouble when I was a kid, as you know, but I'm clean now. Been clean for years. Got a job at Nissan. Making cars. Drive a smart one meself like an all."

Philip took out a small notepad and pen. "I need to make notes," he said indicating the pad. "What kind of trouble?"

"You know, the usual. Shoplifting, that vandalism you helped me get off wiv. We were just bored kids havin a laugh. Nowt serious like."

The term "usual" worried Philip. He pulled up the corner of his mouth.

"It's cool. I'm clean now."

Philip nodded.

"You seem to understand what I need," he said.

Sean Hunt nodded. "Sure. Yer mate gave me the gist. Nice bloke."

Philip had never considered anyone would describe Jack Woods as a "nice bloke."

"Right," he said, deciding to speed things up. "I've got a few questions to ask and then we'll go through the procedure and see what needs to be…done."

"When do I get me money?"

Philip blanched at the question. What am I doing here with this thug? Putting my reputation on the line, along with my career, my home, my whole fucking life! He swallowed and pushed on.

"After you've testified, in court. We'll go through stuff now and then meet up at my office later. You'll meet my boss then. I want you word perfect by the time you meet him."

"Understood," said the big man.

Half an hour later Philip was whistling his way back to the office with a wad of notes and another date to meet with Sean Hunt. Before he was introduced officially into the case, Philip wanted to be sure of him. With Sean Hunt's testimony he could now disclose and push for full settlement at arbitration and if Murphy refused, all the better. Who knows, with Hunt's testimony they might even persuade Ash Patel to come forward.

As he passed the homeless man in the subway he threw him his unopened sandwich. If he screwed this up that could be him.

Chapter 17

"Listen, I've got to be with Jackie and Emma. It's bonfire night. It's for Emma. Besides, I think Jackie might suspect something. She's been…" he searched for the right word, "strange the last few weeks."

"Maybe she's having an affair too," Nikki said, testing.

He thought of the cold tight touch of her lips when she kissed him. Was it his fault he had Nikki?

"No, not Jackie."

She failed to hear the sad tone in his voice and a warm glow of satisfaction suffused Nikki.

"Anyway, you know I'd rather be with you."

Nikki's smile widened into a grin. "I'll be fine. I always am."

Philip's body tensed. What did she mean by that? "What will you do?" he asked, trying to sound casual.

"I'm not sure. I've a couple of invites to get back to."

"With who?" his voice sounded tense and he cursed himself.

"Oh, just people, you know."

"No, I don't, that's why I'm asking." His voice grew angry now.

"Hey, what's this! Not jealous, are we?"

Philip heard the taunting in her voice and fury rose in his chest. Before he knew what he was doing he grabbed her arms and held them tightly, squeezing his anger into her. "Stop pissing me about, Nikki!" he hissed in her face.

"Philip! Let go of me, you bastard," but her voice wavered and he heard it.

"I won't have you making a fool of me," he shook her. "D'you hear me? Do you?"

"Yes. Now let go."

Nikki twisted away from his grip and moved to the other side of the room, rubbing her arms. "What the hell's got into you?" she asked, her voice steadier now he had released her.

Emotions stormed through him, what was he doing with his life? Nothing seemed to work anymore. Nothing. What was he turning into?

"I can't bear this, Nikki," he said, holding his face in his hands.

"Bear what?"

"You. You seeing other men," he slumped into the armchair.

"You can't bear it? What about me? You have a wife and a family. How d'you think I feel about that?"

"That's different, you know it is."

Nikki came and sat opposite him. "It isn't, Phil," she said in a quiet voice. "It isn't at all."

He looked up at her. "But you always knew?" he said.

"We both always knew."

He nodded. She was slipping from him and he didn't want that. He didn't want his life to be without her. Just work and home. He couldn't bear that.

"What if it was for keeps?" he said without a thought. "What would you say then?"

He saw her face struggling with expression. What was she thinking, what was she thinking for God's sake? With Jackie he could read every nuance, he could write the script, but with Nikki he never knew.

"I don't know, Phil," she said at last.

"What d'you mean you don't know? D'you want to be with me or not?" Anger came back into his voice. What the hell did she want?

"I'm not sure it would work."

He jumped from his seat and knelt beside her, a flicker of hope in his body. She was wavering, he could talk her into it. All thought of the consequences forgotten.

"Sure it would. We're of the same mould, you and me."

"What about Jackie?"

"What about her?"

"She's your wife, Philip!"

"I'd get a divorce."

"And Emma?"

"See her every other weekend or something. Thousands of fathers do it. I'm hardly ever there now, she wouldn't miss me. I'd probably get to see her more than I do now." But inside he wavered. They were already so far apart, could he hold onto Emma?

"What about your career?"

"I'll sort it," maybe it was just what he needed, perhaps Nikki could re-inspire him.

Nikki sat in silence. Philip held his breath.

"Come on Nikki, what d'you say?"

"Are we talking marriage, home, the whole kit and caboodle?"

"Sure. Even kids, if you want them." Kids. Was he mad? What the hell was he doing?

"I need to think about it," she said.

Philip took a deep breath and smiled.

Emma lay stretched out on her bed gazing up at the ceiling, tracing the shape of the painted clouds with her eyes. They looked a bit like sheep without legs, she thought. Since the horrible plane thing in America, Emma had been waiting for something else to happen but it had been weeks now and nothing had. Maybe nothing would. Maybe she could relax.

It was six in the evening and they were waiting for her father to arrive so they could go to the firework display in the town park. Lottie had invited her to go with them but her mother had said no. They had to go as a family. Emma didn't see the point.

Her mother changed when he was around. She went quiet and was different somehow. It wasn't just that she was quiet, it was something else. And then it came to her in a single word. Small! That was it. Her mother seemed smaller when her father was there.

Emma watched her mother fold herself up until she could hardly be seen, could hardly be heard, could hardly breath. Emma hated it, watching her mother's glances, her jerky movements.

She searched the insides of her cheeks with her tongue for pieces she could chew off as her mind drifted to the school day.

Alan Metcalfe had stood behind her in the dinner queue and her heart had thumped so hard she was sure everyone could hear. He was messing about with Warren Douglas and bumped into her. He apologised but she didn't say anything. By the time the dinner ladies filled up the various sections of her plastic tray she had lost her appetite.

She followed Lottie to a table. "Did you see?" Lottie asked her, breathless as they sat down.

"See what?" she asked, knowing exactly what Lottie was talking about.

"Alan Metcalfe! Behind you!"

"No," she lied.

"He was looking at you the whole time."

Emma shot Lottie a scornful glance.

"Honest! Cross my heart," Lottie crossed her chest with her finger.

Emma said nothing.

"I think he fancies you," Lottie said airily.

Emma shook her head. "No he doesn't," she muttered, poking through her lunch.

Lottie shrugged. "Suit yourself," she said and then started relaying a story about a girl called Poppy in year six who'd been given a hundred pounds cash for her birthday.

Emma was half listening as she chanced a glance around the room. She jumped when her eyes met Alan Metcalfe's staring back at her, he grinned and she looked down at her tray and kept them there the rest of lunch. Her insides burnt hot with excitement.

It was still there. Perhaps it was true, maybe he did fancy her. Maybe he'd ask her to be his girlfriend.

This is cool, she thought. *I'm in love.*

Donald handed Liz a brandy.

"Mmm, lovely," she said taking the glass. "It was freezing out there tonight."

Donald sat in his winged armchair by the fire. Before they left he'd banked it up and now it was flickering heartily, sending out waves of heat.

"Met my neighbour for coffee the other week. Nice woman. Jackie she's called."

Donald nodded. "That's good. You need good neighbours."

Liz looked at her father, a look of amusement in her eye.

Donald noticed. "What?" he said.

"Ruth Buchas. She was being very neighbourly this evening," she said. "Did she have a good holiday?"

"Yes, as a matter of fact."

"Still bringing you gifts?"

"She's a very generous woman."

Liz laughed. "You've changed your tune."

She had noticed a change in her father. It was subtle but it was there.

"Elizabeth, there are things we need to talk about."

"What things?"

"You know, the things your mother…dealt with."

"You mean my sexuality?"

"Good grief, Elizabeth, do you have to be so blunt?"

"So what *are* you talking about?"

"Never mind."

"Dad!"

"Elizabeth, don't do this, don't push me like this, I'm doing my best."

Liz knew it was true, he was. The fact that he'd even broached the subject was new, and difficult for him. Assuming that was what he'd been trying to talk to her about.

Her heart softened and she considered asking him again about her mother's writings, but he seemed distracted this evening, bothered by something.

"Is there something you're not telling me?" she asked.

Liz watched her father swirling his brandy round his glass. His face blank.

"Something wrong?" she pressed.

Donald looked up and Liz saw the sadness in his eyes. "When your mother died, Elizabeth," he began softly. "I thought I'd never wake up happy again." He paused and leaned forward to pick up his pipe. He rolled the bowl between his fingers. "In time it's become easier. As each month has passed things have come to fill the gap she left. All except one."

Liz sighed heavily. "I miss her too, Dad," she said softly.

"I know you do, that's not what I'm getting at."

"Dad?"

"Elizabeth, I don't know how to say this, but…."

Liz's heart began to speed up and she sat up in her chair. Her father was behaving oddly, he wasn't making sense, was he ill? Oh let it be anything but that. For all his faults and prejudices he was still her dad.

"What is it, Dad?" Why didn't he just get on and tell her?

"I'm not sure how to tell you this...."

Liz held her breath high in her chest, waiting.

Her father took a deep breath. "I had supper the other night with Ruth Buchas."

She saw her father glance over at her nervously. Relief flooded her body, he wasn't ill.

"Is that all?" she said, almost shouting.

"I wasn't sure how you'd take it."

Liz began to giggle with relief. "You getting married?" she asked.

"Don't be ridiculous. It was supper!"

Liz noted the look of distain on her father's face. "Sorry," she said as she pulled in her laughter and stuffed it down. "Dad it's been well over a year now," she added when she regained her composure.

Donald pulled on his empty pipe, hissing.

"It was just supper," he said, his voice hard.

The evening, Jackie decided as she climbed into bed, had been a disaster, but she felt better now. A few glasses of wine were appropriate sometimes.

As she lay, rocking gently in her sea of alcohol, her emotions numbed, she was able to view the evening dispassionately.

The moment Philip walked in the door Jackie knew something was wrong.

"You okay?" she asked.

He nodded and pushed past her in the hall to hang up his coat without making eye contact.

Her body became tight. "Can I help?"

"No."

"Cup of tea?"

"Leave me alone," Philip snapped.

Jackie's insides shrivelled and frustration clawed at her guts. *Why does he speak to me like this? Because I let him,* she thought.

She took a deep breath and followed him into the kitchen. "Don't speak to me like that Philip. I'm only trying to help." She could hear the lack of power in her voice, the tell tale shake.

Philip filled the kettle with his back to her but she could see his face reflected in the dark window, his mouth was twisted into an ugly shape. She held her breath, waiting. Waiting for the avalanche of insults and anger. He always did, so why would tonight be any different?

It would be different because she wouldn't take it anymore.

Philip turned and plugged in the kettle. Still she waited. Nothing.

She began to relax. She'd made her point, he hadn't retaliated. She'd won, a minor victory, but a victory none the less. She glanced at the clock.

"It's six–thirty," she said.

"I know," his voice sounded heavy, tired.

"We need to leave in about fifteen minutes."

"I know."

Jackie stood waiting. She knew he knew and yet still insisted on telling him. Why did she do that?

"I'll just go and see if Em's ready. Are we taking your car or mine?"

"It doesn't matter."

"No I don't suppose it does."

Philip opened the cupboard door and took out a mug. He waved it at Jackie. "Tea?"

"No thanks."

She watched, hypnotised by his hands as they worked. Closing one door, opening another, taking out the tea caddy, after a few moments he stopped.

She knew his eyes were on her and she looked up into his face. It didn't have the usual sneer, the frown, the tightness round the jaw. He looked relaxed, as if he'd been fighting internally all this time and had finally surrendered.

Jackie smiled. She smiled at the face she'd gone to college with, the young man who had tried to do the right thing. Something lurched inside her, he was as much a victim of their circumstances as she was.

And then it shifted. The focus sharpened again, like a cine camera, pulling back and she was smiling at the closed and angry Philip she now lived with.

"Jackie?" he said, the edge back in his voice.

"Yes?"

"Leave me alone, will you?" he sounded weary. "Let me enjoy my tea in peace."

Later, as she watched the colours spread across the sky, her heart jumping at the noise, his words still hurt. Such innocent words really, and yet, they had hurt more than anything he had ever said and she didn't understand why.

She looked at Emma and Philip standing either side of her. There they were, the two most important people in her life, and yet she stood alone. They looked absorbed in the display while Jackie watched from inside a bubble, removed from everything except the noise crashing into her heart. Isolated in a crowd of hundreds, she fought back the urge to weep.

Now, swaying in the sunshine paradise of her imagination she wondered once again why she stayed? Why not just pack and leave? But before the answer came she was unconscious.

Chapter 18

Jackie scrubbed the kitchen floor tiles hard with the mop, the smell of bleach scalding her nostrils, but still echoes of the previous night roamed through her mind. This time an alcohol-induced sleep had not helped. Nothing would. This morning she hadn't woken from a dreamless sleep with a numbing headache remembering nothing. This time she remembered everything. Everything. The dreams of being pursued, the faces from a distant past and the question.

The question echoed through her head. Meeting Liz had stirred something inside her. She had feelings when she was with Liz, she reminded Jackie of Clare. An idea surfaced but before it was fully formed she recoiled from it like a crisp packet on an open fire.

Memories of Clare loomed, like grey clouds, bumping onto each other. She remembered her first meeting with Clare so vividly. Every detail.

She'd been waiting with the other students outside the great hall to take the first paper of their finals. She'd put in late nights, early mornings, reading until the words swam in front of her but her mind always wandered back to the clinic.

And now, as she stood waiting, she knew she was on the brink of failure and panic rose in waves, moving through her with such force she began to feel light headed. Philip spoke to her and sounded as if he were talking through water. Her body swayed and her vision began to close down until it was dark.

She woke up with a headache laying on a couch in a room she didn't recognise. A large office dominated by a wooden desk with walls covered in either shelves of books or framed photographs and certificates. There was a profusion of green leafy plants by a long Georgian window.

She became aware of voices behind her but she couldn't decipher what they were saying. She tried to sit up but her head began to spin so she lay back down, aware of a throbbing in her temples. The voices ceased and the door closed. At first she thought she was alone until a woman came creeping around the sofa. She looked down at Jackie and seeing she was awake relaxed and smiled.

"So, you're awake."

The woman had an oval face, strong cheekbones and short black hair trimmed into the nape of her neck. The severe look was softened by a pair of bovine eyes. She was much older than Jackie, perhaps in her thirties. Probably the age Jackie was now.

"How you feeling?" she asked.

Jackie attempted a smile. "I've been better," she said weakly.

"I'm sure. Want some tea?" The woman gestured to her desk where a teapot and cups stood on a tray.

"I think so," said Jackie attempting to move.

The woman put out her hand, "Please don't move, you had a nasty fall, best stay where you are for a while."

Jackie lay back. "What happened?"

"You fainted. Probably the worry of the exams."

Jackie said nothing.

"How do you take your tea?"

"White, no sugar, thanks."

The woman brought over a cup and saucer. "Now try to sit up but take it slowly."

"I feel a bit groggy," Jackie said as she sat up.

The woman laughed. "Well, apparently you did come a cropper. Hit your head quite hard, so I understand."

Jackie took the cup and saucer from the woman's hand.

"I'm Clare by the way, writer-in-residence."

"What's that?"

"I'm paid to be here for other writers in the area, or aspiring writers, help them out, and I get time to work on my latest book." She smiled broadly. "To tell you the truth it's like having a paid holiday. Not well paid but I'm really enjoying it, shame it's only for a year."

"When's your year up?"

She poured herself tea and took a seat opposite Jackie. "September," she said. "I started last year in the school term—that's when the university thought would be best. Only a few months to go."

"Then what?"

"Not sure really. I have a house in the Dales so I could go back there but I've really enjoyed having all these people around. Very distracting, so I haven't worked as much as I had hoped but hey, life's too short, don't you think?"

Jackie looked at Clare closely. She did have something of the artist's flair about her, that ability to twist a scarf around your neck and look chic, or create seventeen different styles with a wrap and a hairpin.

Jackie took a sip of her tea. It was warm and nurturing.

"I'm afraid you missed your exam," said Clare sipping her tea.

"It doesn't matter, I'd have failed anyhow."

Jackie's eyes filled with tears. Clare said nothing and Jackie was grateful. She didn't want sympathy; she didn't deserve it.

"I couldn't study," she mumbled after a while. "I tried but I just couldn't make it sink in. I've had…other things on my mind."

Clare nodded. "Want to talk about it?" she asked. Clare's thin dark eyebrows arched at the question. "A trouble shared and all that."

Jackie thought for a moment.

"It's a long story," she said.

"That's okay, I can get more tea if we need it."

Jackie shook her head.

Clare sat back and crossed her legs. "Okay, lets talk of cabbages and kings," she said and Jackie started to laugh.

They wiled away the afternoon drinking tea and talking, the first of many. It was the beginning of one of the most important friendships of Jackie's life. *Until I spoilt it all,* she thought.

Jackie brought herself back to her kitchen and scrubbed the floor with a shudder. Another writer in her life. Was this an omen? *I'm not gay*, she told herself. *I couldn't possibly be. I don't look gay. I don't feel gay.*

She shook her head as if to shake away the past. She didn't want to follow this train of thought, what good would it do? In a few weeks it would be Christmas. All this reflection was bad for her, made her feel morose, unsettled. And darker shadows loomed. Memories clamoured for her attention, knocked at her consciousness. But she couldn't open the door. It was jammed shut tight.

Whenever she allowed herself to sink into herself like this she always resurfaced with a restless, uneasy feeling in the pit of her stomach with no reason for it.

She picked up the bucket to empty down the drain outside, pushing down the thoughts and memories, fighting with the familiar urge to reach for a drink.

Chapter 19

Jackie pulled off a piece of sellotape and placed it precisely along the spine of a book. Today Abby and Jackie had been asked to repair the reading books and they were sat in the library with what appeared to the contents of the whole school looming like a mountain between them.

They'd be lucky to get through them all today. Jackie was contemplating whether to offer to come in again this week. She knew Mrs Rayburn, the Head, would snap up her offer and besides, it was the one place where the need for a drink didn't haunt her quite so much. It was almost as if she belonged. Or perhaps it was just that she was useful.

Abby interrupted her train of thought.

"So, what's she like then?"

Jackie looked up. "Who?"

"Your neighbour."

They hadn't been assigned a task together since mounting the pictures and when Jackie had gone to collect Emma from Abby's house Abby had been too busy to sit and chat.

"Oh, Liz? She's okay."

"Found out the mystery of the large house?"

"No. Well, sort of. There's no real mystery. She said it was a new start."

"From what?"

Jackie was reluctant to talk to Abby about Liz.

"I'm not sure."

Abby reached for another book from the pile. "Didn't you ask?"

"It was...awkward."

"Why?"

Jackie shrugged. "Don't know. I just felt uncomfortable asking her stuff when I've only just met her."

"What's she like?"

"Nice. Really nice. I like her."

"She live alone then?"

Jackie nodded. "She works from home so I guess she needs a room to work. And she plays the piano. That's the main reason for such a big house. She's got a grand."

"A grand what?"

"Piano."

"Oh."

"She's good. I hear her through the walls sometimes."

The two women worked in silence.

"How's things with you and Phil?"

"The same." Jackie stopped, sellotape mid air. "That's not true. They're worse."

"Really?"

Jackie nodded. "He's much more distant. I know he's got a big case coming up. In January, I think, but there's something else."

"What?"

"I think," she paused. "I think he might be having an affair."

"You sure?"

"No. Not sure but, oh I don't know, Abby, maybe it's me. I just seem to aggravate him. I don't mean to but ...."

"Are you going to talk to him about it?"

"Maybe."

As she walked home with Emma later that day she wondered why she had said anything to Abby. Saying it out loud like that had made it true and now she considered her options.

If she confronted him he would do one of two things. Deny it or admit it. Either way, what could she do?

If he denied it, it would simply cause a scene and if he admitted it, what then? It would turn her life upside down. Decisions would have to be made. And then there was Emma. In September she would be changing schools. How would she cope with upheaval at home too?

"Mum look!"

Jackie followed Emma's pointed finger and saw Liz stood on their doorstep and the weight of her thoughts lifted.

"Hi! Thought I'd pop round for a cuppa. If you're not busy."

"No. No it's great to see you. Come in."

Jackie went into the kitchen to put the kettle on.

"What are you working on at the moment?" she heard Emma ask Liz as they entered the kitchen.

"Unfortunately nothing ground breaking."

"I'm working on a short story at the moment."

"Good for you."

"Yea, there's this competition I thought I might enter."

"Go for it!"

"Would you read it when it's finished, tell me what you think?" Emma sounded shy.

"Delighted and honoured."

"Great! Well, I think I'll go up to my room and work on it," Emma said as she grabbed an apple and left.

"She loves working with words," Jackie told Liz as she placed two mugs of tea on the table.

"Words are so sensual," said Liz

"Oh?"

"Yes, take the word sixty-nine. When you look at it you see the shape of bodies."

Jackie paused, taken aback by the other woman's candidness but pushed on regardless. "Ah, but that's when it's numerical, not when it's written. A written sixty-nine doesn't have the same shape as a numerical 69," she pointed out.

Liz jumped up and started to stride round the room, her long legs gulping up the ground beneath her. "But that's the whole point. Don't you see? The moment you read a word, any word, you translate it into a mental picture you can view."

"Maybe," said Jackie slowly.

"Every time. Really, try it. If I say pink elephant you don't see the words in your mind, you see a pink elephant. If I say I'm going to post a letter you see the event taking place, not the words. Yes?"

Jackie had never thought about this before.

"And so logically," Liz continued. "It must follow when you read the word sixty-nine you'll transpose it into a mental picture of the bodies in the numerical

69 shape."

Jackie enjoyed the warmth spreading through her body as she listened to her friend speak.

"Listen," Liz said sitting back at the table. "I was wondering if you'd like to go to the theatre. A writer friend of mine has a play on at the local arts centre."

"I'd love to. When?"

"Two weeks."

"I'd love to if I can get someone to sit Emma."

"Can't Philip do it?"

Jackie paused. How could she explain? "Maybe. He's got a big case coming up so...." God how many times had she heard herself say those words!

"Work above everything, eh?"

"Something like that."

The two women sat sipping their tea.

"I'll see what I can do. She might be able to stay over at a friend's."

"Okay. Let me know. I might buy the tickets anyway. My way of supporting the arts and all that."

"I'd really love to go." *And I will*, she promised herself. *I will.*

Philip felt Jeremy Walford's presence at his office door before he saw him and his throat tightened. *Does he know?* he wondered.

"So how's it going, Phil?"

Jeremy Walford stood with his hands in his pockets over Philip's desk.

"Jeremy! Good to see you," he hated Jeremy's smug face.

"How's the Douglas case?"

"It's coming along. Coming along."

"You on top of it?"

"Definitely am."

Philip's hands shook and he put them under the desk out of sight.

"Easy to see why Douglas' passed it our way, eh?"

"It's a tough one," Philip's jaw tightened round his smile.

"Need to bat it out there to get it back, eh?" he clicked his tongue and imitated a cricketer.

God he was a prick, Philip thought.

He had finally come clean at work. The partners had not been pleased initially until they heard what a strong case he had and how he'd negotiated their fee. Now he was the golden boy, or nearly. Much to the annoyance of Walford, he was sure.

"You know how important it is we win this one?"

He means *I*.

"I know. What can I say, it's in the bag."

"Good man," Jeremy said banging Philip on the back. "You're the best we've got."

Philip smiled weakly. *Pompous arse*, he thought.

"I think it's fair to say that there's always room at the top here for a good family man," he clicked his tongue again. "Need I say more?"

Philip felt like an imbecile nodding and smiling as his boss strutted out of the door.

He knew what Jeremy was saying. The facts spoke for themselves. It had been a gamble, still was because everything hinged on Sean Hunt's testimony. To be sure he'd get Nikki to type up a couple of letters on Douglas headed note paper and slip them in where paperwork was missing. Letters countering Murphy's offer, that sort of thing. Of course Murphy would say he hadn't received them, because he hadn't, but what did that matter? In for a penny...

His hands were shaking and he took a deep breath in an effort to abate it. He toiled over the same questions again. When had it started to fall apart? When had he lost it?

Last month he'd lost the Jennings case because he hadn't prepared properly. And he'd been tired. He had been too engrossed in Nikki. This time, this time he had to win. Had to. He rubbed his hands over his face, his shoulders ached, and his head was beginning to thump.

"I can do this," he whispered to himself but the words sounded hollow and Jeremy's words echoed through his brain, the irony hitting him hard.

"Good family man. Good family man."

It was Friday, their night, and Nikki had been through her usual preparation. She was now smooth, perfumed and primped. Tonight was not just any night. Tonight she would give him her answer. She'd kept him waiting long enough.

She applied her lipstick, smacked her lips together and leaned back to survey the effects in the mirror. Perfect.

Nikki strolled through her neat flat, surveying it in its entirety, checking everything was in place. They were eating in tonight. A supper of Beef Bourgoine simmered in the oven. The table was laid. The silver and crystal sparkled in the candlelight. The cushions on the sofa were plumped. Everything was ready.

Tonight everything had to be perfect. Tonight she would say yes.

Neil returned from the bar and put the drinks on the table.

"Blimey it's busy in here," he said as he fell into his seat.

Liz pulled a face. "It's Friday, what d'you expect?"

"I prefer it when we come during the week."

"When it's dead, you mean."

"When you can get to the bar and the loo without it being a major obstacle course."

Liz laughed. "You sound old!"

Neil grimaced and Liz laughed again.

"So, how's your new neighbour?"

"Jackie? She's great. We're going to the theatre next week."

Neil raised his eyebrows. "A date now?"

"Sort of."

"Does she know?"

"It's not that sort of date."

"Be careful," he said gently.

"I like her Neil, I really like her."

"Am I missing something here or did you say she was married, with a kid?" He emphasised the last word.

"So was I. Once. It doesn't mean anything."

"Maybe not to you, but for her it could mean you're barking up the wrong tree."

"She's not happy, Neil. I know it."

"Sweetie, thousands of women are not happy in their marriages. Doesn't mean they're gay."

"I know, I know but...."

"Look, I don't want to rain on your parade. I just don't want to see you getting hurt."

"I know what I'm doing."

"Just so long as you do. Like I said, be careful."

"So, how was your day?" Nikki asked gently as she passed Philip his drink.

"Shite. As a matter of fact, there's something you can help me with."

"Oh?"

"Yea, it's for the case. I need you to type up a couple of letters for me, just to strengthen the case."

"Is it illegal?"

"Only a bit and I promise I won't tell anyone if you don't."

She smiled. "You're a sly old fox."

"All part of the game, my sweet," he smiled back. "So you'll do it?"

"Course, no problem. Just tell me what you want me to say."

"Cheers," he said, raising his glass. "And how about you?" he asked when he finished drinking. "What was your day like?"

Nikki sat beside him on the sofa and folded her legs beneath her.

"Good."

"You always say that."

"That's because it's always good," she lied.

Philip looked at her and his body started to loosen. She was a breath of fresh air. He laid a hand on her knee. "I love being here."

"I'm glad." She paused. "I've been thinking. About what we talked about a few weeks back."

Philip's body stiffened. *Good family man.*

"I've appreciated you backing off and giving me time to think. I needed to. You see, it's not just you who'll have to make changes. I will too. It's not easy. I–"

"I know," he said, before she could continue. "I've been thinking too. You're right. I was talking to Jeremy Walford today. I think the promotion's in the bag, but," he paused. "There's a hitch."

"Oh?"

"Yea. Seems there's a place at the top after all," he paused to take a swig of his drink. The whiskey warmed his chest. "For a family man."

He waited.

"I see," she said.

She seemed so relaxed and composed. Had she been on the verge of saying no? Had he been wrong about them? His jaw clenched. Was he losing her? Would she wait? Had he been right to ask her to help him? Had he disillusioned her?

He regretted his previous outburst but what could he do. She teased him with this talk of her distractions. He needed her and he'd do anything, say anything, to hang onto her.

"No, you don't see. I need this promotion, Nik. It's what I've been working for all my life." He shrugged. "Since I can remember."

"I understand."

"Do you?"

"Yes."

"I still want you."

"Good."

"It's just...."

"It's just not yet."

"No. It's not like that. I just need a little more time."

"And then?"

"Well, once I've got the promotion nothing can stop us. Providing, well, provided you'll have me."

Nikki threw back her head and laughed.

"What?" Philip felt angry. Was she laughing at him?

"Oh Philip, you're so funny."

"What's so funny?"

"We're so alike, you and I. I was going to say the same thing. Why rock the boat when you're so close."

"Really?"

"There's plenty of time."

"Yes!"

"And besides, I have my other... distractions."

Philip went cold all over. "What other distractions?"

"Friends."

"Men?"

She leaned over and kissed him softly. "None of your business," she said. "I've got to go and look at dinner."

He watched her move across the room. He wanted her, wanted her so much. Was he making a mistake making her wait? It was only temporary, just till the case was over and he had his promotion. It was only a few months.

Once he had his promotion he could start making changes in his life, he'd tell her everything; about Sean Hunt, the letters, everything. The truth, the whole truth and nothing but the truth. He shook his head. In his life the truth was as rare as rocking horse shit.

Nikki reached the kitchen and clung onto the sink, taking gulps of breath. Thwarted by a fucking job! She slowed her breathing down. She couldn't let him, refused to let him see her pain, her disappointment. How long before his promotion? How could she be sure he'd leave his wife? How could she bear to go on like this?

The answer was simple. She had to.

Chapter 20

Jackie was folding laundry from the dryer when she heard Philip's key in the door. She swallowed hard, running the rehearsed speech about the theatre trip through her mind. It would depend on his mood, but if he were receptive then she was ready.

One look at the deep lines across his forehead told her he wasn't. She smoothed out Emma's pink cotton sweater and placed it in the laundry basket. Ironing. It seemed never ending. How did women who work manage?

"Steve and Bridget phoned today," she said

"Who?" Philip was flicking through his post.

"You remember. Steve and Bridget? From college?"

"Oh right. What did they want?"

"I didn't speak to them, they left a message. For you. Wanted you to call them back."

"Right."

"Will you?"

"What?"

Jackie sighed as she pulled out Emma's rhinestone jeans. She'd left them in the dryer too long and they'd be hell to iron now. "Phone them," she said as she laid out the jeans on the kitchen table trying to smooth them out.

"Yea. I'll go do it now."

Jackie watched Philip retreat to the hall and pick up the phone. How long had they had this distance between them? Was the distance caused by his affair or vice versa? Affair. Listen to her! She was talking as if she knew for a fact Philip was having an affair. For all she knew she was creating something that didn't exist. She had once read in a woman's magazine that when a woman suspected her husband of having an affair she was usually correct. She heard Philip's laugh from the hallway and slammed the door of the dryer with more force than necessary.

When he returned to the kitchen he looked pleased.

"Good news?" she asked cautiously.

Philip nodded. "Bridget and Steve are coming to dinner."

Irritation scratched at her. Typical of him to make arrangements without asking her. "When?" she asked.

"Next week. It'll be good to see them again, won't it? Catch up on the news and reminisce about old times."

The last year of college roared up inside Jackie, creating nausea. *Why would I want to reminisce about that?* she thought.

"Tea?" she asked.

"I'll make it," he said, smiling. He looked genuinely happy for once and Jackie was sorry she couldn't share it. She dreaded seeing old friends from college. She'd had so much promise back then. She had been a shinning star, had been expected to do so much...*Now look at me*, she thought.

She forced herself to smile and decided to take advantage of his change of mood.

She coughed. "I have a favour to ask of you," she said.

"Mmmm?" he said as began opening his post.

"Our new neighbour, Liz, has asked me if I'd like to go to the theatre in a couple of weeks time and I wondered if you'd look after Emma for me."

"What, you, go out?"

"Yes." His surprise reminded her how long it had been since she had been out in the evening.

"What night?"

She pulled her mouth to one side. "It's a Friday."

She saw Philip falter.

"Look I know you usually work late on Fridays, but I thought maybe, just this once, you'd make an exception. Or get your secretary to come here and work?"

Philip put down the letter he was reading to look at her. "Jackie, this case—"

"I know, I know, I just thought...couldn't you could work from home? Just this once. Would it be so difficult?" Her voice had the pleading quality she hated but she noticed a little shift in his stance. He was thinking about it.

116

"Okay," he said.

Jackie threw her arms around his neck and hugged him.

The following week when Bridget and Steve came to dinner the tensions between Jackie and Philip had returned.

Bridget and Steve were passing through on their way from London to Edinburgh. Steve looked the same. A great lanky thin thing with a hooked nose and rugged complexion. But Bridget had changed a lot. She'd lost weight and her greasy hair was now a shining block of thick chestnut that swung when she talked. Steve was a consultant at Guys hospital and Bridget ran her own PR company, which, according to her, was incredibly successful and might even "float" next year.

I could have done that, thought Jackie. *Couldn't I? I was an ace student at college right up to the last year. Right up until...* She pushed it aside. It had no place today. She had Emma. It was irrelevant. It was ancient history.

All through dinner Jackie sensed him watching, waiting for her to make a mistake. For once couldn't he just give a small compliment, a gesture, something, anything? Her breath became shallow from his scrutiny.

Am I paranoid? Is this a sign I'm losing my way? Am I falling apart or emerging? Weren't the two things one in the same? Surely in order to emerge you had to fall apart. When she was revamping a room she stripped it down first. *That's me, a stripped room. Bare. Exposed. Is this hypersensitivity, clarity or am I quietly going mad?*

After dinner they sat round the table chatting aimlessly. A lot of wine was consumed and Jackie was feeling relaxed, unaware of Philip for once.

"D'you remember Stuart Peacock?" Steven asked.

Bridget nodded. "He walked like Frankenstein."

Jackie giggled. "Not like Jennifer Wright. D'you remember her?"

"Oh God yes," said Bridget, snorting red wine out of her nose and Jackie warmed to her.

"She sashayed," Jackie said, laughing as held her arms above her head and swayed her body from side to side in her seat.

"Sashayed!" Philip shouted.

Jackie looked at him and saw the scorn building, he was ready, his lip raised in a sneer, his brow creased.

"Is there such a word?" he asked, raising his eyebrows.

Jackie stuck out her chin in defiance. "Yes," she said. "There is."

He turned to the others, unphased by her response, "Is there?"

Bridget copied the motion of Jackie's and repeated the word. She sounded sexy and looked, to Jackie, fantastic. She was unmoored and proud. She breathed fully.

It's because she doesn't have children, Jackie thought, *she wouldn't look so fantastic then, silly fool.*

She watched as Philip threw back his head and laughed. His eyes sparkled and she recognised a playful glint as he looked at Bridget. *Did he ever look at me like that?* The question pulled tight on her chest making her catch her breath. *It doesn't matter, I don't care, not really. I'm not going to care.*

She pulled herself tighter still, pulled her heart right in until it was a small compact bundle in her chest, like a car that's gone through the crusher. Hard, compact, solid. No-one was going to get in. She allowed her breath to come again, she was safe now. She was numb.

Jackie, her head swimming, was pulled back into the room.

"You must come and stay at our place," Bridget said to Philip. She glanced towards Jackie. "Both of you," she added as if the original invitation hadn't included her.

Jackie's face smiled. Her response as genuine as the invitation. "That would be lovely," she said.

"Seriously," added Steve. "We'd love to have you both."

"Los dos," giggled Bridget.

Jackie was puzzled until Steve said, somewhat wearily, "Bridge is learning Spanish."

Jackie nodded.

"So how about it?" Steve grinned, showing a discoloured tooth on his right side.

"Well, the problem is Steve," Jackie told him. "We're not two, we're three."

Now Steve looked confused.

"She's talking about our daughter," Philip explained. "Emma, but she won't be a problem," he waved a dismissal and an impotent pot of red hot rage came bubbling up through Jackie. *Bloody typical*, she thought.

"We can always get her minded."

What he means is I will. I'll run around begging and pleading to get someone decent to take care of her whilst he swans around being the

118

wonderful father, solicitor, bread winner, son, husband, lad about town shag factory shit head. He'll be everything to all people by delegating to me. God, he's a real arsehole. She giggled out loud. Philip shot her a familiar warning look and the others looked at her.

"Sorry," she said and smiled as she refilled her glass and hiccupped. "We won't be coming to *your place*. But thanks for the invite." She raised her glass. "Cheers!"

Chapter 21

Jackie was dressed and ready to leave. She wore an old dress she used to wear when she and Phil entertained. A simple two strapped black dress that stopped just above her well-shaped knees. The stiletto heels were dated but she preferred them to the more fashionable cubed heels today because she enjoyed the tip-tap-tip-tap sound they made when she walked. She piled her hair on top of her head and wore long slim gold drops in her ears. Her make-up had been applied subtly and with care. She thought she looked very much like the old Jackie before… she decided not to finish the thought.

She was thrilled about the evening and wondered whether it was the theatre or Liz. The idea frightened and excited her.

She walked downstairs and put on her coat, as she was collecting her lipstick and keys into a small black dress bag Emma came out of the living room.

"Mum!"

Jackie spun round. "What? What's the matter?"

"You! You look beautiful!"

Jackie smiled. "Thank you." She blushed at the unexpected compliment.

"Dad! Come and look at Mum," Emma shouted.

"No Emma please…" but it was too late. Philip appeared in the hallway before Jackie could say or do anything.

"Look at Mum, isn't she beautiful?"

Philip's eyes roamed over her and she held her breath.

"She scrubs up well, eh, our Em?"

Jackie smiled. Philip appeared in cheerful mood considering he was babysitting.

"Thanks," she said. "I won't be late."

As she pulled the door close behind her she reflected on how different she felt tonight. Sexy. She felt a flutter of anticipation. She couldn't pin it down, it was too elusive a feeling, like a butterfly flitting about inside her making her feel like a child on Christmas Eve.

"I have a work colleague coming this evening," Philip told Emma as he handed her the clean plates from the dishwasher.

"Who?" she asked, sensing a new nervousness about her father.

"A lady called Nikki."

"Okay."

"Thought you'd like to meet her."

"Why?"

Why indeed, thought Philip. What was he thinking? "I just thought you might. Do you want to?"

"Alright."

Her response irritated him. He had made an effort and she behaved as if it meant nothing. He had hoped for more…enthusiasm.

"She'll be here in about half an hour."

"Okay. Is that everything from the dishwasher?"

Philip nodded.

"Okay. I'll come down when she gets here, shall I?"

"Don't fancy watching some TV with your dad?"

"I've got homework."

"Course you have. Go on then, sooner you get started the sooner you'll have it finished. I'll call you when Nikki gets here."

He watched with disappointment as she disappeared from the kitchen, taking his heart with her. It wouldn't be as easy as he thought. None of it.

Emma closed her bedroom door and sighed. What was wrong with her father? He'd been edgy and fussy over dinner, smiling too much and the last couple of weeks he'd tried to strike up conversations with her. Who was this woman he wanted her to meet? She hated the way he was behaving. It made her feel weird. And she didn't want to meet this woman. She would say or do the wrong thing and look stupid. She knew it. He had never wanted her to express an interest in his working life or the people in it before. Why now? Mum going to the theatre, Dad bringing work friends home. Maybe this was normal family life, maybe they were finally becoming a family. Maybe.

She sat down at her desk. Mrs Fishfart had given them a ton of math homework to do and it was such a pain. She hated Fishfart. She was always shouting and she never ever gave you a chance to explain anything. Emma's mind drifted to Andrew. He'd bumped into her three times this week. She smiled and opened her math book with a sigh. When her father called her the homework remained undone but her pencil case was decorated with hearts.

In the interval the two women sat at one of the pine circular tables in the foyer enjoying a glass of white wine. They agreed the play was wonderful and well written and Liz had offered to introduce Jackie to the writer at the end of the evening.

"You look gorgeous tonight, Jackie," Liz said.

Jackie smoothed out her dress. "Thanks. It's really old but you know what they say about a classic."

They caught each other's eyes and smiled. Jackie was the first to look away.

"You know," Jackie said, once the moment had passed, "I love your hair."

"Thanks. Fortunately curly hair's in. Hasn't always. Back when I was a teenager it was all Farah Fawcett Major."

"Oh god! I remember that. I had huge flicked out waves held board rigid with a can of hairspray."

"You were lucky. I was Cleo Lane! Not very cool."

Bubbles of happiness fizzed through Jackie's body and she began to giggle. Liz joined in and the two women shrieked with laughter drawing attention to themselves. When the bell signalled the start of the second Act they linked arms and walked back into the auditorium, the wine unfinished on the table.

Nikki was taken aback by the beauty of the lounge Philip led her into. It was a sumptuous room decorated in deep reds and dark greens that gave the feeling you had gone back in time and walked into a Georgian drawing room.

She walked over to the mantelpiece and studied the photo of her rival. A fresh face dotted with freckles looked back at her—Jackie. She could see why Philip had been attracted to her back then. She had button brown eyes, a rich generous mouth and a warm smile. The woman Peter Douglas had introduced Nikki to at the charity ball last year was a shadow of her former self.

"Here we are," Phil announced as he entered the room.

Nikki turned round to find herself confronted not with the small child she had expected, but a young girl on the cusp of womanhood. A beautiful one at that. Nikki noticed with envy her smooth unlined skin. She had the same chocolate eyes of her mother, a large sensual mouth and thick dark hair.

"Hi," said Nikki with a smile.

"Hello," the girl replied.

"I'm a friend of your father's. My name's Nikki."

"This is Emma," said Philip, fussing at her collar. They both looked at him. "Well, I'll go and get something to drink. Em, you want a Coke?"

"Mum doesn't let me have Coke this late at night."

"Well, what she doesn't know won't hurt her, eh? Just a bit of a treat to celebrate, no harm in that."

Emma smiled and nodded, though she felt sure there was harm, somewhere.

When Philip left she turned to Nikki. "Who are you?" There was a polite tone in her voice.

"I'm a friend of your dad's."

"How do you know him?"

"Work," Nikki lied.

Emma sat down on the sofa and left Nikki standing by the mantelpiece. She could see the child's eyes flicking round the room, taking it all in, working it all out.

"What are we supposed to be celebrating?" she asked.

Nikki hesitated. What do you say to children, half children, like Emma, almost grown? Would she guess?

"How old are you?" she said, deciding to avoid the question.

"Eleven."

"Boyfriends?" She held her breath, regretting the question. It might put ideas into Emma's head about her and Phil.

"No."

"D'you like school?"

"It's alright."

God, where was Philip with the drinks? This was like extracting teeth.

"What's your favourite subject?"

"Creative writing."

"How wonderful! I'm in PR, so we use a lot of that."

"I want to be a writer when I'm older."

"Really, how lovely! I do quite a bit with the company I work for, you know, press releases, brochures, that kind of thing." Nikki's mind went blank.

"I want to be a proper writer."

"Yes. Hard business though."

"If it's worth having, it's worth working for."

"It's good you know your own mind."

"I like observing people," Emma told her, and suddenly Nikki felt exposed and crossed the room to sit in the armchair. "It's vital for a writer," Emma continued.

"Yes, I suppose it is," Nikki said, tugging at her skirt.

"Here we are!" Phil boomed, pushing the door open and entering with a tray. The glasses tinkled as he carried it across the room and put it on the coffee table.

"Coke for Emma," he passed her a tall tumbler full of the brown bubbly liquid and poured wine for himself and Nikki. He raised his glass, "Here's to us," he said.

Nikki threw him a glance and they both looked at Emma sitting on the sofa. "To friends!" he added.

They drank in silence for a few moments. "So have you two been getting to know each other?" he asked.

"Yes, Emma's been telling me how she'd like to be a writer when she gets older."

"Really!"

It occurred to Nikki that this was as much news to him as it was to her.

"And I was telling her about the PR work I do for my company."

"Yes. That's how Nikki and I know each other. Work."

Emma nodded.

"Got your homework done then?" Philip asked.

"Some. I've still got a lot to do."

"Maybe it's a good idea you get on and finish it. Take your Coke with you."

"Okay," she said and left.

Nikki turned to Philip. "Think she guessed?" she whispered

"What, Emma? No."

"I wouldn't be so sure." Nikki returned to her normal voice tone. "She's a bright one."

"Don't be silly." He grinned at her. "You seemed to get on."

She agreed, not wanting to disappoint him. "The fact that I'm sleeping with you made me feel uncomfortable but yes, we got on."

Philip pulled her towards him. "Good."

Nikki leaned away from him. "Philip, I don't think it's a good idea."

"It's fine. Jackie won't be back for hours and we won't see Emma again tonight."

Nikki extricated herself from his arms. "Still, better safe than sorry, eh?"

"How about a little kiss then? No harm in that."

Nikki smiled and moved closer. "No. I don't suppose there is."

❖

Half way up the stairs Emma sat listening. The pieces fell into place now. The time her father spent away from home, his nervousness this evening. It wasn't her fault. There wasn't anything wrong with her. He had a girlfriend. That woman in there was his girlfriend! The one who was drinking Mum's wine in the living room. *No wonder Mum is so unhappy*, she thought. But why had her father invited her here? Were they going to tell her mum when she got home? Did this mean divorce? The thought sent her scurrying to her room to hide under the duvet and cry.

❖

The following morning Emma crept into the kitchen. Her mother wasn't hung over, which was unusual, but apart from that everything seemed normal.

125

Nothing was mentioned. Emma waited all through breakfast, thinking her mother would tell her after she'd finished so as not to put her off the most important meal of the day. Nothing. *If I say nothing too*, she decided, *maybe everything will be okay.*

Chapter 22

It was ten days before Christmas and the snow fell heavily.

"Mum, look!"

Jackie was kneading bread on the table and smiled at her daughter's excitement. *Only children could get excited at snow*, she thought. All she could see was cold and wet, dangerous driving and dark nights, months of them. Still, it was nice to be tucked up inside her warm cosy home. Safe.

"D'you think we'll have a white Christmas?"

"Maybe, but I wouldn't count on it. Have you got everything you need?"

Emma nodded, gazing out of the French windows into the white garden beyond.

"Won't be long now," Jackie reminded her.

Emma was off for the evening to stay at Lottie's. There was talk of sledging and Jackie shivered at the thought, glad she wasn't included.

"Mum d'you think I'm pretty?"

"Course I do," Jackie said without hesitation. "Why do you ask?"

"There's different kinds of pretty, isn't there?"

Jackie stopped kneading and looked at Emma.

"You know, I'd never really thought about it but yes, I suppose that's true."

"Well, d'you think I'm the gorgeous pretty or the nice pretty."

Jackie laughed. "What's brought this on?"

"Y'know when you went to the theatre with Liz?"

Jackie nodded, pulling at the soft warm dough with her floury hands.

"Well this friend of dad's came. A woman."

"I know." Jackie's heart thundered in her chest. She licked her lips, focusing hard on her hands. "She works with him or something," she said, her voice casual.

"Well, she was pretty, but a different pretty to you."

"Oh? What was she like?"

"She had long red nails and long blonde hair. She wore make-up and had this dress that was really, well, posh."

"And I don't." Jackie tried to smile through a concrete face.

"No, you don't. You have a different prettiness and I wondered which I was."

"Which do you want to be?"

"Don't know. Which do men prefer?"

Jackie bit her lip hard and turned to put the dough into the tin to prove.

"I'm not sure I can answer that," she said after a few moments. "You see, I've only ever really gone out with your dad. I'm assuming he likes my kind of pretty because he married me." She stopped herself saying anything more. The contented warm feeling she had gathered to her today was evaporating.

"Do you think men change their minds?"

Jackie clapped her hands together loud in an attempt to remove some of the flour from them.

"I don't know." There was an edge in her voice and Emma looked round at her.

"You okay, Mum?"

Jackie smiled. "Course, why shouldn't I be?"

"Don't know, you just seemed a bit…cross just then."

"No. Now, run upstairs and get your bag, they'll be here in a minute and you don't want to keep Abby waiting, do you?"

As Emma left, Jackie covered the dough in the tin and put it on the shelf above the boiler to prove. She started to clear up, desperate for Emma to leave.

It had been over a week since she went to the theatre with Liz and since than her drinking had reduced considerably. Now the keen in the back of her throat roared. Something dark and moist was trying to claw its way out of her belly only this time, she wanted to drown it.

Philip sat in his office pouring over the case again, looking for any other way than the route he had chosen. Was he mad? But unless he could find another way he had no choice. He had assured both the partners of his firm and Peter Douglas that a win was on the cards, now he had to deliver. If he didn't…

Then there was Nikki. She had been odd since coming to the house. Boy what a mistake that had been. She had become aloof, difficult to get hold of, evasive. He didn't understand what was going on and these silent scenes, for that's what he'd named them, were getting him down. He was beginning to think she was more trouble than she was worth!

The only place he had some breathing space was at home. Ironic but true. There had been a change in Jackie over the last few months. A change so slight he barely noticed it at first. Maybe it was striking up this new friendship with their neighbour, what was her name now? Lynn or Liz or something.

He was beginning to wonder if he was doing the right thing by leaving. The upheaval and all. There was a time when he couldn't wait to get out but now…

And then he remembered how crazy he got when he didn't know who or what Nikki was up to. He didn't have a right to know where she went, what she did, who she was with but it drove him mad just the same. Sometimes he wished he'd never met Nikki.

Love. Drove you mad. Drove him mad. He had never felt this way about Jackie. He and Jackie were just him and Jackie and if she hadn't got pregnant at Uni they never would have married. It was the least he could do. He had blamed himself back then, but surely he'd paid his dues by now?

He had found love and as hard as it was sometimes, as much as he wanted to walk away or wished it had never happened, it had. And he needed to be with Nikki. And to be with her he needed to win this case. It was impossible to imagine doing anything else now.

Arbitration had failed, as he knew it would. Peter could be so stubborn sometimes. Him and Murphy both. They were going to court. He was risking everything but he had to. If he lost he wouldn't just be losing a case, he'd lose everything. Nikki, his job, the family home, money, his reputation, maybe even his freedom.

He sighed. Losing was the least of his worries, if he was found out… He could go to prison.

Liz caught herself doodling on a piece of paper. The screen in front of her still blank. She had a deadline and she had never failed to meet a deadline before but now she was in danger of doing so.

The two boxes of her mother's writing stood on the floor of her office. They were responsible for her predicament.

She threw down the pen and put her fingers on the key boards. When suffered from writer's procrastination she knew the best thing to do was to write through it, to just start writing anything, but she was out of ideas. Her mind tight and blank.

Over the past few weeks she had spent some time every day reading her mother's words, her voice coming back, the scent of roses lingering. It made Liz ache when she lifted her head from them. They were her escape, but she'd spent too long escaping recently and she had to, *had to* finish these pieces.

The trouble was that today they hadn't given her that escape. Today they had disturbed her. She picked up the red notebook from the desk beside her. She had found it at the bottom of one of the boxes. It was her mother's diary and she reread the piece that had disturbed her so much earlier in the day.

"It has always been painful to me not to have my own children. Like a hole that can never be filled no matter what Donald does for me. I fear I am unable to produce novels in the way I am unable to produce children. I have a barren mind and a barren womb. Well, perhaps the hole will be filled. The things Donald will agree to, the things he will do for me never cease to amaze me."

What did she mean? Was her mother writing in character? If so, why use her father's name like that? Perhaps it was the only way she felt she could really get into the skin of the character. Still, Liz had a knot of apprehension in her stomach.

As she wrestled with her thoughts, trying to make sense of what she had read, the doorbell rang.

"Shit!" she said, standing up and throwing her pen down. "If it's Jehovah's bloody Witnesses I'll shove my brolly up their arses," she muttered walking down the hall.

"Let me in, it's freezing out here," Jackie said. As she pushed her way into the hall Liz was aware of a powerful aroma emanating from her. It took her a moment to recognise it as alcohol.

"You are such a baby," she said, deciding to ignore it.

"I know, I know. I'm sure I was swapped at birth. I was born to live somewhere where they don't even know what freezing is, let alone snow! Got time for a cuppa?"

"Sure. Writings going shit at the moment." She considered showing Jackie what she had found but decided against it.

Jackie held up something in her hands. "Brought you some home made bread."

"Mmmm lovely! I'll get the bread board out and we can have toast and jam."

"So, what do I owe the pleasure?" Liz asked as she set out the mugs.

"Emma's gone off till tomorrow with her friend and Philip's at work and I was alone. Needed the company really."

"What's up?"

"Oh something and nothing."

"Isn't it always?"

Jackie smiled. "It's something Em said this morning about this woman who came to the house."

"What woman?"

"When we went to the theatre Philip had a work colleague round only...."

"Only you're not so sure she was work?"

"Right."

"Have you thought about asking him?"

"Yes but...it's complicated."

"In what way?"

Jackie took a deep breath. "Honest?"

Liz nodded.

"I'm afraid."

"Ahh."

"I'm afraid of rocking the boat, of what I'd do if he was seeing someone else, of managing on my own, of being weak and staying in the relationship anyway."

Liz listened quietly as she busied herself slicing bread and getting the teapot ready.

"You don't sound as if your heart's breaking," she said. "If you don't mind me saying."

Jackie watched Liz put out the butter, jam and a couple of small plates on the table then she sat down. They sat in silence. The toaster popped and Liz got up and brought the toast over.

"We don't love each other," Jackie said at last. "Never have."

"So why did you marry him?"

She shrugged. "I'm not sure."

"And Philip?"

"That's easier. Guilt," said Jackie as a memory surfaced of them in the Railway Bridge café talking over a yellow Formica table.

"So you don't want the baby?" she asked.

"Yes, yes I do."

They both knew he was lying.

Jackie shook her head. "It doesn't matter now." She stopped and looked intently at the toast in front of her. The bread like small brown mountains with black peaks.

"What happened?"

Jackie looked up at Liz. Her green eyes so warm and full of concern. *I could lose myself in those eyes*, she thought.

She looked down and coughed. "I failed my exams and Philip felt responsible, wanted to take care of me I guess. That's why he married me." It was almost the truth.

"Maybe that's why you agreed to marry him too. Perhaps you were scared of being on your own."

"You're probably right," Jackie said, pushing down thoughts of Clare. "You know what really gets to me though?"

Liz bit into her toast. "What?" she mumbled with her mouthful.

"That he brought her to our home. Fucking hell, that really pisses me off!"

Liz raised her eyebrows. "Whoa, I never thought I'd ever hear you swear."

Jackie flushed. "Sorry."

"Hey, don't apologise to me, I can swear with the best of them—I'm just a little surprised you can." She picked up the milk jug.

"There's lots of things I can do," Jackie said like a mantra.

"I know."

"It felt good," Jackie giggled.

"It sounded good," Liz put the milk jug down and looked at her friend. "You Jackie Lawson, are a good swearer," she announced and they both burst out laughing.

"I think my parents are going to get a divorce," Em told Lottie later that day.

"Really, how cool!"

"It's not cool!"

"It is. You'll have two homes and you'll be able to play one off against the other. You ask Rebecca Swinton. She says she gets stacks of stuff since her parents divorced. And then there are your grandparents of course. They get paranoid that the other grandparents are doing more for you and seeing you more so they give you loads too. Oh, it'll be like Christmas every day."

"I don't want stuff. I want to live in the same house as Mum and Dad!"

"But you told me you never see your dad."

"So?"

"So what does it matter? In fact, you'll probably see him more."

"You think?"

"Yea course, 'cause he'll be feeling all guilty about you coming from a broken home. They both will."

"You make it sound fun."

"It is. Talk to Rebecca. She says she's much happier now."

"D'you want your parents to divorce?"

"No chance of that even if I did. They cuddle all the time. It's disgusting," Lottie wrinkled her nose. "They're so old now you'd think they didn't need to do that anymore."

"Mine don't."

"D'you think they still...you know."

"What?"

Lottie lowered her voice to a whisper. "You know...have sex."

"I don't know!"

Lottie giggled.

"It's disgusting. Shut up."

Lottie started to pick bits off her duvet sulking. It didn't last long.

"Why d'you think they're getting a divorce anyway?"

"Dad brought this woman home. I heard them talking."

"Wicked! He brought her to the house?"

"I think she's his girlfriend but I don't think my mum knows. At first I thought she did but now I don't think so."

"Sometimes wives turn a blind eye."

"What's that?"

Lottie shrugged. "I'm not sure, but I think it means they pretend not to know."

Emma remembered her resolve to say nothing. Was that a blind eye?

"How do you know about it?" she asked Lottie.

"I heard Mum talking to Ruby who lives next door. Her husband ran off with someone for a while but he came back and she let him."

"My mum wouldn't do that. If she finds out they'll get a divorce."

"Don't worry about it. Yer mum might not find out."

Chapter 23

Liz sat at her desk fiddling with a piece she was writing on the Euro. It was being introduced into twelve different countries this month but no matter what she did it wouldn't read right. She was trying to make people see the possibilities of manipulation and corruption that its introduction could engender, but the piece sounded hysterical, even to her, as if a mad woman had written it.

She rolled her neck to ease the ache. The truth was, she didn't think many people in this country were interested, as long as the sterling didn't change. And even that was more to do with their discomfort of change rather than a loyalty to the pound. *Am I being fair?* she wondered.

Over Christmas she had argued with her father about it. She had insisted it was a ruse to increase prices and take control to a central point. He told her she was talking nonsense; he hated to be considered old and consequently often took the opposing view of his generation. They'd argued about a lot of things but not talked about anything important. Big world issues yes, but not about themselves. Not his feelings for Ruth, her life choices, or the box of her mother's writings and the diary she'd found. She had told herself her mother probably wrote it before she was born, maybe she had an irrational fear of not being able to have children but when she worked out the dates her mother would have been on the verge of having her. There was bound to be some perfectly logical explanation for it. So why hadn't she asked her father about it? What strange unconscious force was stopping her? What hidden irrational fear prevented her from broaching the subject with him?

She shook her head and brought her thoughts back to her work. That was the trouble of working on your own. No distractions other than the sound of your own thoughts circling like vultures looking for something to pick at.

Maybe her father was right about the Euro, she reasoned in a determined effort to work. After all, she'd been wrong about attacking Afghanistan. That whole sorry business was forgotten now, almost. Travel insurances had gone up, British Airways had used it superbly to ditch extra staff and the West had used it to confirm the Middle East as the new threat, but apart from that everything was back to normal. Well, for everyone except those in Afghanistan.

She read the piece through again but it was no use. Now it just seemed like a meaningless string of words. Babble and nonsense. She saved it and decided to go and pay Jackie a visit, she hadn't seen her since before Christmas. The thought lightened her and she smiled.

She hadn't felt this way since Jenny, she thought, allowing her mind to wander as she waited for the computer to close down so she could switch it off. Jenny. She sighed. She and Jenny had lived together for eight years. For Liz it was the real thing, they were going to be together forever. Had even discussed the possibility of children. When it broke up Liz was devastated.

She was drunk, distraught and confused at a party a few weeks later when she slept with Todd. He'd pursued her for years but it was the only way Todd could have ever got her into bed, them both drunk, and her not having a clue. She could laugh about it now but what a disaster! Who'd have thought, pregnant on a one-night stand? No, that wasn't fair, they had been more than that, not much more and not for long, but more.

The computer beeped, bringing her back into the room and the imminent visit to Jackie. She leaned over and switched it off, looking at her reflection in the dark screen.

"What are you doing?" she said, shaking her head. She leaned towards herself. "Making another whopping mistake…or moving on?" she whispered.

Nikki and Philip sat in an exclusive restaurant on the outskirts of town. Candle light sparkled off the crystal glasses, expensive fabric swathed the walls, the room was filled with the cosy hum of conversation and a discreet string quartet played elegant music in the corner.

Nikki was oblivious to all this luxury as she dallied with her food, unsure how to play it with Philip. He seemed distracted the past few weeks and small insecurities were surfacing in her. *This is why I promised myself never to fall in love*, she thought. *Still, it's too late now.*

She glanced at him across the dinner table. He looked tired but she didn't know why. Not long ago he told her everything.

"Philip, you okay?" She kept her voice light.

He looked up, his eyes far away. "Yes."

"You seem…distracted this evening."

"Sorry, Nik, I was thinking about work."

"Want to talk about it?"

She watched him struggle, holding her breath, waiting patiently until he let her in.

Finally he shook his head. "I want to forget it." He picked up his glass and sipped the wine, the faraway look still in his eyes.

Was this what he was like at home? How did his wife stand it? How could any woman stand being shut out like this?

She slipped off her high heel. "I know just the thing to take your mind off it," she said in a sultry voice. Philip's eyes flicked back to focus on her. Small frown lines appeared across his forehead and her body tightened.

Undeterred she reached out under the table with her bare foot and began to work her toes under the hem of his trousers. He jerked his leg away and Nikki sat upright.

"What?" her voice was tinged pink with anger.

"I'm sorry, Nik, I'm just not in the mood."

"What do you mean you're 'not in the mood'? Not in the mood for what?"

"For all this," he gestured with his arms to include the restaurant, her, their meal.

"Well pardon me for breathing. Perhaps I should find some more amicable company in future." The moment the words were said she regretted them.

Philip's eyes turned on her, their usual rich blue turning to a shallow grey. "Is that the best you can do?" he asked, his voice rumbling low.

"What?"

"These threats of yours, these little games, I'm tired of them. At least with Jackie I know where I am."

Nikki dropped her cutlery onto her plate with a clatter. "Why don't you go home and fuck your wife then, you dick head," she hissed and stood up, knocking her chair over.

"Nikki wait!" She paused. "I'm sorry," he said.

But he had refused her, again. It cut deep.

"Fuck you, Philip," she said. "Call me when you've got more to say than sorry," and she strode out of the restaurant shaking.

"So how was your Christmas?" Liz asked. They were sat at the table in Jackie's dining room.

"Oh the usual, quiet. Just me and Emma. Philip was about but we rarely saw him. I swear the man's a workaholic, either that or he's shagging that woman. What about you?"

"Quiet. Spent it with Dad. It was nice," she lied.

Jackie looked out into the black garden and saw her reflection staring back at her. How long before she would be able to see snowdrops and crocuses, how long before the days became longer? She ached for some sunshine.

"Haven't spoken to him then?" Liz asked.

Jackie shook her head. "Wouldn't know where to start," she said.

"It was the same for me, when I found out about Todd. I ignored it for months."

"What changed?"

Liz shrugged. "Me, I suppose. I just couldn't go on with it anymore. I suppose that's your answer. If it doesn't tear you up why bother to do anything about it?"

"Why did you buy such a big house?" Jackie asked, changing the subject.

"I needed the space."

"On your own?"

"Sometimes I think I bought it for my mum."

"I thought she died?"

Liz nodded. "She did, but she always wanted a big house. She used to tell me she wanted 'a big house, to fill it with kids and write all day'." Liz smiled. "Sounds crazy, I know, but it's true. Of course, I can justify it all. The front room is my living room and houses my grand piano. The smaller back room is my office. You have no idea what a luxury it is to have a room to work where I can simply close the door at the end of the day."

Jackie nodded. Did Philip feel like that? Shame *he* didn't come out and close the door on it once in a while.

"Then upstairs of course I have the largest bedroom at the front, the middle one will be for guests or Dad. He's on his own now and not getting any younger. There's going to come a time when I'll need to take care of him."

Jackie watched her friend wander for a moment. What would it feel like when her mother died? She was ashamed by the answer—relieved.

"And then I'm going to convert the small back bedroom into a dark room when, if, I ever manage to get it done."

"A dark room?"

Liz nodded. "It's a hobby of mine, photography. Started in college. Really useful sometimes too. Helps me sell pieces, although it's primarily for fun. Besides, I find it relaxing." She took a drink of her now cold coffee and grimaced. "So I can justify it, but I think it's for Mum. Ironic, buying my own place was supposed to be a way of moving forward since Mum's death, and yet…"

"Want another one?" Jackie nodded towards Liz's mug.

"No thanks, only usually drink one cup a day and this is already my second."

"It is decaff?"

"Makes no difference really. Still as poisonous to the body—all the chemicals they use to pull out the caffeine."

"So why drink it?"

"Simple. I love the taste but my system can't stand the caffeine. I flip out. Get all hyper. So I drink decaff."

"Doesn't bother me." Jackie could hear the boast in her voice and it made her cringe. She hoped Liz hadn't noticed.

"Your system's probably used to it," Liz told her. "Our bodies are extremely good at adapting, even to poisons. At least, to a certain extent."

Liz's next words made Jackie stiffen.

"Take alcohol for example, or any form of drug for that matter. The first time a person tries it they don't need much. After a while, however, it takes more for it to have the same effect. Hence addictions."

"Alcohol isn't a drug though, not really."

"Course it is."

"Not in the same way."

Liz nodded. "Did a piece for one of the Sunday Broadsheets last year. Did you know that nicotine is more addictive than heroine? And there are more alcohol-related deaths, diseases and accidents than there are from any other drug?"

"No!"

Liz nodded. "You'd be surprised how many alcoholics exist in the world."

Jackie shifted uncomfortably in her seat. She had a sudden desire to eject Liz from her cosy dining room.

"There's a new buzz word now, 'functioning alcoholic.'"

"Really?" Jackie said, praying for Liz to shut up.

"Yea. Apparently normal everyday people, people like you and me, have a drink problem and no one knows about it." Liz stopped and leaned back into her chair. "Anyway," she said, spreading her long pianist fingers over the wooden table. "I should be getting on."

Jackie stood up.

"I get the feeling I've said something wrong." Liz said as she rose. "Have I?"

"No," said Jackie leading Liz into the kitchen. "Don't be silly."

Liz stopped and pointed to a large group of empty wine bottles. "I wasn't inferring anything," she said.

Jackie waved her into silence. The bottles looked frightening lined up like that. She would have to get rid of them today. "Of course not…recycling's overdue."

Liz nodded and smiled. "I wouldn't want to cause offence," she said at the front door.

"You didn't," Jackie reassured her.

It wasn't offence, thought Jackie as she closed the door. It was something much worse.

Emma heard the front door close downstairs and knew Liz had left. Her mother would be up in a minute to check on her and she quickly closed the note book and pushed it under her pillow. She didn't want her mother to see her holding it in bed in case she teased her. There had been enough embarrassment for one Christmas.

When she and her mother had returned from the supermarket on Christmas Eve they found the present on doorstep. She had been embarrassed and delighted to discover it was from Alan Metcalf.

They would be back at school on Monday and she wondered how she was going to face him. Her mother had insisted she write a thank you note, as if she were seven.

She didn't mind writing letters to her grandparents and uncles and aunties, but to have to write a thank you to Alan Metcalf. It was so uncool. And how on earth would she be able to give it to him without Lottie noticing? If Lottie noticed the whole school would find out within a couple of hours. She adored Lottie but she had a big mouth and she would tell everyone Alan fancied her, there would be no shutting her up.

Emma sighed heavily. It was a dilemma. She didn't want Alan to think she wasn't grateful but at the same time she didn't want the world and his wife to know about the present.

It was such a perfect gift. A neat notebook for her writing with a silver hologram cover which caught the light like a disco ball. Her mother said he must have been asking people questions to find out about her in order to buy something so thoughtful.

She was sure he would ask her to the spring dance now and it didn't frighten her anymore. Instead it made her whole body tingly and her heart jump. She would say yes. Now that she had found out about her father's girlfriend she knew it wasn't her. It wasn't. It was him.

Alan Metcalf. Emma Metcalf. Mrs Emma Metcalf. It sounded fantastic.

If only she could get over the thank you letter business. Of course, she could always simply drop the letter in the bin on the way to school. Her mum was unlikely to find out and if she did, well, then Emma would just have to get her to understand how uncool it was. That settled, she smiled and hugged herself to sleep.

Chapter 24

"Of course, I haven't done half the things I planned to do with the place and I've been in there what, nearly five months."

They were walking along a country lane. To their left stood bare and barren fields. On the right, a wood. Liz noted the destruction wrought by the high winds of a few days ago. Numerous branches were broken and trees uprooted, their roots clawing the air like hags' fingers. It changed the landscape, shifted everything and for some reason it riled her. So did her father.

Donald Mullard laughed at his daughter's impatience. "These things take time. You can't have forgotten how long it took your mother and I to fix up the house? And it's still not finished."

"Well obviously I have!"

"We're in a mood today."

"I've got a lot on my mind right now." Liz missed her mother now more than ever. She'd always been able to bounce things off her without fear of judgement. But it was more than that today. It was the diary too. Those words. Her mother barren. How could that be?

Her father interrupted her thoughts. "Want to talk about it?" he asked, discomfort in his voice.

"I'm not sure it would do a lot of good," she said softly. Unsure of whether she was referring to her dilemma with Jackie or the diary.

"How d'you know if you don't try? I know I'm not your mum, Elizabeth, but, well, maybe I could help?"

She shrugged. *In for a penny*, she thought, unsure which problem she was going to broach. "It's Jackie," she heard herself say. The diary was probably nothing anyway.

"Your neighbour?"

Liz nodded as she picked up Benjy's stick and threw it ahead of them.

"What about her?"

"I'm afraid she might have a drink problem."

"What makes you think that?"

Liz plunged her gloved hands back into her coat pockets.

"I've always thought she drank a lot but I thought it was just social occasions or the evenings, but recently I've smelt it on her during the day too. She tries to mask it with chewing gum or toothpaste but there's that methodol aroma, y'know what I mean?"

Donald nodded.

"The other day I was talking about addictions, and I just sensed her becoming really uncomfortable. Trouble is, I don't know what to do about it. I want to help her but I'm not sure how."

"If she does have a problem there's no one who can help her but herself."

"I know, but I can't just stand by and watch her drink herself to death."

"Is it that bad?"

Liz grinned. "Probably not."

"Know why she's drinking so much?"

"She's not happy in her marriage." Liz wanted to say more but bit her lip, reminding herself she was not talking to her mother now.

"Tell me, is this…" he coughed. "Is there something more going on? No details," he added hastily.

Benjy had found a way through the thin hedgerows and was sniffing round in the field. They stopped as Donald called him.

Liz looked at her father. He held himself tightly as he waited for the dog to come. She decided to give it a try, after all, he was reaching out and it wasn't easy for him either.

"I do like her," she ventured.

"As a friend?"

Liz rocked her head from side to side and pulled a face again.

They passed the field with the large chestnut tree where she went in search of conkers with her mother and father when she was small. Her mother's voice rang in her ears, and she sighed. Donald followed her gaze. The scent of roses hung in the air.

"I miss her too," he said.

"I think…I think I might be falling in love with Jackie," she said quickly. Benjy loped ahead his tail spinning like a helicopter.

"Ah," said Donald as they continued their walk in silence.

"But I'd want to help her anyway," she added eventually.

He reached out and patted her shoulder the way he used to. "Of that, my darling, I have no doubt."

They walked, watching Benjy until he said, "What I'm concerned with however, is that you've fallen in love with a woman who is not only married, but has a child, not to mention a possible drink problem. It's a lot to take on."

"I'm not taking anything on."

"No, I know but you would, given the chance, you're just like your mother."

"Maybe."

"How does this woman feel about you?"

"I don't know. I haven't told her I'm gay. Not really. I've hinted."

"So she doesn't know how you feel about her?"

"She knows, Dad, she might not know she knows but there's something between us."

Liz waited, unsure how far she could go in this conversation. It was unique, they were both swimming in depths they had never swam in before.

"Are you sure this isn't just a case of wishful thinking?" he asked finally. "Our minds can play terrible tricks on us if we want them to. They get us to see all sorts of things that simply aren't there."

"True, but I really think she cares about me."

"I'm not disputing that she cares about you. All I'm saying is that she may not care about you in the way you want her to. It's more than possible that she sees you merely as a close and loving *friend*."

Liz stopped. "Dad, isn't that what you're hoping for?"

He dropped his eyes to the ground. "Maybe," his voice was quiet.

"And don't you realise that just because it doesn't work with one woman, doesn't mean I'm going to start going out with men?"

He nodded, his eyes sad, and Liz immediately regretted her bluntness. She moved closer to him.

"Dad," she said in a softer voice. "I know this is difficult for you but I'm gay and I think it's more than friendship with Jackie."

He looked at her. "You have some sort of system for detecting each other?" he asked, surprised.

"Don't Dad, this is important."

"I know. It's difficult for me not just because you're…gay but because I want you to see how foolish all this could be."

They walked on quietly side by side.

"So what do I do?"

"I think it's very laudable that you want to help this unhappy woman…"

"But?"

"But I feel strongly that you have to do it for the right reasons. Otherwise it could all go terribly wrong." He sighed, "What would your mother say?"

Liz shrugged. "She'd say what she always says. 'Tell the truth.'"

He smiled. "Bloody good advice. So perhaps it's time to come clean, let her decide how she feels about it."

"But what if…."

"What if she rejects you?"

"Yes," Liz said quietly.

Donald stopped walking and put his arm round his daughter. She looked so sweet and vulnerable, his heart hurt for her.

"Then you'll have your answer and if you still want to help her, and she wants you to, it will all work out right."

Philip emerged from his study needing a cup of tea to find Jackie sorting through seed packets in the kitchen.

"Hi. Planning the garden?"

Jackie didn't look up. "Thought I might try growing some vegetables this year."

"Really? Baking bread, growing vegetables, it's like living in an episode of *The Good Life*."

"How's the case?" she asked deciding to ignore his jibe.

He sighed. "Long and difficult."

She listened as he moved around the kitchen. She admired women who could simply carry on regardless of whether their partner was in the vicinity or not. She couldn't. It was like he was pulling on her energy when he was around. Tugging at her. Especially now. Now she had all these images of him with the woman with the painted nails. She imagined her digging them into his back when they made love and she hated it.

Why? Why did it bother her so much? She was glad when he wasn't at home. He disturbed her equilibrium. She was like some finely balanced trapeze artist riding a bicycle across a tightrope. Everything was fine then he would arrive like a weight on one side pulling her off balance, threatening to plunge her head first off the rope.

Radish, she thought, trying to pull her mind back to the task in hand. All the books seem to agree that they, along with onions, were the easiest vegetables to start with. She liked the idea of the sweet peas because of the smell in the summer. She closed her eyes, trying to conjure up some summer feeling inside her but there was nothing. Nothing but the cold, damp bleakness of winter.

"What are you doing?" Philip's voice broke into her thoughts.

"Just thinking," she said her face flushing.

"Don't think too hard, you might strain yourself," he said laughing and retreated back to his study.

As she heard the door close she heaved a sigh of relief. Tears welled in her eyes. Why did he do that? Why did he have to trample on her, her ideas, her dreams, her little plans. She dropped the seed packets on the table. It was pointless, what was the use?

She would be too ashamed if she planted the seeds and they didn't grow. An image of shrivelled failures replaced her earlier picture of lush nutritious vegetables and she knew that once again, she wouldn't follow through with her plans.

"And what about you?" Liz asked when they were back at the cottage.

Donald was slicing a granary loaf while Liz fried bacon on the stove.

"What about me?"

Liz pushed the bacon round the pan with a fork wondering how to broach the subject. Finally she took a deep breath and plunged in. "I mean you and Ruth."

She saw Donald hesitate momentarily cutting the bread. "I told you, there is no me and Ruth."

Liz flipped over the bacon.

"How you doing with that bread? Bacon's nearly done."

"Do you want butter on yours?"

"No. Brown sauce."

Liz watched her father move across the kitchen to the cupboard.

"I don't mind, you know?" she said.

146

He opened the cupboard and took out the sauce bottle without responding.
"Did you hear me?"

"Keep an eye on that bacon, I don't want mine burnt to a crisp."

Liz took out half the bacon and put it on a plate. She placed the plate on the table and stood in front of Donald with her hands on her hips. Eventually he looked up.

"What?" He looked irritated.

"We talked today, Dad, got closer I thought. Had a real conversation."

Donald's shoulder slumped in defeat. "I heard you. I know you don't mind," he said. "But I do."

Liz wrapped her arms round her father's robust body and held him. She'd broach the boxes of writing and her mother's thwarted dreams another day. Enough was as good as a feast, as her mother would say.

Chapter 25

Nikki sat in front of the computer screen on her desk, clearing emails with half a mind on her work.

Bastard! Fucking bastard, she thought as she stabbed at the delete button, sending the email into cyber space or wherever the hell it went. Who the fuck did he think he was? She hadn't heard from him since the restaurant scene over three weeks ago. She had to do something.

She sat back in her chair and took a swig of her tea, weighing up her options. She could cause him a lot of trouble. She knew where he worked, where he lived, his wife. It would be easy to pick up the phone and call him, or her.

She put down her tea. But what would that accomplish? She wanted him, her body ached for him. Two nights ago she dreamt he was there, his arms encircling her. She actually felt it! Then she woke up to an empty bed and a lonely hollow feeling in her chest. How did people live with this love thing? How?

Perhaps he just needed some time. He was right in the middle of the case for her boss Peter and there was a lot riding on it. Perhaps he'd been overwhelmed by that? Still, a quick call, that's all she asked. It wasn't unreasonable.

Or had he decided he'd had enough? Finished it but didn't have the courage to tell her? Maybe he'd decided to stay with his cardboard cutout wife after all. Anger rose again. That would be just like him. He was weak, like all men! They always took the path of least resistance.

How could she find out without blowing it altogether? It could be he needed some time and space to get the case out of the way before he made his decision. If she went barging in on him now, at such a crucial time, it could destroy any chances she had.

Oh shit, how did it all go so wrong when it seemed to be going so right? How had he escaped? The telephone on her desk rang and her heart leapt, but it was just a routine call.

The truth was, she decided, when she'd dealt with the call and replaced the receiver, all she could do was wait.

Philip had been in the court room for two days and things were not going as well as he would have liked. This was the final day and any second thoughts he might have had about using Hunt's testimony were long gone. He couldn't afford not to, they would lose the case without him.

Hunt was their last witness and as he was called Philip watched Colin Murphy's face twitch into a frown. He was worried. Hunt was an unknown entity and it was obvious some of the things Mr Patel had said in his statement were true. Murphy had reason to be nervous. He was now a respectable business man using the courts to sort out his grievances, but he hadn't always done that. Philip's body relaxed a little. It wasn't all made up, just exaggerated a little.

"Mr Hunt—you say that Mr Murphy had some unusual business practices."

"Objection."

"Overruled."

"But my Lord, what knowledge does Mr Hunt have of business practices? He is not an expert and so his opinion is merely that, an opinion."

"His opinion is worth quite a lot as he was employed by Mr Murphy for two years and has since had other occupations. I suggest, my lord, his opinion is relevant, your honour," said David Price, their barrister.

"Continue," said the judge. He turned to the witness, "Please answer the question."

"Well, he liked to put pressure on people, sort things out in his own way."

"I see. And what form did this 'pressure' take?"

"You know, he would send out the lads, we'd pay a little visit so to speak."

"No! That's not true," Murphy shouted.

The judge's heavy gravel pounded on the granot. "Order. Mr Murphy, you will not shout out in my court room."

When it was quiet, David Price tuned to Hunt. "'Send the lads round,'" he said slowly as if he were tasting the flavour of the words by rolling them round his mouth. "Could you explain for the court, Mr Hunt, what this means exactly."

"If a punter wouldn't pay up he'd ask us to go round and rough 'em up a bit like, you know, put the frighteners on them like."

"Do you mean threaten them?"

"Yea."

"Your honour, I admit as evidence the statement of a Mr Ash Patel. Document no 6."

The barrister passed the statement to the judge and then turned back to Sean Hunt.

"Mr Hunt, did you know Mr Ash Patel?"

"Not personally, no, but I remember his name."

"In what capacity?"

"What?"

"How do you know his name?"

"It was a few years back now. Mr Patel owed Murphy a few bob and we were instructed to go round and threaten him."

"Who is 'we'?"

"Me and a bunch of other blokes. I was really young at the time, led astray you might say, but I'm clean now. Drive a car and I've got a job."

"In your opinion, Mr Hunt, what kind of man is Mr Murphy?"

"Objection. Speculation."

"My lord, I am merely asking the witness his opinion of Mr Murphy. He worked for him for over two years."

"Overruled, but be careful, Mr Price."

"Thank you, your honour," Price turned back to Hunt. "I'll repeat the question. What kind of man is Mr Murphy?"

"He scared me. I think I'm tough but he was tougher. He was a hard nut. It was the worst job I had. It was my first job, so I thought all bosses were like that. I thought that's how you did business like. Now I know different. He's a thug and a criminal."

"Objection!"

Murphy stood up and shouted and the judge banged his gravel again. "Order! Order!"

Things settled down quickly and the judge turned to David Price. "Objection sustained. Mr Price, your witness cannot call people thugs and criminals without evidence. Strike Mr Hunt's comments from the record."

"I'm sorry your honour, it won't happen again."

"It better not, Mr Price, for your sake."

"Thank you, your honour."

"But he threatened me," Hunt said aloud. "Said he'd ruin my chances of ever getting another job if I didn't do what he said. He's a criminal."

"Mr Hunt, that is hearsay and is not permissible," the judge told him. "Strike it from the record."

"No more questions, your honour."

Philip relaxed as David Price sat down, with Hunt's and Ash Patel's testimonies it was in the bag. The witness had played his part beautifully, earning every penny of his ten thousand pound fee. In a few hours it would all be over and Philip could breathe a sigh of relief and start to figure out what he wanted to do about his future.

Liz strode over the hill, her camera bouncing against her chest. The dark room still wasn't set up and Liz had been reluctant to do any photography without a place to develop them quickly, but she needed to relax and for her there was no better way.

She had toyed with the idea of a digital camera, especially recently with her dark room all packed away, but the picture quality suffered and besides, with the house move, money was a little thin on the ground right now.

She'd been focusing too hard on work since the move. She made a promise to herself to get the dark room set up soon. Maybe she'd call Neil and see if he wanted to come over at the weekend and help her.

She crouched down and framed a small bare tree against the pink sky behind. The contrast between the bones of the tree and the warmth of the sky excited her. She pressed the button gently under her finger and heard the reassuring click. That was what photography was about, the reassuring clicks when you took a photo, and you didn't get that with a digital camera. And she liked the wait. She loved the anticipation of watching the photo emerge before her in the dark room. It was too easy to erase photos with a digital. Often she would look at a photo and put it to one side thinking it wasn't what she had wanted to capture only to discover later it had captured so much more.

Art, like life, was often at its best unplanned.

Liz had decided to tell Jackie she was gay and, depending on her response, her emerging feelings for her. Most certainly she wanted to approach her about her drinking. Explain her concerns and ask if she could help.

She tried to imagine how Jackie would react but couldn't. She simply couldn't. Whenever she thought about it she got through her speech and then, blank.

Often as Liz got to know people, the topic of sexuality would come up and it gave her an idea of how the person would respond to her sexuality but with Jackie it never had.

Her musing turned to her father. She could see something happening between him and Ruth, even though he denied it. She wished she could ease his conscience. She knew her mother wouldn't want him to be alone. He was the kind of man who needed a woman around the place. He'd withered until recently and Liz had been worried about him. She should be glad of what Ruth had done for him. She should be.

Damn those boxes of writing and that diary. They had churned up so much in her. So many memories of her mother. The writings and the big house. The house was supposed to be a step forward, a new start. Instead it had enmeshed her even further into her grief. She hadn't realised the real reason for buying the house until that talk with Jackie.

She turned back home. She would set the dark room up, and once she'd talked to Jackie she would clear the air with her father and talk to him about the diary. It was silly to try and keep finding reasons when she was sure a quick chat with him would sort it all out.

Chapter 26

It was Saturday and an inch of snow lay snug to the ground. The sun shone casting long blue shadows against the clean white.

Jackie and Philip sat at opposite ends of the breakfast table reading the weekend papers as Radio Four burbled in the background. Emma was watching Saturday TV in the front room.

Philip concentrated on his paper with difficulty. He had won the case due to the false testimony of Sean Hunt but he had none of the elation he had with other cases. He had cheated and there was the possibility of blackmail. Sean Hunt was not a clever man, but even he could understand Phil's role in all this and its implications for him. Perhaps Hunt would come back for more money.

He went over the steps he had taken to cover his tracks for the umpteenth time. When he was corrupting Hunt's evidence he had always met him where it was unlikely there could be any witnesses. He had paid the fee in cash. There was evidence of the withdrawal of the money from his savings account. But other than that he was clean.

Jeremy Walford had called in his office to congratulate him. There had been a lot of hand shaking. It was a big win. The firm stood to make a substantial figure from the 1.2 million awarded. Twenty percent of that figure to be exact. The publicity was phenomenal too and Peter Douglas had offered them all his legal work in the future. Murphy's was being investigated and Philip's job was safe. In fact, his promotion looked assured. He smiled at the thought of Walford's face when Phil won. Excellent. Worth all the agro these past few months.

It was all over. He had phoned Nikki when he got out of court and left her a message to tell her he'd won and he would be with her soon. Should have gone last night but he really hadn't been in the mood for the sexual acrobatics they always found themselves in. And after losing the last case because he was so enmeshed in her he'd decided to avoid her until the trial was over. And now it was. Finished. Finally.

He looked across at Jackie sitting in her dressing gown in a little world of her own. What did she think about, he wondered? What filled her mind, her days? She'd lost all the verve and sparkle that had first attracted him at college. Then she'd been a mini dynamo, with the tenacity of a terrier. Now she just seemed empty and flaccid.

It made him cringe to admit it, but she bored him. He could never think of anything to talk to her about. Her body wasn't soft and yielding like Nikki's, she didn't take care of herself, she drank too much and seemed so…so…desperate to be looked after. And he was tired of looking after her. Weary from the years of being responsible for her happiness and never quite managing it. He wanted to be happy and he had a chance with Nikki. It was Nikki he wanted and he was sorry now he hadn't been to see her after all. Yes, it was Nikki. It was just a matter of when, and how.

The fear of blackmail reared and Philip saw himself in the dock declaring his innocence with Nikki, his mistress, by his side. It wasn't good. The same picture with his wife and daughter standing by him was better, much better. And always, always the presence of his parents lurked in the background.

He rubbed his face with his hands. He could feel a headache coming on, again.

Nikki rewound Philip's message again and pressed play.

"Hi! We won! Isn't it fantastic! I'll call you. Soon."

She hit rewind again. No apology, nothing. It was like the last three weeks of silence never happened.

She hit play again. Listening to the joy in his voice, imagining him going home and swinging his wife round, hugging his daughter. Only now his wife wasn't the woman she met at the party, she was the one in the photo.

Nikki had expected him last night, she'd cooked supper, everything. He hadn't showed, he hadn't even called.

She rewound the message and pressed play. Listening, as if it would change something. Tears streamed down her face. *What do I do?* she thought. *What do people do with all this pain?*

There wasn't any reason why I can't have it out with him now, Jackie thought. The case was over and he'd won. Now it was time to sort things out between them. At breakfast that morning it was amicable between them. This could be their future. Not a torrid love affair perhaps, both setting each other on fire, but a companionship that would stand them in good stead as they grew older. But she didn't want to settle. Not anymore.

She wanted to be filled with pulsing red and gold instead of this grey dampness that permeated her being, pulling her down, and tripping her up at every turn. She didn't want this half-life anymore and if they were to be together she had to face him. Had to tell him she knew, or rather thought she knew, he was having an affair. And it had to stop.

They had just finished dinner. It was time. Her mouth dried when she went to speak but she forced the words out.

"Philip?"

"Excellent food, thank you."

"Philip, I need to talk with you."

"Shall I help you clear, then I can pour us a couple of brandys?"

"I don't want brandy."

"Suit yourself."

He got up to leave and she felt the moment slipping from her.

"Philip, I need you to listen."

The acid in her voice made him pause, half out of his chair. He sat back down with a thump. "What is it now, Jackie?"

"We need to talk."

"No. We don't need to talk. I am perfectly fine not talking. It would appear that you need to talk ergo, I need to listen."

Why did he have to be so pompous?

"Whatever," she said, dismissing him. "Philip...I know you're having an affair."

She watched him. Waiting. He didn't look at her.

"Aren't you going to say something?"

"As I said, I have no desire to talk."

"Oh for fuck's sake, Philip!"

He shot her a look. "Emma," he hissed.

"What about her? Since when did you give a stuff about her? About either of us, for that matter."

"I love Emma and I married you, didn't I?"

"Yes you did and I've been quietly paying for it ever since."

"You've what! *You've* been paying for it? *You*?"

Jackie and Philip glared at each other across the expanse of a table.

"Yes. You've always made it quite clear you did your duty but you'd be damned if you'd do anymore."

"What more do you want? Look at this place!"

"It's not about that. Things."

"Then what is it about? As far as I could tell it wasn't about sex!"

It was Jackie's turn to be concerned for their daughter. "Keep your voice down."

"What? Afraid of some home truths?"

"Philip, please."

"So what if I have an affair? I am a normal man with normal desires. And you, you're a cold fish in bed. It's a wonder I haven't done it before."

Jackie blushed.

"You hate sex, I love it. I had to marry you. Had to," the years of frustration emphasised these last two words. "But that doesn't mean I had to go without sex or love."

"Love! You don't even know the meaning of the word. You ignore our daughter–"

"And why? Because I can never get in. You shut me out, Jackie, long before I went elsewhere."

"That's not true."

"It is and you know it."

"You're a contemptible bastard."

"No. I'm just some guy who woke up and found his life empty and half gone and is trying to make the best of it."

"What about my life!"

"I can't be held responsible for everything, Jackie. You're grown up now, you've got to do it."

"How can I? You won't give me any freedom."

Philip stood up. "Rubbish. You slosh around in your own little world. You've no idea of reality because of this stuff," and he swept the bottle of wine off the table, smashing it against the hard tiled floor, making Jackie jump. "I didn't love you when we got married. No more than you did me. But at least we liked each other. Now, now there's nothing."

He began to stride from the dining room.

"Where are you going?" she demanded.

"Out," he said, slamming the front door behind him.

Jackie bent down and through her sobs began to pick up the pieces of the broken wine bottle.

Emma lay in her bed with her fingers in her ears, her eyes shut tight. The cold space surrounding her growing into a huge expanse stretching far out into the night. And there she was, lying on a raft cut loose from its moorings drifting out to sea—miles from anyone.

"I'm sorry I called you."

"It's what friends are for," Liz told her.

"It was awful."

"What happened?"

"We had such a fight, such a cruel and hideous fight."

"Want to talk about it?"

It took another two glasses of wine before Jackie could form the words.

"I had an abortion."

The words hung, heavy, like wet washing on a clothes line.

"When?"

"Years ago, but it's inside, eating at me. I've never…I've never told anyone and I need to," Jackie was sobbing now. Liz pulled her into her arms and held her as Jackie's body wracked with sobs.

When Jackie pulled away she picked up her glass and gulped the wine.

"We went to a family planning clinic after we got married. I'd done home tests," she laughed, it had a hint of hysteria. "I did three! Just to be sure. Found out two weeks before our finals. That's why I failed, I went to pieces, couldn't concentrate. Didn't know what to do."

Liz was having difficulty following Jackie's ramblings.

"You had the abortion after you were married?"

Jackie nodded and began to cry again.

"Shush now," Liz said, patting her arm.

Jackie took a deep shuddering breath and stared in front of her. "After I found out I was pregnant," she began, calmer now, "I failed the exams. I couldn't concentrate on anything. Once the exams were over we got married. His parents weren't pleased about it, I didn't want to, neither did Philip. It was madness but it just seemed the right thing to do at the time." She reached for the glass and drank deeply.

"After the honeymoon we told his parents. They insisted on paying for us to go private." Jackie snorted. "NHS wasn't good enough for their grandchild. They took over." She put the glass back on the coffee table and stared down at her hands.

"The clinic was bizarre," she said. "I thought I'd made a mistake at first. It was like a hotel. It had thick dark carpets and soft deep chairs, beech wood furniture in the reception. It had that expensive exclusive air really posh hotels have. I didn't feel comfortable. It was like a health clinic for pampered wives rather than a hospital. I suppose they wanted to make it nice for me but I felt like chattel. Weird, huh?"

Jackie slopped more wine into her glass.

"Haven't you had enough?" Liz asked softly.

"Oh I've had enough alright," Jackie said. "Enough of everything. He said he'd be with me every step of the way. You know where he was? In a café down the road. Ha! Fucking typical."

Jackie drained her glass and bashed it down onto the glass coffee table, making Liz jump.

"They asked me questions. Questions, questions, questions. They were lovely. Nice people. I had to pee in a bottle and they examined me with their latex gloved fingers. Pushing and probing. That was the worst, those probing fingers. They gave me a scan. Asked me the same questions over and over again and then we waited. After all that and hours of waiting, you know what they said?"

Liz shook her head, unable to trust herself to say anything constructive.

"They said, 'Mrs Lawson, we're sorry but the baby has died.' Can you believe it! Just like that. It's called a 'lost abortion.' That's the medical term for it. Lost abortion."

Jackie sniffed and focused on the pattern in the carpet. Brown swirls melted into orange ones. It had been a mistake, this carpet. She had hated it from the day it was laid.

"I had to go home and wait until the next week for the...." she emitted a small whimpering animal noise. "Had to carry a baby corpse around inside me for a week. Until they aborted it. I had to sign a form agreeing to the abortion. I was four months pregnant. Just starting to show.

"When they put me under the anaesthetic, I started to cry. A bald man dressed in the green theatre stuff held my hand and hushed me. He told me to count to ten slowly. I felt so close to him I didn't want to let him go. I reached four and I don't remember anything else until I woke up, on one of those steel trolleys. The nice man in green was gone. There was a nurse there but it wasn't the same. All I had to remind me I'd had been pregnant was a thick wad of blood-stained cotton between my legs. And a marriage certificate.'

The two women sat in silence for a long time.

"Philip came to collect me," Jackie said. "As soon as I saw him something inside grew hard and angry. I don't know why. It was like I blamed him. Stupid really. They offered me counselling but Philip said no. He said we just needed to put this behind us and try again. As if it were that simple. Like we'd bought a faulty car or something. I wanted him to pay after that. We drove home in silence and it's never been mentioned since. Not even alluded to...until tonight."

Jackie looked up at Liz. "It was like some horrid dream. It all happened so quickly. You can snuff out life so easily," she stopped and sighed. "You see, there was a part of me that was relieved. We didn't have to stay married, see? I could escape. We both could. I didn't want the baby, I wished it away. And then I signed that paper, so they could abort it, perhaps they'd made a mistake. Perhaps it wasn't dead but I just signed anyway, didn't even ask if they could be wrong."

Liz smiled. "They don't make mistakes like that Jackie. The baby was...gone. It wasn't your fault."

"I'm not so sure." Jackie filled the glasses and handed one to Liz. "That's why my life's like this. Full of shit. Full of nothing. It's what I deserve." She drained her glass again and put it on the coffee table gently this time.

"I signed for an abortion," she whispered. "And what's worse, we felt so guilty at the relief that instead of getting out, instead of us getting the hell away from one another, we tried for another one. It was two years before Emma came."

It all came back to her now. The rasping breath and stale alcohol. They had to get drunk to do it in the end. To numb them to each other. The worst part, the bit she hated the most, was the weight. It squeezed the breath from her. Once she was sure she was going to suffocate before he'd finished. His grunting and gasping shudder was a relief for both of them. Something had died between them, along with their unborn child.

"You see, when the baby had gone I realised I had nothing. I'd failed my exams and then there was Clare...." she stopped.

"Clare?"

Jackie shook her head. "Doesn't matter."

Liz placed her wineglass down on the floor, moved closer to Jackie and took hold of her hand.

"Listen to me. You didn't have an abortion. The baby was already dead. They can't tell you that it if it's not true."

Jackie wiped her face and sniffed.

"You have to stop tormenting yourself like this, Jackie, it's not healthy."

Jackie looked up into the face of this new and very dear friend. "I feel as if I've known you forever," she said.

"Me too."

They looked at each other for a long moment. Jackie's body softened as she felt drawn to Liz, unable to pull herself away from the magnetic force drawing them together.

Their lips met. A hot searing electric current ran between them, taking Jackie by surprise. She had never felt such thirst, such need. Liz's lips were warm and gentle, so smooth. No man's face, no matter how closely shaven, could ever feel this soft, this yielding. Liz's tongue gently probed her mouth, leaving her breathless and desperate for more.

Small bursts of energy exploded between her legs. It sent waves of heat throughout her body, stiffening her nipples. Liz's hand reached out and brushed against Jackie's breast, creating a hunger in the pit of her stomach. With no thought of what she was doing, Jackie reached out to Liz.

Jackie found herself gasping small breaths as she gently kneaded the softness of Liz's small breasts. She wondered with excited surprise what it would feel like to pull the nipples into her mouth and suck gently.

She heard Liz groan into her mouth and Jackie responded by kissing around Liz's lips and along her neck. Jackie caught a sob in the back of her throat as she began to unbutton Liz's shirt, desperate now to explore the woman's body.

The smell of her skin was heady as she pulled the hard nipple into her mouth. The small pink explosions between her legs turned into deep red throbs. Her head swam with excitement, never had she had so much power pound through her body.

From some deep far distant land called reality she heard a familiar sound. The clunking of a door far away. The sound moved closer to her until she realised it was her daughter going to the bathroom and Jackie was pulled back into her body with a snap of realisation.

She sat up, horrified by what she was doing and where she was going.

"I'm sorry," she stammered and stood up, the powerful feelings that flooded her moments ago melted.

"Jackie, it's okay," Liz's voice was hoarse with desire as she buttoned up her shirt.

"No, no, it isn't, I was upset, I'm not sure what I thought I was doing I've never done anything like this before, please go, please just leave. Go."

"Okay okay but really, don't worry. I need to talk to you–"

"Just go, Liz."

"But it's–"

"Go!" Jackie couldn't look at her friend. She said in a whisper, "Please, just go. Please."

When Jackie heard the front door close she reached for the bottle of wine and emptied it into her glass with a shaking hand.

What had happened to her? She had behaved like an animal. She had never ever felt like that. She couldn't think about it anymore, it made her feel sick. She poured the liquid down her throat, choking on her tears.

When the intercom buzzer sounded Nikki jumped with fright. It could only be Philip and she was in a mess. She had no make-up on and was sat in her towelling dressing gown, painting her toenails. She hobbled to the buzzer, wads of cotton wool stuffed between her toes and pressed the button.

"Yes?"

"Nik let me in, it's me, Philip."

"Philip, I can't, I…." Nikki considered telling him she had someone here.

"Listen I need to talk to you," he said. "I'm leaving Jackie."

Nikki froze, taking in his words, allowing them to engulf over her.

"Nikki?"

"Philip, I'm in a bit of a mess," she glanced round the flat. Cushions were flat, magazines were strewn on the floor, along with her dirty plate from her lean cuisine supper.

"I don't care about that, I want to see you."

How could she let him in?

"Where have you been these past few weeks?" she asked, buying for time as she ripped out the cotton wool from her toes and ran over to plump up the cushions.

"The case, you know. It was really heavy. Look, let me in and I'll tell you all about it."

She ran back to the intercom. "Give me five good reasons why I should," she said and then ran to collect up the magazines, stuffing them under a cushion.

"Well, first and foremost I just told my wife I'm leaving her."

She picked up the plate and ran into the kitchen with it.

"I won the case so I'm getting my promotion, that's two. And I need someone with style to celebrate it with, that's three."

He paused and Nikki ran back to the intercom, took a deep breath and the pressed the button. "So far so good," she said then dived into the bedroom to apply her make up. A little lipstick and some mascara was probably all she'd be able to manage in the time she had left, though base foundation might be better.

"Four is that I want to be with you and five well," he stopped. Nikki paused, her mascara wand held in the air, suddenly held captive by the silence.

"The fifth reason is that I love you."

She caught her breath in the back of her throat. He loved her. She had heard the words often, from many men, but they had never held this magic before, had never made her body tingle like this.

"Nikki? Can I come in now?"

She dropped the mascara on the table and rushed to the intercom to open the door below. She flung open the door of the flat and stood waiting.

When he appeared her heart leapt. She pointed to her face.

"No make-up," she told him.

He smiled at her. "Better," he said, taking her in his arms.

Chapter 27

Jackie drove through the rain. Fast. Needing to be gone. Needing the space between her and the house. Between her and her life. Between her and last night. Between her and the event. The event. Was that how she was going to refer to it? The event? How about the kiss? It would be more real. But it was more than that. A kiss. A kiss. It made it sound insignificant, childish even.

The rain was lighter now so she flicked the wipers from constant to intermittent. Intermittent. A strange word. She rolled it round her head as the grey countryside passed by unseen outside. Anything to keep the facts at bay.

Intermittent. Every so often. Once in a while. Now and again. Occasionally. Her head felt full and dangerous. Dark clouds loomed, threatening to burst inside her.

When had her life become a confusing ball of tangled wool? When had she lost her way? How had she come to kiss a woman? A friend. The roads were empty and she pushed the accelerator down hard, listening to the spray from the tyres.

Everyone else, she thought, would be getting on with their lives. At work, shopping, at home cleaning or preparing lunch. She glanced at the clock. One-thirty. Maybe not lunch. Maybe a cup of tea and a chat with a friendly neighbour. She laughed out loud. How friendly? As friendly as she had been? She doubted it. She saw a sign for Hamsterly Forest. The car suddenly seemed claustrophobic. The air stale. She turned and followed the signs.

Jackie parked the car in a car park devoid of other vehicles. As she stepped out and locked up the sight of her car alone made her sad.

She followed a trail by the river. The rain was dying off and the air smelt clean, washed. The trees held out their bare skinny arms like ballerinas. Fat drops hung heavy. It was quiet but for the gurgling river and the squeal of small children from somewhere in the distance.

The path was squelching mud. She had small heeled Italian leather shoes. Her feet would be sodden by the time she returned, the shoes ruined but she didn't care. What did it matter? What did anything matter when you've kissed a woman?

Was her soul tainted black? Black tar stuck to her soul like smoker's lungs. She looked at her muddied shoes.

Wasn't her soul already thick with her crimes? Wasn't the murder of an unborn child enough to send your soul to purgatory? What was a kiss after all? Simply the meeting of one person's lips with another's. Did it matter who those lips belonged to? Maybe not, if it had only been a kiss.

She breathed deeply, desperate to inhale some of the newness, the freshness, cursing that the rain had stopped. It would have cleaned her, wash away her sins. Standing under a deluge would clear the past, wash away the grime of all she had been, all she was.

What am I? Who am I really?

It wasn't just a kiss. It wasn't. It was so much more. It had pulled forward a part of her she had pushed away. It had awakened some depth inside her untouched since Clare.

Clare. How she haunted her now. Regurgitating unpleasantly like breakfast eggs. Jackie shook her head hard, trying to find some space somewhere.

Emotions choked her. Too much. Shut up. Stop! She wanted to scream, she wanted to shout, she wanted to release something, anything. Make space. Understand. Instead she walked. Put one foot in front of the other. As she had done all her life. Keeping to the path no matter how unsuitable the shoes. Outwardly calm, putting one foot in front of the other. Plodding. Treading water, Liz had called it.

Didn't Phil do the same? Wasn't that why they stayed together? It was safe. They knew the rules in the confines of their relationship. Knew their roles.

She doubted he was any happier than she. No that wasn't true, he had his career, his affair. Their relationship didn't have to fill him, he could get that from elsewhere. Not her.

Was that why she kissed Liz? Did I kiss her or did she kiss me? Did it matter? She knew she had wanted too. It didn't matter who started it, she had continued it.

She breathed again. The smell of wet soil clogging her nostrils with longing. I want to be clean, she thought, not sure how it would feel, unsure of what she meant.

Slowly, as she walked, the tornado of emotions subsided and she began to calm. As she approached her car, joined by others now, she was less restless but no nearer a conclusion.

She glanced at her watch. She'd been walking for nearly an hour. She had to get home for Emma.

She started up the car and put Tosca on full. The noise intruded into the woodland but she didn't care. Why should others walk around undisturbed? She wanted to cause ripples. *It is childish,* she thought as she pulled away, *but it is the only thing I've the strength to do right now.*

"Liz, we still haven't been to see *Lord of the Rings*," Neil said reaching for another piece of pizza.

"I know."

"Fancy going next week? It's still showing at the multiplex."

"Okay."

"Well don't bowl me over with your enthusiasm, will you?"

"Sorry."

"Come on then, spill the beans."

Liz hesitated.

"Come on," said Neil through a mouthful of pizza. "It can't be that bad."

"Wanna bet?"

"You mugged some old lady then?"

"I kissed Jackie."

Neil sat upright, dropping pizza in his lap. "Whoa, when did this happen?"

"Last night."

"What, you just leaned over and kissed her?"

"Sort of. She leaned too."

"She kissed you back!"

Liz nodded. "And there's more."

"You didn't?"

"No, but we were on the way."

"Shit, Liz, I don't believe it. What happened?"

Liz shrugged. "She backed out."

"Did she say anything?"

"What was there to say?"

"Good point." Neil returned the pizza to its box and sat back.

Liz twinned her fingers together in her lap but remained silent, nibbling her lip gently.

"You did tell her."

She shook her head.

"I thought you were going to tell her. Get it all out in the open."

"I was but she'd had this huge argument with Phil and she was upset and, oh Neil it all happened so fast."

"So what are you going to do?"

"I don't know."

Philip drummed his fingers on the steering wheel as he waited for the lights to change. He'd told Nikki he was leaving Jackie and now he was driving home with the intension of smoothing things over with his wife. What the fuck was he doing? He loved Nikki, yet he needed Jackie, at least, he did for the next few months, till he could be sure of his promotion, till he was safe from Sean Hunt, till he could speak to his parents.

What had possessed him to lie like that to Nik? But he knew. He'd been afraid she wouldn't open the door, she'd turn him away and he'd have to scuttle back home. Besides, it was true, he did love her. He sighed as the lights changed and he pulled away.

And what had possessed him to react like that to Jackie? It was as if years of holding back had been building a pressure under him. It had just come up, out of his control, like striking oil. Great black stuff gushed from him and spilt over then, their history, their relationship.

He turned into Bromwich Street. And now he was going home and he had no idea what he was going to face or how he would deal with it.

Jackie sat on the sofa when she heard Philip's key in the door. Her body stiffened as she waited.

"Hello," he said, standing at the doorway as if he were waiting to be invited in.

"Hi."

After a few moments he came in and sat on the other sofa, his keys jangling on his hands.

"Not stopping?" she asked looking at the keys.

"Am I welcome?"

Jackie looked at the pictures flickering on the TV.

"I thought we should talk," he said.

She hadn't wanted to be in this room when she saw him again. Thoughts of what happened here the previous day rose and she could find no words.

Phil misunderstood her silence. "Don't sulk, Jackie. We won't get anywhere like that. I'm sorry I said the things I did, I was out of order."

She nodded to acknowledge she'd heard him. She wanted him to stop talking now.

"It's just the years of frustration, and, if I'm honest, the guilt. I don't want you to believe I didn't give you and Emma a thought when I was…well, you know."

Jackie looked down at the carpet and noticed it needed hoovering. Shame seeped through her body and she was convinced her crime, her infidelity, was written all over her face.

"Why now?" she asked. "Why tell me all that now? After all these years of silence."

"I've been under a lot of pressure at work. More than you could ever know."

And he told her the story of Sean Hunt, of the letter, of hiding the case initially from the partners, of everything.

"You fabricated evidence?"

"No. Not really. Just embellished it a little."

They sat in the silence until it pressed down on the two of them so hard it was unbearable.

"And the woman. Is it the one you brought here?"

"Oh God, Jack, I'm sorry."

"Don't call me Jack, you of all people should know not to call me that."

"Sorry."

"But that sums up our relationship really, doesn't it? It's always on your terms."

"That's not fair."

It wasn't, she knew, but she was on the high ground and she wanted revenge. Was that what the thing with Liz had been about? Revenge?

"The whole thing was about you. Where you wanted to live, when you wanted to come home. You've had this separate little life all along."

"You had choices."

"When? When did I have choices? I was so grateful you married me I went along with everything and never once did you give me a choice."

"Jackie, people don't give you choices, you take them."

"No Phil. No. That's just you."

Chapter 28

Jackie pushed the hoover round the living room. The noise filled her head enabling her to escape the implications of her life for a while without the use of alcohol.

Since her talk with Philip the previous week Jackie had made some decisions. That conversation had shifted things for her. That conversation and her "encounter" with Liz. The encounter. The event. The thing. She was still to face Liz and it was a meeting Jackie kept putting off.

First she had to sort out her head, rearrange the new information and realisations she had made over the past week. When Philip told her how he had won his latest case it rocked Jackie.

In all the years they had been together she had supported Philip in his work because essentially she felt they both believed in the same thing—justice. It had sustained her when she failed her exams, to watch him striving forward and doing what they had discussed they would both do. When she came home from the clinic she silently cheered him on. When the house and Emma were all she had left she took consolation from the fact that Philip was out there making a difference for both of them. Even when she found out about his affair, even then, their shared belief in justice helped her. When she asked him why, he simply said he needed to win. Needed to win!

That information led her to a shocking realisation. She was stronger than Philip.

In spite of the alcohol dependency and all external appearances it was she who had held the family and the home together. She had raised their child. It was she who had kept their vows…well, until recently anyway. *Did it count with a woman?* she wondered as she dragged the coffee table back into place.

She straightened up and switched off the hoover. That was better. Cleaning helped her regain control. It always did. As she wound the cord round the vacuum cleaner she heard the doorbell.

Liz stood on the doorstep, her usually wild hair tucked behind her ears and held in a ponytail. Her face looked drawn and tired.

"Hi," she said with a small smile. "Can I come in?"

Jackie's cheeks burnt as she took Liz though the kitchen to the dining room, avoiding the room of the incident. Liz followed in silence.

The kitchen seemed brighter, the white snow reflecting the sunshine into the windows.

"Coffee?"

"Best not. I'm not sure how long you'll want me to stay when you hear what I've got to say."

Jackie walked over to the French windows. "White is a very misleading colour," she said. She gazed out at the fresh layer of even snow. "It makes things look cool when they're not, small, when they're not, and innocent, when they're not."

"Jackie, I've got something to tell you. It's important."

"What?" she said without turning.

"I know I should have told you sooner. I tried," Liz paused then added. "I'm gay."

All the air left Jackie's body. *I was seduced,* she thought, *it wasn't my fault.* All this time she had believed they were two women caught up in the moment, felt guilt in case she had instigated it, but that wasn't it at all.

"I was going to tell you only, well, that night you seemed so upset and—"

"And you thought you'd take advantage instead."

"No! It wasn't like that."

Jackie turned round to face Liz. "So what was it like?"

"You needed me to hear you not listen to my confessions and what happened," she shrugged. "It was an accident."

"Don't you dare do that, Liz. Don't you dare reduce it to an accident."

"Well what was it then?"

"It was seduction. I was vulnerable and you—"

"Me! Can I remind you who instigated it?"

"What?"

"I came here to apologise for my part in all this mess but I'll be buggered if I'm going to play the scapegoat because you're ashamed of what you did."

"You seduced me!"

"That's bollocks! You reached for me and I responded. I was wrong to do that under the circumstances, I'll admit that, but I refuse to take the blame for it all"

"Get out! Get out of my house!"

"I'm going. Just think on one thing, Jackie—whose breast was in whose mouth?"

When Philip returned that night he was surprised to find Jackie warm and welcoming. She slipped her arms round his neck and whispered in his ear.

"Would you like to go to bed with your wife?"

Her words sent him into a storm of conflicting emotions. At first, over-riding everything was confusion. He had been sure after all that had happened, after his affair with Nikki, after his confession of fabricating evidence, after all that he was sure that if anything, Jackie would grow colder towards him.

He felt a flicker of revulsion too, if he were honest. She had no self-respect throwing herself at him like this, even when she knew the truth. Nikki wouldn't.

But the emotion that surprised him the most was guilt. He loved Nikki, it was her he wanted and as he followed his wife up the stairs he wasn't sure he could respond to Jackie's invitation.

But surely this change in Jackie was a good thing, he reminded himself. It could mean a future for them. It could be a turning point, an opportunity to cement them as a couple and so cement them all as a family.

They were in the bedroom now, connecting at the mouth but for Philip nothing else was happening. Perhaps this first time would be difficult, it *had* been a long time. Like an automaton he began to remove her clothing.

There was a desperation coming from Jackie. It was as if she too felt the need to go through this façade. He knew all he had to do was take a step back, pause them for a moment and it would end and yet, something compelled him to go on.

He had an erection growing but it was more from knowing she didn't really want to do this. He felt like a powerful master taking what was owed to him and the thoughts roused him further. She was a young virgin and he the Lord and master.

By the time they were naked Philip's erection was tight and hard. He didn't have to take his time, he didn't have to make love. Taking his fantasy to the next level, he realised he could take her for his own satisfaction.

Philip pushed himself into her. She was tight and dry and whilst it hurt him a little it excited him too. She gave a little cry as he pushed himself into her but he didn't stop, he couldn't. Not now.

Slowly he pushed deep and then began to work into her unresponsive body, shoving hard, heaving quickly to a climatic quiver. His lust sated, it was immediately replaced with revulsion with himself. He felt dirty. He had been out of control and he had hurt her.

He kissed her on the forehead. "Thanks love," he said then turned over, facing the other way whilst he tried to understand what had just happened. Reaching no conclusions but deciding he would make it up to her, sleep came quickly.

After, as Philip lay sleeping beside her, fear roared in her belly and large silent tears rolled down Jackie's face.

The following morning Philip whistled his way through breakfast and kissed Jackie before he left. As he travelled to work he decided he had some serious reflecting to do.

He had lost his way but Jackie had forgiven him his sins and if she could, then why couldn't he? No, they didn't love one another but they had been through a lot. They were a strong team and with Jackie's new found confidence, her opening up to him sexually and her determination to knock the alcohol on the head then maybe...

It had been a close call. He had pushed himself to the brink. He had risked everything. His career, his family, his home, his freedom, everything. He had been lucky. Perhaps it was time to clean up his act.

Maybe what he had with Nikki had been part of a madness. Love—who needed it? He could do without the emotional roller coaster she put him on. Or could he? Could he settle for life without Nikki?

He had so much. A family, a wife, and a career that was back on track. They could take up Bridget and Steve's offer and go on holiday with them. He would ring Steve and ask if they could take Emma too. Their first family holiday. He'd be mad to let it all go now. Wouldn't he?

"Mum?"

"Emma, come on, we're going to be late if you don't get a move on."

"Mum. Are you and dad getting a divorce?" She noticed her mother hesitate.

"What makes you think that?"

Emma shrugged. She couldn't tell her mum what she had overheard.

"We're fine. You'll see. Grown ups argue sometimes but it doesn't mean very much. Now come on, pick up those feet or we'll be really late!"

"So, how did she take it?"

"Mmmm?"

Nikki leaned over the table and pulled at the newspaper Philip held in front of him.

"I said, how did she take it?"

"Take what?"

"Oh for Christ sake, Philip! Keep up."

"Sorry Nik I was reading the paper."

"Really. I would never have guessed. Are you trying to avoid me?"

Philip smiled. "Don't be ridiculous, how could I do that? This place is too small."

"D'you think we need a bigger place?" She heard an unfamiliar whine in her voice. What is happening to me?

"Maybe."

"Philip!" Was he deliberately being evasive or was she becoming paranoid?

"What!" he snapped.

"Answer my question."

"Which one?"

"How did Jackie take the news?"

Philip folded up his newspaper, aware he could not put off the inevitable any longer. "Not too well I'm afraid."

"What did she say?"

"Not a lot it was…well, it was awkward. I—"

"You didn't tell her, did you? You didn't tell her you were leaving?"

"No. Sorry. It wasn't as easy as I thought. She's vulnerable, Nikki, she's, well, she's not like you."

"What's that supposed to mean?"

"You're so tough and independent. Jackie isn't like that. She's always depended on me. I think the idea of her going it alone frightened her."

"Oh boo hoo."

Nikki caught the sharp look Philip shot her. "I'm sorry," she said quickly. "That was unkind."

"Yes it was. You've got to understand my position. I have a wife and a child. I've always had a wife and a child. It's not as easy for me as it is for you."

"You think this is easy?"

"That's not what I meant."

"You do still intend to leave her, don't you?"

"Yes, of course, just—"

"Just not yet."

Philip leaned forward and covered her hand with his. "Just give me a little more time, darling, that's all I ask."

Nikki forced a smile onto her face. She was so close, she didn't want to blow it now. Besides, she knew Philip, she should have been prepared for how much he would dither when push came to shove.

"It's okay," she heard herself say. "I understand. Take as much time as you need." What was she doing?

She was beginning to understand her mother.

Chapter 29

It had been nearly two weeks since Jackie had seen Liz. Relations between her and Philip had improved. He'd stopped the affair, at least, that's what he told her, and he did spend a lot more time at home so she supposed it was true. Sex was difficult for her. His penis an intrusion in her body, but she endured it. What was the alternative? Besides, Liz's last words haunted her.

Just think on whose breast was in whose mouth.

And there were the thoughts. The thoughts of those few brief moments when she'd abandoned herself to desire. A desire that even now, amongst the shame of it, caused her body to heat up and yearn. An orange pulsing that began between her legs and would take over her whole body if she let it.

She stood with the other mothers outside the little scout hut and wondered how they would react if they knew the thoughts that echoed inside her head. Would they smile so politely if they knew she'd had a woman's breast in her mouth?

Had she been at fault? Had she been the instigator? It was true the kiss had unlocked something inside her, but hadn't she been in a vulnerable place?

She stamped her cold feet, needing movement to dislodge the thoughts circling in her mind. Today had been glorious, full of sunshine and bird song. An unexpected gift breaking through the gloom of the long winter. Now with the setting sun the air pierced through her clothing.

It had been July when Clare had told her but it had been cold then too, but worse than this, much worse. A cold that seeped into your bones and froze the marrow. A freak weather cycle from the North. They'd escaped it in a pizza place in town. It wasn't there anymore. Now it sold car parts.

"Cheese and tomato," Jackie insisted.

Clare laughed. "You always have that."

"I like it."

"Have something a bit more exotic, like an Hawaiian."

"I don't want anything more exotic, I want cheese and tomato."

Clare laughed again, placed the order and lay her hands on the table. Jackie could still remember the thin fingers, nails short, resting against the plastic red and white table cloth. A small ruby ring nestled on the fourth finger of Clare's right hand.

"We need to talk," Clare said.

"Oh, sounds ominous. What have I done?"

"Nothing. It's about me. I know you must have heard rumours."

It was true. On several occasions people had whispered in Jackie's ear but she had refused to listen, refused to believe.

"I don't take notice of gossip," she said, feeling superior.

"No, I know, but there's something I need to clear up with you. I've been waiting for the right time but it never seems to come."

Jackie felt an awkward ache in the pit of her stomach, a terrible foreboding rose from it and began to spread to her chest, making her breath shallow.

"It's not a big deal, you understand, not to me, but…" she shrugged.

The pizza arrived and Jackie began to breath again, believing the conversation at an end, but Clare picked it up again as soon as the waiter left.

"I feel a bit silly making a deal of it like this," Clare suddenly looked much younger than her years. Vulnerable and childlike.

"Pizza's good," Jackie said quickly. "I'm glad we came here. Good idea."

Clare smiled. "Jackie this is important. I'm…I'm gay."

The room seemed to shift when Jackie heard those words. She'd heard them whispered before, often, but wouldn't believe, couldn't believe.

But here Clare was, telling her and the pizza became a tasteless mulch in her mouth, her blood rushed to her feet and she was unable to say anything.

Thoughts tumbled over her. *I've talked to her about my poor sex life with Philip, listened to her advice. I've stayed at her home. She's seen me naked. I've watched her undress. We've held each other close. I've felt her breath against my cheek, looked into her eyes, admired her smile.* Jackie shook inside as thoughts thundered over her, engulfing her.

In the distance she could hear Clare's voice, see her bovine eyes pleading, but she was unable to respond.

"It doesn't change anything. We're friends, that's it. I don't come on to my female friends," she laughed. "Wouldn't have many if I did."

Finally a silence descended between them and grew, it was Jackie's turn to say something.

"It doesn't matter," she lied, pulling the corners of her mouth into a smile.

Clare looked down. "I know it does a little, I'm sorry I didn't tell you earlier, it's just…" she shrugged. "Sometimes people can be funny about it and I like to know a person well before I, well, you know," she took a breath. "We've only been friends for a few weeks but I feel I've known you forever." She smiled.

Jackie nodded, regaining her composure. "It's a bit of a shock, but it's cool."

"Good. You going to eat that?" Clare pointed to Jackie's pizza.

Jackie shook her head. "Not really hungry. It was the warmth I needed more than the food."

A flicker of something Jackie didn't understand crossed Clare's face as she reached over and took the pizza.

Over the next three weeks Jackie was too busy to meet up, then too busy to take Clare's calls, always reassuring her it was nothing to do with her sexuality. She was just busy. Jackie was angry with Clare, and began to refer to her as "that old dyke." The calls lessened and then stopped all together. Clare got the message.

Jackie was stood under the town clock waiting for Philip, a light rain whipped round her by the wind and as she hunched her shoulders in an effort to ward off the rain her mind wandered. Decisions had to be made; about her future, Phil, her career, the list seemed endless. Did everyone feel so confused about life? She looked round at people hurrying by, wrapped up against the weather, they knew where they were going.

Unlike me, she thought. There was no certainty in her life, no moorings, no anchor. She was just bobbing about on the verge of drowning. Everything seemed so difficult. She was three months pregnant now, unfocused and frightened.

Phil had asked her to marry him and she knew it was out of duty; for the baby and because he felt responsible for her dropping out of college. He was responsible, she reminded herself. She knew why he'd proposed and yet, she heard herself telling him she would think about it. Think about it – what was there to think about? She didn't love him and she knew he didn't love her.

She stood waiting, chewing her lip.

She had shared everything with Clare. Well, almost. She had been her confidant, her heart closed, a frozen and angry lump in her chest. And then she thought she saw her, across the road, head pulled into her collar. Jackie turned to face the other way, her heart lurching. It couldn't be, it was her imagination. She was afraid, ashamed, disgusted, angry, her heart beat in her ears as she waited, praying that the other woman hadn't seen her.

When she felt a tap on her shoulder she jumped and spun round, and there she was, Clare, with a deep welcoming smile, forgiving her everything, and Jackie shrivelled inside.

"Hi, haven't seen you around for ages," Clare said. "How are you?"

"Okay. Thanks."

Clare looked around. "Waiting for someone?"

"Philip."

"Right."

They stood in silence for a few moments.

"Any particular reason you haven't returned my calls?"

Jackie's face reddened but she said nothing.

"Ah, I see." Clare laughed. "It's okay. I've been through this many times." She paused and took a deep breath. "I did expect more from you. I thought we had...something deeper."

Still Jackie said nothing.

"Look, do you want to go somewhere warmer? Talk about this?"

Jackie shook her head.

"Okay," Clare sighed. "I'm gay. So what?"

Jackie finally found her voice. "It's not that, I've just been really busy." *I told her about Philip and me. I told her about our...our sex problems.* Her insides convulsed.

Clare stretched out and laid her hand on Jackie's arm. "I'm sorry you feel this way," she whispered.

Jackie shook her hand off as if the woman had some infectious disease and looked around horrified. She didn't want people to see her like this, with this gay woman's hand resting on her arm, whispering to her.

"Get off me!" she shouted. She hadn't meant to shout. People turned to look as they passed.

Clare began to laugh. "Jackie, don't be so foolish, this is ridiculous!"

Jackie rounded on the woman who had betrayed her. "Foolish! Foolish! I tell you what's foolish—me. Yes, me," her eyes began to water from the wind. "Coming to meet you, chatting to you, letting you into my secrets, it's disgusting. You're nothing but an old lecherous dyke!"

Clare turned away, took a deep breath and turned back. Her face looked tight and pinched. "I'm sorry you feel that way, Jackie. I can assure you I had no ulterior motive, I had no intention of 'seducing' you. I think, I think this said a lot more about you than it did about me. You know where I am if you want me." And with that Clare turned and left.

Jackie watched Clare walk down the street, feeling foolish and embarrassed. What if people thought they had just had a lover's tiff? Anyone would feel threatened by a friend like that... wouldn't they?

Three weeks later, Jackie and Phil emerged from the local registry office as Mr. and Mrs. Lawson. The bride looked drawn, but then, her friends remarked, she always looked like that these days. The bridegroom looked terrified, but he'd had that look for about the same length of time, so no one commented on that either.

Now she knew. It was like a roaring in her ears. It could no longer be ignored. She had always known why he married her but now she knew why she had married him and it choked her. She had married Philip to run away from what she was. She had used Philip. Poor man. She had used him and then blamed him all these years for her unhappiness.

Poor Emma. Jackie looked round at the groups of women quietly chatting. Normal. They were normal. I'm not, she thought, the panic grabbing at her chest. I'm gay. What would happen to her, now there was no escape from the truth? And there was more, so much deep dark pain, memories banging and demanding her attention.

As the scout hut doors opened and children spewed out, Jackie choked back her unshed tears, the pain searing her throat. She didn't deserve the relief of tears.

"You were right," Liz said down the phone to Neil.

"Aren't I always? But please, enlighten me, in what particular area would this be this time?"

"Neil, you can be a right pain in the arse."

"That is also true."

Liz said nothing, tightening her grip on the receiver.

"Sorry. Jokes aside. Tell me."

"I should have told Jackie weeks ago."

"Yep."

"Dad told me to. I was just on the verge of telling her when–"

"When she jumped your bones."

"Neil!"

"What? Isn't that what happened?"

"Sort of, but don't put it like that."

"So what you going to do?"

"I don't know," she sighed. "I tried going round there but we just ended up having a big ruckus."

"Then leave it. She knows where you are."

"It's such a mess, Neil. How could I have been so stupid?"

"We all do silly things sometimes, especially when we're in love."

"Love!"

"You don't love her?"

"Maybe. I don't know. I just don't know anything anymore."

"Evidently. I know what you need."

"What?"

"A night out with a friendly shoulder to cry on. We still haven't been to see *Lord of the Rings*. Come on Liz, I want to see it on the big screen."

Liz looked at the boxes of her mother's writings. What she really wanted to do was sit with them, to feel her mother's presence again. Her mother's voice came to her so clearly but perhaps Neil was right, a night out was probably exactly what she needed.

She sighed. "Okay then."

Chapter 30

Over the next week Jackie struggled to push back down the avalanche of Clare memories, but the woman haunted her. Clare slipped into the next aisle of the supermarket, was ahead of her in the queue at the post office, she was among the crowds of shoppers in the town or she was driving a car that passed Jackie as she was waiting at the pedestrian crossing. Everywhere there were glimpses of her.

At night Clare's face began to mingle with Liz's in her dreams. The ache for a drink intensified, clawing and scratching up through her body, making her body ache and shake. She said nothing to no one. Who could she confide in? What would she say? She wasn't even sure she knew exactly what she was fighting. The drink, or the memories?

That weekend Jackie sat at the dining table, her mother's letter in her hand. It had arrived that morning but Jackie had waited until the evening to open it, bracing herself, feeling weary from the week's battle.

It seemed once you opened the door to memories they all came tumbling out, like an overstuffed toy cupboard. And the letter seemed to wrench that door all the way open.

Jan. Princess Jan. It was full of the exploits of dearest darling Jan and her offspring. There was a photo. Two little girls with blue eyes and blonde hair and Jackie's heart ached for them, for all of them. The years peeled back, ripped from her like the skin from raw chicken. Painful memories of her childhood forced their way up with implications that skewered her.

Jackie had watched her sister sit on their father's lap night after night and ached to be there instead. Jan could make their father set back his big head and roar with laughter. He only ever scowled at Jackie, at least, that was how it felt.

She watched his hands rubbing Jan's back, patting her bottom and landing soft kisses on her ears and sometimes her pretty button mouth.

Her mother bit at him. "Tom, stop it! It's indecent."

"I'm just showing her a little affection, isn't that right, poppet?"

Jan lowered her eyes and battered her lashes and Jackie hated her. Hated everything about her. She wanted some of that affection.

She heard her father visiting her sister's bedroom at night. They talked in low tones and Jackie would lay on her bed and pray he would visit her. He didn't. She prayed her mother would bite at him again and chase him out. She didn't. It seemed God, like the rest of the family, wasn't listening to her.

The mornings after her father visited Jan, her mother would make her sister an extra special breakfast of bacon and scrambled eggs.

"Your favourite, my lovely," she said. And she would stand and stroke Jan's hair while she ate it, as if she'd been away somewhere for a long time.

Jackie stopped asking for the same. There wasn't enough for her. Instead, her mother would let her help herself some of her special jam.

The full implications of those events came back to her now. She had realised years ago but it had been filed away along with everything else.

Jan visited regularly…with her kids. Her daughters. And Jackie felt tears threaten. She thought of Emma, just the idea that anyone would do the same to her made her roar with rage inside. If Philip ever…but no, he hadn't, she had watched him closely in the early years, made sure he didn't get too close. She wouldn't turn a blind eye. She wouldn't let it happen to Emma. Never.

Maybe Jan had wiped all memory of it from her mind as Jackie had for so long? Part of her wanted to force Jan to remember, to react, if only for the protection of her children, but a bigger part didn't want anything more to do with them. It was over.

She had never belonged and now she was pleased. Maybe God had been listening after all, only he had the bigger picture. Kept her safe.

She thought of Emma again. So young, so fragile, so naïve still. How could a grown man do such things and her mother, the breakfasts? But then, she reminded herself, perhaps it was all her imagination. After all, she'd never actually *seen* anything. Never. Which was another good reason not to rock the boat. If she did, if she tried, they'd say it was jealousy. And maybe it was. No. Let them all get on with it without her.

It could have all been different if I'd been a boy. The thought caused a glitch in her heart beat, like a scratch on a vinyl record. Maybe I could have distracted him if I'd been a boy. Saved her. And maybe nothing happened she reminded herself. She had to believe that, otherwise how could she live with her parents' blood in her body?

She tore the letter in half and put it in the bin. Now, with memories lapping at her throat she needed a drink. She owed them nothing. Nothing. And at that moment she knew, right down to her DNA, that she would never contact any of them again.

Later that night Emma came down for a drink.

"I'm sorry," Jackie slurred. "Could you get it? Mummy doesn't feel good."

"Why do you drink so much?" Her daughter's question took her by surprise.

"I don't know."

"Are you unhappy, Mum?"

"I...I suppose so."

Emma sat down beside her mother. "Mum, I love you."

"I love you too," Jackie's words sounded deformed and tears sprang to her eyes. She didn't want Emma to catch her like this.

"Will you stop drinking, Mum? Please?"

Jackie looked into the wide eyes of her daughter. They pulled hard at her and shame flared up inside her.

Jackie nodded and put her hand over her daughter's. "This time I'm going to get some help and really really try."

Emma took hold of her mother's hand. "I think you're really really brave, Mum."

Jackie smiled. "Make me a coffee, sweetie."

In bed Emma lay thinking over the evening's events. It had frightened her, seeing her mum so drunk. But she'd promised to stop and it made Emma feel better. It was different this time. She had seen her mother struggling not to drink in the past but Emma had never asked her. It had never been spoken about. Something was different now. She could sense it.

Something had happened. Something to her. Something was missing. Inside her. She closed her eyes to try to figure it out. She was different. Something had changed and in a good way.

And then she knew. The hard rock she carried inside her had gone. The heavy foreboding she had always had was no longer there. No. It hadn't gone but it was smaller. She didn't know why, and she didn't care. It left her lighter. Happier. Braver.

She could face anything. Well, not *everything,* but she didn't feel so scared about the things. Alan Metcalf, her new school, making new friends, even the possibility of her parents divorce. She was wobbly but not the gut-wrenching panic she had once had.

Smiling, she curled up in a ball and stuck her thumb in her mouth, allowing sleep to lap at her until it finally claimed her for its own.

Chapter 31

Philip clipped another paper clip to the chain he was making. His case load sat in his tray on his desk untouched. It was decision time. It had been over a month since the case ended. If Sean Hunt was going to blackmail him he would have done so by now. It looked like he'd got away with it. He could breath, at last. It was all behind him now and he could look to the future. The trouble was, with who?

Jackie and Abby met in the staff room for their morning coffee together. It had been two weeks since her mother's letter. Two weeks without a drink. Her mother had left a message, asking her to call, but Jackie wouldn't. There was a loose feeling in her body since her decision; she had space to breath and the thought of contacting her parents filled it up.

"How's it going?" Jackie asked.

Abby nodded. "Good. I'm listening to Year two's read. They are so sweet. Shame they lose all that innocence really." Abby sipped her coffee. "You look good"

"Do I? God, I feel like crap."

"Your hair looks great."

Jackie had to admit she was beginning to feel better without the drink. At least, physically. Emotionally was a different matter.

"How's things with you and Phil?"

"Okay I suppose. The affair's over."

"So you were right?"

Jackie nodded.

"Okay, so how come I get the feeling you're not over the moon?"

"Probably 'cause I'm not."

"Jackie, it'll take time. To build things up–"

"It's not that."

"Then what?"

"I've met someone."

Abbey's eyes went round as saucers. "Who? When?"

"It's something and nothing."

"Well it can't be nothing otherwise you wouldn't have mentioned it."

She wished she hadn't.

"Have you…" she made a motion with her head and raised her eyebrows.

Jackie hesitated.

"Well, have you?"

Jackie smiled. "We've kissed, but nothing else."

Abbey looked gleeful. "Good for you," she said as the bell signalled the end of the break. "Serves the bastard right."

Jackie wondered how Abbey would react if she found out it was a woman.

"Big news, Mum, huge!" said Emma dancing beside Jackie as they walked home.

"What's that?"

"It's so big I can hardly bring myself to say it."

"Well if you don't I can't share it with you."

"It's Alan Metcalf."

"He's the one you've got a crush on right?"

"Yep."

"He's the one who bought you the note book for Christmas right?"

"Right."

"So, what's the big huge news?"

"He asked me to the school dance."

"Oh that's great! That really is, sweetie."

"I think I'll wear my sparkly jeans. The ones with the rhinestones in."

"Sounds great." Jackie was only half listening as they approached Liz's house.

"And the pink Lycra top, or should I wear the turquoise one? Mum?"

"Sorry, Em."

Emma followed her mother's gaze. "We don't see Liz anymore."

"No."

"Have you two had a falling out?"

It was usually what Jackie said to Emma when she didn't want Lottie round. Jackie smiled. "Sort of."

"Well, why don't you just do what you tell me to do."

"What's that sweetie," Jackie said as she pushed her key into the lock.

"Call her and say you're sorry."

Nikki stood in the kitchen taking it in. She was numb. Nothing. She heard what he said but it wasn't getting through.

"This isn't an easy decision for me to make," he told her.

"No, I don't suppose it is."

"We've had some good times. No. Great times."

Nikki smiled. "Yes we have."

She turned her back to find a vase for the roses he'd brought with him.

"Those are just a peace offering."

"They're nice."

"I thought so," he said. "Pink."

She hated pink. "Yes," she said.

Nikki pulled out the white ceramic vase she'd bought at IKEA and placed it on the table in front of her. She moved mechanically.

"So you won't be back then?" She unwrapped the flowers from their paper, peeling back the cellophane so their stems lay exposed.

"Well, I think it would be more painful to draw it out. Don't you?"

She heard the apprehension in his voice and toyed momentarily with the idea of making this harder for him. She walked over and took her clippers from the drawer. On the way back to the table she chanced a glance at him. He stood with his hands clasped in front of him, his dark hair flopping into his eyes.

"You need a hair cut," she said as she picked up one of the stems and stripped the leaves away, careful to avoid the thorns.

"Yes," he said, pushing his hair from his face, his eyes rooted to the floor. "Can we be friends?" he asked.

Nikki's heart somersaulted. It was typical of Philip. So typical.

"What do you think?" she said as she sliced through the first stem.

Nikki woke the following morning to an empty bed and decided Philip Lawson could not get away with treating her like this. She would get him back. She would not be used. She was not her mother.

Liz sat bewildered by what she had read. She had spent most of the day and early evening reading through her mother's writings and something about the two boxes struck her hard.

The first box, the box she had regularly dipped into over the last few months, whenever she had needed to call her mother to her side, was very clearly her mother's voice. Soft, lilting, comfortable, poetic even. But the second box was different all together.

It had less writing in, being only a third full. The problem for Liz was that it had a harder edged voice, an aggression Liz didn't recognise. A street wise tough tone that came from a woman who had seen life, not the kind of woman who had baked bread, made jam for the county fairs and looked after the doctor's surgery.

Here was a woman who had seen the darker side of life, had been stripped and laid bare of everything she would later appear to be. It was written by someone else. She scrutinised the handwriting again. Liz was convinced of it.

Chapter 32

Jackie climbed into the bath. She'd put in too much foam bath and as she lay back the water enveloped her like thick chocolate. The house was still. She recalled her conversation with Abby and wondered what her reaction would have been had Jackie told her it was a woman she had kissed.

Suddenly anger rose, making a tight band round her head. She had to stop this, it was eating her up inside, all this anger.

Her life was such a mess. A shambles. When had things gone so horribly wrong? When she failed her exams? When she left Clare behind? When she married Phil? When she had the abortion? Miscarriage, she corrected herself, although it still didn't feel right yet. Or did it go back further, to her father? Her mother?

She thought marrying Phil would be the solution. Everything would settle into place. She would have a baby and knuckle down to her new life. That was the plan.

She told herself at the beginning that it would get better, that time would heal but instead the pain had been driven down deeper. Each year was like another pillow over her face and she was slowly suffocating.

Pain clenched her heart at the betrayal she had suffered and her loneliness. She had no one. She was alone. It tore at her, she was incapable of easing the pain.

So much betrayal. Her father, her mother, Phil. And then both Clare and Liz . She had drawn not one, but *two* gay women into her life. Both had a profound effect on her and both had lied to her.

And the guilt. The guilt of it all.

Her head began to throb and the familiar feeling of helplessness rose inside her. If only she could have a drink, that would numb it all. But she'd promised herself and so far, she'd kept that promise.

Everything was wrong. The thought was accompanied by a tiredness, a deep heaviness that permeated her every cell. Tears burned until she was unable to fight them any longer.

Without warning she sat up, drew her legs up to her chest and began to weep. It echoed round the bathroom, a sad hollow sound that sang of desperation and loneliness.

After a few minutes the pain in her chest subsided and her tears turned to hiccup sobs. It was so hard to face life square on like this. How did people do it? Nothing to soften life. Nothing to blur the edges of reality. Life was tough without that beautiful burning sensation in her throat, her relief.

The urge to tell, to shock, to break out and be different, be herself seized her. It was over. She couldn't fight anymore. Not sober anyway.

She lay back and touched her nipples peeping above the soap suds. This was her body. The body that gave birth to Emma. The body she gave to Philip. The one she had wanted to give to Liz. And Clare. The thought sent out an electric shock of excitement. Without the drink there was nothing to stem these images and her body burned.

Tentatively she moved her fingers down to touch herself. It was warm, soft, an open wound, exposed to the elements. A bunch of red raw quivering nerves open to all external stimuli. Too tired to fight any longer she closed her eyes and finally succumbed to the delicious fantasies. To Liz, to Clare. She moved her fingers experimentally around, finding what pleasured her most. The feelings were intense, building, she opened her eyes in surprise and an involuntary cry escaped her lips as an explosive orgasm pulled at her, tightening her body, holding her rigid. Just as quickly her body relaxed and waves of relief flooded from the central point between her legs, reducing in intensity until there was nothing.

Nothing. Only a hollowness left inside her, a deep dark hole of loneliness and fear of what she was, who she was. She was gay. She was gay. Still she recoiled from the words. From the truth. She was gay and she was attracted to Liz, maybe even in love with her. She was gay and she had been in love with Clare. Had tortured her friend. She was gay and she had been unkind, mean, spiteful. 'You're an old lecherous dyke,' she'd called her. Clare. Dear sweet Clare. She remembered her sweet forgiving smile the last time they'd seen one another, and the pinched worn look on her face as she walked away. So disgusted with herself, Jackie had done everything in her power to avoid it and had hurt people in the process, maybe even destroyed them.

She sat up. It was too much to contain in a still body.

Then there was Emma. They were close when Emma was a baby, but in the last year, with her daughter on the cusp of exploring her own sexuality, of understanding exactly what sexuality was, Jackie had pulled away. *I'm afraid*, she thought.

She rubbed her face hard with her wet hands. Now she had surrendered there was no way back. The future extended out in front of her like some arduous lonely trek full of obstacles and fears. Like a pilgrimage.

She lay back and pushed her head into the water until it covered her face. Laying still she heard the silence and in it came a voice. *You need help.* She heaved herself out of the water splashing it regardless round the bathroom and smiled as the water poured down her face.

She knew where to go.

Nikki had almost plucked bald her chenille cushion. Her mouth set tight and hard. She had been blind. Foolish. That was what came of falling in love. Well, she'd done it once, but never again. And she would make sure Philip would never forget her. He would not be allowed to cast her aside as if she were some plaything.

After a week of plotting she had finally worked out how she could exact revenge on Philip. How she could pull him back to her. She would hit him were it hurt the most. His career.

But first, she would play with him. Torment him the way he had tormented her. He was going to be sorry he ever met her. Either that, or come crawling back.

"Philip, a word?"

Was this it? "Sure thing, Jeremy."

Philip followed Jeremy Walford down the hall to his office his heart pounding, his throat dry, he needed to go to the toilet. He followed Jeremy into his office and sat down in the chair indicated for him.

"I've talked to the other partners. As I said before, we're all very impressed with the job you did on the Douglas's case and it looks like they are too."

"Oh," Philip's body relaxed and he smiled.

Jeremy Walford smiled and nodded as he leaned back into his chair. "They're sending more work our way and they want you to front it."

"That's great!"

"There's more," he pointed at Philip and clicked his tongue. "We want to offer you junior partner, see how things work out."

"That's fantastic!"

"You deserve it. We can't let a good man like you go, can we? If we don't offer it to you then some firm somewhere will come along and grab you."

Phil heard the underlying message. Walford didn't want to give him this, his hand had been forced. Strangely it made it all the more sweet for him.

"A word of warning, Phil," he paused. "Our reputation is paramount. I'm a man of the world and I'm well aware of your little, shall we say…dalliance? No problem there as long as it's kept discreet. No scenes. Divorce we can cope with but, well, affairs are a different matter. Understand?"

"Completely. No need to worry on that score, Jeremy. That's all in the past now."

"Glad to hear it. Continue to impress Douglas' and you know what you can expect in the future."

Philip grinned. He'd made the right decision.

So why did he hurt so much?

Liz sat opposite her father, a mug of rooibos steaming between her hands. Donald was talking but Liz wasn't listening. Instead she was still trying to understand how she could broach the subject, how she could question her mother, her father, the foundation of everything she stood for, everything she believed in.

"Elizabeth, you haven't listened to a word I've said, have you?"

Liz shook her head. "Sorry."

"What's on your mind?"

Liz paused, anxiety gripping her. The most difficult part of all this was she didn't know what made her so nervous. It just didn't feel right. There was probably a perfectly natural explanation. But what?

"Is it…is it this woman?"

Liz smiled at her father's attempts. She loved him so much when he waded out of his depth like this.

"No Dad, it's not that."

She saw his body relax. "What then? Come on, out with it."

Liz took a deep breath. "It's those boxes, of Mum's writing that you sent over." She saw him tense up again.

"Ah, yes, that. Bit of a mix up that, just assumed they were yours you know."

"So you didn't know they were Mum's?"

"No." She watched him play with his beard, tugging at it and stroking it.

"I sat down and read right through it all, both boxes."

"I see," he scratched the side of his face.

"And I found a diary too. Mum's diary."

He stopped scratching and let his hand and eyes drop.

"Is there something I should know?" she asked.

He pulled his upper lip into his mouth and drew his lower teeth over it a couple of times before answering. "Tell me what you know, or what you think you know."

Liz sighed. "Not much. Two boxes. Some excellent writing. You can hear Mum's voice coming through. But the diary really bothers me."

He nodded but said nothing.

"There's an entry I don't understand. The last one in it as a matter of fact. Something about mum being barren and unable to have children."

Donald sighed. He nodded but seemed reluctant to say anything. The silence was thick and choking.

"How could she write about being barren when she had me? I mean, at first I thought it was before I was born but I worked out the dates and it was when she was pregnant with me. It just doesn't add up."

Donald stared at his hands.

"Dad! Please, say something."

He stood up. "How about a nice drop of brandy or something?"

"I don't want any brandy or anything else. Sit down, Dad, and talk to me."

Donald sat back down and looked at her. There was a deep sadness in his eyes.

"Dad? What is it?"

He shook his head and then looked down at the carpet for a long time before he spoke. "We should have told you, I know we should have told you. Don't know how the years slipped by the way they did but before we knew it you were a woman and it seemed…cruel in a way, cruel and pointless."

"What?"

He sighed. "And then of course I could have been struck off for Malpractice. It was all kept in the family and we moved to the village when it was all over. Registered you there. It was all lined up. The job, the house, everything all organised." He stopped and shook his head again. Two pink spots appeared high in his cheeks, Liz recognised them as signs of stress and her body tensed up. Whatever he was rambling on about was not good. Not good at all.

She took a breath of the dense air, unsure whether she wanted him to continue. It was like watching a horror movie and wanting to press the pause button, go and make a cup of tea and calm down before it continued. But this was real and there was no control panel in real life.

"If it hadn't been for that diary," he said. Liz was shocked to see tears gather in the corner of his eyes and spill down his pink cheeks.

"Dad please, what is it?"

"She should be here to help me now. We didn't mean any harm."

Liz went and crouched by her father's chair, laying her hand on his arm for comfort. She had never seen him like this and it made her feel unsafe, unsteady. Like a small row boat on the open sea.

He pulled a starched white handkerchief from his trouser pocket and mopped the tears from his face before turning to her and covering her hand with his.

"Before I go on, Elizabeth, I want you to know that your mother loved you dearly. There wasn't a day went by when she didn't thank God for the gift of you. Promise me you'll remember that."

"Okay."

"I mean it, Elizabeth, promise me." He squeezed her hand hard.

Her heart beat hard in her chest. "Yes, yes I promise."

She watched her father take a deep breath. "Your mother wasn't your birth mother. She didn't carry you or give birth to you." He took another breath and then added quickly, "She was your mother in every other sense of the word."

His words made the flesh of Liz's body retract from her skin. She felt shrunken and distorted, oddly shaped, like a candle burnt in the middle.

"But my birth certificate? There had to be adoption papers, something. It isn't possible."

Donald sat in silence for a while and then in a heavy slow voice he told her the story.

Her mother's sister, May, agreed to carry a child for them when they discovered Margaret couldn't have children. Donald was her biological father but May, not Margaret, was her biological mother. May lived with them and registered herself under Margaret's name. Elizabeth was born at home with Donald as the named doctor and a private midwife who didn't know the true identity of Donald's wife. A few weeks after the birth, when May was fit enough to leave she returned home to Birmingham and Margaret and Donald moved to the village Elizabeth knew as home.

"It was very simple and straight forward."

Liz's voice came out as a whisper. "You would never have told me, would you?"

Donald shook his head. "We did intend to, but there seemed no point once you were grown. And your mother was so…ashamed. When we got you she refused to write anything. It was like she'd traded you for that dream of hers."

"I…I…is this real?" she found herself asking.

Donald nodded. "I'm sorry sweetheart. Your mum was very jealous of the fact that you were my daughter, biologically. I believe she felt you were more mine than hers. Initially at least. I took a step back, encouraged her to bond with you."

Liz stood up and made her way haphazardly across the room to collapse into the chair opposite. Her body was automated, she was numb, unsure what to say, how to feel, how to react. Her mother was not her mother.

"My mother isn't my mother," she said aloud.

"No, that isn't true," Donald said, his voice stern. "Your mother couldn't have been more a mother. In fact, sometimes when I watched the pair of you I thought she was closer to you, loved you more, because she hadn't conceived you."

Liz remembered her mother's soft voice, her gentle hands, the bedtime stories and lullabies, the giggles and tickles, snuggling and cuddling in her mother's warm bed with pillows that smelt of her mother's rose perfume. The birthday cakes she baked, the party costumes she sewed, the long letters they wrote to each other when Liz went off to university, each needing them to supplement the long telephone conversations. The shopping expeditions, the cups of coffee and laughter, the tea and sympathy, the years of listening and laughing and drying her tears. The years of love and understanding. She was worth a million when her mother looked at her. Her mother. Her mother? She recalled the two boxes of writing and the two different voices. Now she understood.

Finally Liz turned to her father. "I need to go home."

"Don't go, Elizabeth. Let's sit and talk about this."

"I'm sorry I can't, Dad. I need to think. I want to go home," and for some reason the last sentence tore at her chest. A roar of pain rolled up and she found herself sobbing, feeling lost, unanchored, afraid.

And for the first time in her life her father wound his arms round her and rocked her, shushed her, comforted her. He felt big and strong and safe and it made her cry more.

Chapter 33

Jackie sat in the lounge sipping hot coffee, watching Clare move around the room, sorting piles of books and papers. She felt a mixture of relief and discomfort to find Clare here, after all this time.

When she had woken that morning the realisations she had made in the bath the night before had come crashing in on her. There were things she had to lay to rest before she could make decisions about her life, about her sexuality, and Clare was one of those things.

Many times on the drive up she had almost turned back and when she approached the gate, it was like wading through water, but she forced herself on until she'd reached the front door and knocked.

Clare blanched when she opened the door, her eyes wide and her face pale and drawn. She hadn't changed much, thought Jackie. Her hair was greying and there were more lines round her eyes but she was still beautiful and Jackie's heart quivered at the sight of her.

"Clare?" It came out as a question.

"Jackie?" echoed the woman in front of her.

"Can I come in?"

Clare opened the door wide and led her down the hall and into the front room on the left.

"You've caught me at a bad time," she explained.

"Should I go?" Jackie asked, reddening, wishing she hadn't come, realising what an intrusion her presence must be after all these years.

Clare's arm shot out and held onto Jackie. "No," she said and quickly withdrew her arm again. There was an awkward pause as each relived their last meeting.

"If you could just give me half an hour," she said lightly. "Just make yourself at home. The kitchen's down the hall if you want a drink." She smiled and turned to leave but stopped. "It's good to see you," she said as she turned and left.

Jackie stood and took in the room. It was snug with a small fire burning in the open grate. The thick white washed walls were littered with sketches of ballerinas. The tiny latticed window allowed little light in and so a wooden standard lamp had been switched on in the corner. Bright orange curtains and cushions with bright blue sofas gave the room a modern but comfortable look. Rag rugs were scattered over the floor, a TV cabinet stood in one corner and a desk in another. The desk was swamped in paper and books. It hadn't changed a bit and she felt the old feelings of warmth envelope her.

Clare came in babbling. "Please sit down, put the TV on if you want. Reception's not great I'm afraid, I need to get the aerial fixed, blew off in those horrid winds a few months back and I still haven't got round to getting it fixed. Still, it's one less distraction!"

She walked over to the desk and picked up a bundle of papers. "Last lot to sort," she said, lifting and waving the pile in her hands.

Jackie smiled and took a seat, suddenly unsure why she was here.

Eventually Clare came and sat next to Jackie, with two mugs of hot coffee. "White no sugar, yes?" she asked, handing Jackie a mug.

Jackie nodded and took the mug.

"How did you know I was still here?"

"I didn't."

Jackie smiled again, unsure of where to start. She took a deep breath. "I'm not really sure why I'm here. My life is such a mess and I have no one to talk to. I was sitting at home this morning feeling so lonely, feeling adrift. There's so many things I've got wrong, so many wrong turns I've made," she stopped.

Clare said nothing.

"I hope you don't mind. I suppose it's a bit cheeky after the last time...." Jackie trailed off and cast her eyes down. "I don't know what happened."

"It was a long time ago now. I can't say I wasn't hurt at the time but, well, it's water under the bridge. What's going on with you?"

Jackie took a deep breath. "I'm not sure where to begin," she said.

"Well, as the old cliché says, why not start at the beginning?"

And so Jackie told Clare everything.

She talked about her father and Jan, her problems with Phil, her relationship with Liz, her battle with alcohol and finally, and most difficult of all, her confusion about her sexuality.

"All these years it's been bubbling inside me and I never knew it." Tears began to trickle down Jackie's face. Clare said nothing.

"I never understood why everyone raved on about sex," Jackie continued. "With Phil it was okay but nothing spectacular. I thought there was something wrong with me.

"Phil would shout at me, blame me, say it was my fault. He was struggling with the work at Uni. He said I was so frigid he couldn't concentrate. I thought it must be true because I was coping well, even enjoyed the challenge."

Jackie was distant, absorbed in her own thoughts. The full force of the memories and the battles came back to her and she didn't want to share it now. It was too raw, too new.

God, what a mess. She lay her head onto the back of the sofa and closed her eyes, feeling weary. Sometimes it was too much!

Clare sat beside her quietly. They sat like this for a long time. Nothing was said, nothing needed saying. Jackie started to cry and Clare moved closer to put her arm around her shoulder. Jackie moved round to face Clare and they just looked at one another for a long time. Wondering what could have been and mourning what had been lost. Eventually Jackie leaned forward and buried her head into Clare's shoulder to cry again.

"It's okay," Clare said, stroking the other woman's hair. "You're safe."

Liz had slept over at her father's last night in her old bedroom. They had sat up late talking. He had answered her questions, held her when she cried, apologised when she stormed around in anger and explained his misery at the distance that had formed between them over the years. He told her how proud he was of her and how much he loved her. She had seen a side of him she had never seen before, had felt closer to him than she had ever felt before. And she had left him this morning as if some Perspex wall had been removed from between them.

This morning, as she sat at her desk she felt at peace about her mother's death. The tears and tantrums of the night before seemed to have cleansed her. She had grieved. Finally she had grieved. She felt the pain of losing her mother not once, but twice.

She picked up the diary. "What a tangled web we weave," she said aloud to the teddy her mother had given her and which occupied a place on her desk.

She walked over to the boxes of writing and opened one up, putting the diary inside and closing the lid. She couldn't throw this out. She'd never be able to do that, but she was ready to store it. Maybe in the attic. She could let go that much. It was time. She turned her attention to her work. She had a deadline to keep and she wanted to make sure her mother would continue to be proud of her. She smiled—her father too.

Liz had been given her own comment column in the monthly woman's features section of the local paper. Her brief was to keep it topical and short. She read the piece over again.

Is the Monarchy really privileged? That is the question I found myself asking as I watched the Queen disembark from her plane in Jamaica. Here is a woman in her seventies who is scheduled over the next few weeks to make not one long haul flight, but six, and at a time when life has had a fair amount of stresses for her recently.

Last November Prince Edward and Sophie went through the pain of losing their unborn child through an eptopic pregnancy and it is only days since she buried her sister. In addition, she leaves behind an aging and ailing mother.

Her personal grief, family rifts and squabbles, joys and traumas are put on display not only for the people of this country, but worldwide.

We observe and deal out our judgements, often failing to remember that what we are witnessing is real people, real events and real emotions. And she endures all this not because she sought publicity and fame as many young people have recently on Pop Idol, but because she was born to that family.

I am not a royalist but I am a humanitarian and when I watched our Queen arriving in Jamaica this week dressed in black and looking sombre, I couldn't help but see all she represented about Britain. That stiff upper lip, duty before everything mentality. And whether I agree with it or not, I couldn't help but admire her.

If that is a life of privilege I know I'd fall way short of the necessary skills to carry it out and perhaps it would do us all good to meditate on the privilege of anonymity.

She'd have to check on the Queen's age but on the whole she was pleased. She sat back, satisfied.

Thoughts of Jackie rose immediately and her heart was a stone in her chest, constricting her breathing. She was sad to lose the friendship but if they could have parted on good terms she would have found it easier to handle. This rift and the way they left things made her body feel dirty.

Had she been deliberately deceitful? Had some part of her unconscious held her back from telling Jackie until it was too late? She shook the thoughts from her head. It made no difference now. It was too late. Still, it didn't stop the tears of regret crowding her eyes as she clicked on save.

Jackie stood with Clare in the kitchen as she washed up. Her heart beat like a wild bird trapped in her chest and her throat was tight. She took a deep breath and asked the question quickly as if it might escape if she didn't get it out.

"Why didn't you ever try to kiss me?" she blurted out.

Clare arched her perfectly shaped eyebrows for a moment and then smiled. "What makes you think I wanted to?" she said with humour.

Jackie blushed and looked at the kitchen lino, studying it as if her life depended on being able to memorise the brown criss-cross pattern.

Clare leaned closer. "As a matter of fact I did want to." She rinsed a glass and put it in the rack to drain.

"Then why didn't you?" Jackie said, agog at her own audacity.

Clare considered the bubbles in the sink for a few moments as if the question had sent her off beat and then she looked at Jackie. "I don't know what you think being a lesbian means, Jackie, but perhaps I should clear up a few misconceptions here. We're not out to recruit and swell our numbers. Lesbianism is about sexuality and that's it. Nothing more, nothing less. It doesn't mean your morals fall into the gutter nor sadly does it raise them, lesbian or not. I'm still the same person."

They were silent for a few moments as she washed a breakfast bowl. "I still want all the same things as anyone else. A home, someone special in my life," she laughed lightly. "I even wanted kids," she shrugged. "Too late now of course. Being a lesbian is just one aspect of my life. I don't mean to come on heavy it's just...." she paused, holding the bowl aloft.

"People always assume the worst?" Jackie said.

"I wouldn't say *always* but well, yes. When people find out my sexuality they change their opinion of me. Well, most do." Jackie coloured as she listened.

Clare rinsed the bowl and put it with the glass then stopped. "It's like you become a different person all of a sudden, as if everything you were is suddenly cast aside and a new definition created. It might be that you're more interesting, you're a threat, anything. It can be positive as well as negative but their view of you changes and that saddens me because I haven't changed." Clare continued to wash up.

Jackie thought back to her reaction when she discovered Clare was gay and shrank from the memory.

As if she had read Jackie's thoughts she said, "Remember that day in town?" She waited to get a nod from Jackie before continuing. "I told you then that I had no intentions of seducing you and I meant it. You were upset, you needed a friend. Seducing you, assuming I could," Clare laughed, "well, it would have made your situation ten times worse. I'm not that kind of person, gay or not!"

Jackie looked at Clare. Her face was flushed, although Jackie wasn't sure if it was the heat from the water or her emotions. It added a prettiness to her. Her dark hair, still beautiful with its shots of grey, shone under the light as she moved, her dark eyebrows rose up and down as she spoke. Sincerity was stamped across her face.

"What if I'd wanted you to?" Jackie asked quietly.

Clare looked thoughtful before answering. "I don't know. There's more to a relationship than sex."

Jackie smiled. "To be honest, I'm still not sure."

"I know."

"It's all so confusing."

Clare nodded as she pulled out the plug. The water drained away noisily.

"Did you always know?"

"No. For a while I just didn't fit it. I had sex with boys, but like you couldn't understand what all the fuss was about."

"Exactly!"

"Ah, but have you had sex with anyone other than Phil?"

Jackie shook her head.

"Then it could be…" Clare sighed as she dried her hands. "Look I really like you, but I've no interest in games. I don't want to confuse you further but, well, before you try a woman you might want to consider that Phil is just really bad in bed."

Jackie laughed.

Clare smiled. "Look, I'm not suggesting you sleep with anyone else, male or female, but before you declare yourself gay think about it." Clare's voice took a sharp edge as she said, "It's not an easy option, even in these supposed days of enlightenment."

Jackie rolled her mug between her hands as she considered what Clare had said. *Maybe I'm not gay, maybe…* But inside, deep in the very core of her being she knew the truth.

That evening at home Jackie rinsed her cup at the kitchen sink and stood it on the draining board. She looked around at the modern white units trimmed with grey. Clean, spacious, uncluttered. Not a bit like her life. When they had replaced the old battered dark mahogany kitchen they had purposefully put in a breakfast bar for when their children were older. The white worktop swerved round and curved out, supported by one white pole underneath. Two ash stools were tucked away neatly. They were to have two children. Two little bottoms sitting here morning after morning, chatting about the day ahead of them or arguing over the last piece of toast. Movement, noise, life. And here they were instead, in this huge house. This huge empty house, with only her and Emma.

She thought about Clare. It had been good to see her, to understand things more clearly. She had wept on and off for most of the visit, but when she left there was a peace within her.

She had been thinking over her options and decided she did have choices, she saw that now. Philip was right. She always had choices. Perhaps they weren't the kind of choices she would have liked, but she had them. And now she had made a decision. She would seek out a counsellor to help her deal with the past and talk to Philip about the future.

Chapter 34

"We need to celebrate!" Philip announced the following day as Jackie pushed the iron over his best blue shirt. *He did look handsome in blue*, she thought.

"What are we celebrating?"

He stopped, suddenly aware of how much he'd shut her out of his life. She had no idea of the stress he'd been under, sticking his head above the parapet in the hope that rather than being shot off, it would be noticed and promoted. And he'd done it. He'd bloody done it. Yes, he'd confessed about creating evidence but he hadn't explained his motives for doing so. He pulled her into his arms.

"I've been offered junior partner, Jackie. Isn't that great! Everything's going to be different from now on, Jackie, you'll see."

She smiled. It was good to see him so happy. He was right, for once they agreed.

She unwound herself from his arms. "Philip, we need to talk."

"What about?" he asked, his brow frowning. She could tell by his tone of voice she had deflated him.

"Us," she said quietly.

"And I haven't seen her since," Liz told her father. They knelt side by side in the garden digging compost into the beds round the lawn, the sun warmed her back, easing her aching muscles.

"I'm sorry."

Liz smiled. "Thanks for listening and not saying I told you so."

"Not my style," he chuckled. A genuine warmth had sprung up between them.

"No." She turned over the soil with the small trowel.

"I've been seeing a bit more of Ruth these last couple of months."

"And?"

"It still feels strange. I was with your mum for so long and we were so happy. It feels like I'm being unfaithful somehow."

Liz stopped digging and turned to her father. "What…have you—"

Donald bustled. "None of your business!"

"*I* told you about my little flirtation with Jackie."

He paused for a moment and then said, "Our generation is not as free and easy about discussing our sex life."

She wondered if he'd had to have sex with May, her birth mother, but pushed it aside. "That means yes," she said, instead as she returned to her digging.

"It means no such thing and as a matter of fact we haven't!"

"Only asking."

"Well don't."

Liz saluted. "Message received and understood, Captain!"

They worked in silence. Benjy, who had explored the garden earlier, now lay out on the patio in the dim afternoon sun.

"So?" she ventured eventually.

"It's difficult, Elizabeth. I thought I'd moved on, built a new life and now…." he raised his gloved hands in a hopeless gesture, the trowel spilling soil onto the lawn.

"Dad, can I give you some advice?"

"Probably."

Liz laughed. "You're thinking about all this way too hard. Just get on with it and see what happens."

205

"I'm worried for Ruth. She's a lovely lady and I don't want to play with her feelings."

Liz sat back on her heels and scratched her nose with her wrist to avoid the dirty fingers of the gloves. "Then be honest with her, be up front. I wish I had."

Donald smiled. "I think that's very good advice," he said. "When did you get so smart?"

She gave a wry smile. "When I started listening to my old dad."

Nikki dialled Philip's office number.

"Yes, I'd like to make an appointment to see Philip Lawson please."

"Has he seen you before?" the receptionist asked.

"No. I'm a new client. But I have spoken to Mr Lawson previously. Actually, the case is complex and when I spoke to Mr Lawson he suggested I make an appointment when Jeremy Walford was in the office. In case we needed to call him in?"

"I understand but it means that unfortunately I can't book you an appointment until next week."

"Next week will do fine, thank you."

"Can I take your name please."

"Mrs Hunt."

"Philip, I want a divorce."

They sat at the dining table, the remainder of the chicken chasseur congealing on the plates.

"Jackie, that's ridiculous," he laughed. "Things are just going our way."

"No, Philip, they're going *your* way."

"Look if this is about that silly fling I had—"

"It's not that. I'm unhappy, Philip, I always have been. So are you if you'd only have the courage to admit it. This marriage is a sham."

Philip's jaw set tight. "I'll admit it's been tough in the past but there's evidence that things are improving now."

"Oh Philip, listen to yourself! This isn't one of your cases. This is our lives!"

"Jackie, you're becoming hysterical."

"Philip, I've not even raised my voice. If you mean I'm getting emotional then you're right. And under the circumstances it's not surprising."

"But I don't understand. What's brought this on?"

She pushed her fork through the leftover food. "Nothing specific. I'm just fed up with it all."

"With all what, for Christ sake!"

"This! This constant fighting for my space."

He stood up. "You're being irrational, Jackie. Look, this is a difficult time for you right now. You've just stopped drinking. It's like a grieving process. You know what they say, don't make any big decisions in the first year."

"Philip–"

"No. I said no, Jackie, and that's final. It's nonsense," and he strode out of the room before she could say anymore. He was sure he was doing the right thing. She'd come to her senses eventually, even if she hated him right now. If he could leave Nikki, if he could make that sacrifice, then she could damn well put in the effort to make this thing work.

Jackie considered following him but decided there was no use, instead she began clearing the table.

Chapter 35

When Liz opened the door she was surprised to see Jackie standing on the step in the sunshine.

"Come in," she said, her body tensing, pleased to see her but unsure, the memory of their last meeting still clear in her mind.

Liz led Jackie into the front room. The sight of her polished grand piano a comfort. She indicated the large white sofa for Jackie to sit on and then took the matching armchair.

"It's good of you to see me," Jackie said, her eyes lowered.

Liz's body loosened. Perhaps it would be okay. She jumped up and walked across the room.

"Want a drink?" she asked shaking a bottle in the air.

Jackie shook her head.

Liz crossed the room and sat back down in their chair.

"I'm curious as to why you're here, after the last time," she said after a few moments.

Jackie clasped her hands in her lap and stared at them hard. "I came to apologise."

"I see."

"And to try to explain."

It was obvious this was difficult for Jackie and Liz softened. "Your apology is accepted. There's no need to explain."

Jackie looked up. "But I want to. I need to. I know that might sound selfish after... after everything but, if you don't mind?"

Liz shook her head, feeling her curls swing around her head. "No, if you need to I'm all ears."

Jackie started to laugh lightly. "I don't know where to start now. I've spent days practising this little speech and now…."

"Jackie, it doesn't matter."

"But it does. It does to me."

Liz held up her arms in defeat. "Okay. Fire away."

"I think I'm gay," she said. "It wasn't just the …thing that happened between us, it's lots of…things." Liz raised an amused eyebrow and Jackie laughed. "Not like that."

Jackie took a breath. "I've asked Philip for a divorce."

Liz said nothing.

"Was your husband the only man you ever slept with, Liz?"

Liz laughed. "No. No, he wasn't. I had a few boyfriends before him, a few girlfriends too."

"Really?"

Liz nodded. "I was really confused. Sex with men wasn't bad, I enjoyed it. But it was better with women. I felt…it just felt right. Like I was being myself." She picked her nails for a few moments before continuing. "If I'm honest, I was a bit like you. Didn't want to admit I was gay. It was a different climate all together then too. Very hush hush, the whole business," she shrugged. "When I got pregnant I thought it would solve the problem, decision made, end of story."

Jackie nodded. "I've stopped drinking," she announced.

Liz nodded and smiled encouragement.

"Philip doesn't want a divorce. He's worried about his career."

Liz smiled. "I'm sure it's not just that."

"No. Maybe not. It's probably more to do with his parent's approval but he doesn't see that. Or perhaps he just won't admit it."

"We simplify other people's feelings sometimes."

Jackie wrapped her hair round one ear. "Have I done that? With you I mean?"

"I can't answer that."

"Do you *think* I did that with you?"

"Perhaps. It doesn't matter now." Liz stood up. "You sure you wouldn't like a drink? I mean tea or coffee?"

Jackie shook her head.

She sat back down again. "So, does Philip know why you want a divorce?"

"No. I didn't have the courage to tell him. He thinks it's because of his affairs."

"It's a good enough reason, for now."

Jackie nodded.

"What you going to do?"

Jackie shrugged. "I'm not sure. I've got to tell Emma yet."

"Tough one."

Jackie nodded.

"I've always been gay," Jackie said quietly. "I didn't know it until recently. No, I always knew it, I just wouldn't admit it to myself."

"There's no shame in that. It's a scary concept."

"Yes."

"Especially when you have children."

"How d'you think she'll respond, Emma, I mean?"

"To the divorce?"

"No. To me...the gay thing?"

Liz thought for a moment. "She's your daughter. You probably have a better idea than me."

"But don't you see, I'm too close. I'm too scared."

"From what I know of her she's a very mature young girl."

"And that's it. She's a girl. A child."

"You do have another option you know. It doesn't have to be all or nothing."

Jackie looked hard at Liz. "It's always been like that with me. Always. I'm just beginning to realise that."

"But it doesn't have to be," Liz said softly.

"How d'you mean?"

"Don't tell her. Don't tell anyone at the moment. Deal with the divorce first. As time passes and you get more used to the idea then talk to others. It doesn't all have to be done in one go."

"Is that what you did?"

Liz nodded. "I got through the divorce first, then told my parents. Well," she laughed, "I told my mum first. She was great about it and broke it to my dad. He was shocked at first but he's come round." She thought fondly of the day recently in the garden when they'd been able to talk comfortably for the first time.

Jackie couldn't imagine telling her family. Besides, she didn't need to anymore. It didn't matter what they thought of her. It didn't matter if they knew or not. The thought freed her.

Liz moved onto the sofa and took Jackie hand. "But the point is you don't need to tell anyone. You'll wake up one day and know it's the right time but for now just take one day at a time. You've enough to do getting through the divorce and staying off the alcohol. Spend some time getting to know who you are before sharing yourself."

"I suppose so."

"What do you want from life?" Liz asked her.

"I don't know. I don't know what I want. I only know something in my life has to change."

"Why not get a job?"

"I can't. I've never worked. I wouldn't know where to start."

"You're an intelligent woman. Finish your degree, retrain in something new, teaching for example, there's a national shortage, I'm doing a piece on it." She laughed, "They'll take anyone these days."

"Thanks," said Jackie, smiling.

"Seriously though, you could do anything you wanted to you, just need to set your mind to it."

Jackie nodded and smiled. "Maybe," she said.

Janet, Philip's secretary, opened all his mail except the rare letter marked private so it was with some interest that he picked up the long cream envelope this morning.

It felt like a card and Philip's curiosity was aroused as he ripped it open. His heart sank as he removed the cream card. On the front was a silver heart and inside the words '*missing you*'. It wasn't signed but it didn't need to be, he knew who it was from. First Jackie's little scene and now this. It seemed his world was threatening to crumble...again.

It was like building sand castles with the tide coming in. He'd just think he'd finished when whoosh, some bastard wave came along and swept it all away.

He had hoped that their last meeting would be the end of it. And yet, a part of him still ached for her, still wanted to feel her in his arms, touch her, smell her heavy perfumes. Abruptly he tore the card in two and threw it into the waste bin. He had promised himself a fresh start with Jackie, he'd made his decision. He'd made his decision the day they'd married. His mother had disapproved, told him they were far too young. Well, here they were, fourteen years later, a little shaky perhaps but they were getting through, and they'd continue to get through, he was sure of it. He'd show them. Jack would come round, she always did.

Chapter 36

I suppose I could, Jackie thought. She had been reflecting on Liz's comments for the past week. She pulled out a loaf of bread from the carrier bag full of shopping on the table and put it in the ceramic bread bin.

Philip had still not agreed to a divorce and had refused to even discuss the possibility of a separation. It was ironic, all these years she had wanted him to be home, to make a life here instead of with his work and now she didn't want him anymore she couldn't get rid of him.

She didn't really mind the procrastination. She was afraid. What would she do on her own? How would she and Emma manage?

I could get a job, she thought. I had a brain once. A long time ago now, but I was top of my class before…before the miscarriage. There. She'd said it. And it felt right this time. It needed to be said. These ghosts needed to be exhumed from her mind.

She stopped, holding a tin of baked beans in mid air. "I," she said out loud, "had a lost abortion." Lost abortion. That was the medical term for it. But Liz was right, it hadn't been a real abortion.

"I had a lost abortion," she said again but it wasn't right. "I had a miscarriage." That was better. "I had a miscarriage." That was the truth.

There. She'd said it out loud now and nothing had happened to her.

This wasn't so bad.

"I, Jackie Lawson, am gay. Hi, I'm Jackie Lawson and I'm gay," she squeezed involuntarily and her shoulders came up when she said it. Again she waited. Again nothing happened. What she was waiting for she wasn't sure,

213

but something. Something horrid. She exhaled. Still nothing happened.

Jackie turned to put the beans in the cupboard and began to whistle. As soon as she had unpacked the shopping she'd phone the local college. You never knew what they might suggest.

Her thoughts turned to Emma. The class was visiting the secondary school this afternoon and Jackie's anxiousness returned. Emma had been unhappy about changing schools. It was another reason not to push Philip for the divorce too quickly. *Can Emma manage with so many changes? Can I?* Still, like Liz said, there was no rush.

This morning he held the envelope for a few minutes before opening it. She'd left a message every day this week with his secretary. He'd have to do something, otherwise it would look like he wasn't returning his clients calls or, worse, he was having an affair. He remembered Walford's warning. The firm could take a divorce, but affairs were something different. They disturbed the equilibrium. He'd have to do something…but what?

It was the same long cream envelope and he knew it would be the same card inside. He contemplated tearing it up straight away, without opening it, or simply returning it unopened, but his curiosity got the better of him.

He tore it open and smiled. He'd been right. Same card, silver heart on a plain background. Inside she'd written, *'see you soon'*. See you soon…what did that mean? He felt a flutter of fear and his hands shook as he slowly tore the card in two and dropped it into the bin.

"So it was okay?" Jackie was stood at the cooker warming a tin of beans through for Emma who had returned from school starving.

"Mum it was fantastic! They have their own swimming pool and the computer room is twice the size of ours."

"That's great."

"And the drama department is fantastic. They put productions on every year. Big ones, not like the little things we do."

"Oh Emma, I'm so pleased."

"And the best news of all is…."

"Come on, don't keep me in suspense."

"Last week Lottie told me that Alan Metcalf was going to that school but I didn't believe her, you know how she likes to wind me up, but then today he was there!"

Jackie tipped the beans onto the buttered toast, put it in front of Emma and sat down at the table with her.

"So, things aren't so bad after all?"

Emma shook her head as she picked up her knife and fork. "And there's more."

"Oh?"

"Lottie's mum picked her up so I sat next to him all the way back on the bus."

"Did he kiss you?"

"Murm!"

She smiled. "So you two are an item then?"

She shrugged. "We'll see," she said, cutting into the toast.

"I'm really pleased, honey."

"Things couldn't be better," Emma declared with a big grin.

Jackie gazed out of the window while her daughter ate. The apple tree looked burdened with blossom, the branches bending under the weight. Everything was emerging, waking up, growing. She watched the daffodils dancing in the garden. They were past their best now and beginning to brown at the edges. They would need tying down soon to ensure they'd come up next year. Next year, would they be here next year? Was this the right time to talk to Emma about it?

"Mum?"

Jackie turned to her daughter.

"Are you and dad going to get a divorce?"

Jackie looked down at her hands, tracing the cuticles with her eyes. They needed some moisturiser.

"Are you?"

Jackie looked at Emma. "It's a possibility," she said.

"Apparently there's loads of kids at the new school whose parents are divorced."

"Really. Does it bother you?"

"A bit but, you know, change is sometimes good. Sometimes it's…best."

Emma filled her mouth with beans. "Can I go and tell Liz about my new school when I've finished this?" she said with her mouth full.

Jackie smiled at her daughter. Perhaps it would be okay, after all, change was sometimes a good thing. As her daughter had said. Sometimes it's best.

Chapter 37

"That was fantastic," Liz told her father as she licked her fingers clean.

"Yes, Ruth is a great cook."

"Ruth made this!"

Donald nodded, looking proud.

"How are things between you two? Am I allowed to ask?"

Donald frowned at her but he was smiling too. "Good. I talked to her as you suggested."

"And?"

"We're going to take things slowly."

"At your age I wouldn't take things too slowly."

"Hey!"

Liz laughed. "Seriously Dad, I'm made up for you."

He grinned and scratched his beard. "I'm rather pleased myself. Life in the old dog yet."

"Got anymore of that cake going spare, you old dog?"

"Yes, but there's something else I'd like to give you first."

"Oh?"

Donald moved across the kitchen, opened the drawer of the Welsh dresser and took out two photos.

"Here," he said, handing one of them to Liz. "I thought you'd like this."

She took it from him. "What is it?"

"A photo of your Aunt May. You never met her so I thought you'd like a picture of her."

Liz looked at the woman in the photo and caught her breath. The similarities between this woman and her mother astounded her. It was a black and white head and shoulders posed photo of a woman in her mid to late twenties. Her curly corkscrew hair came just past her chin in length and was drawn back off her face with an Alice band. She had a clear complexion, a wide toothy smile and a small dimple in her right cheek. She wore a round neck sweater with the lapels of the shirt underneath folded neatly over the collar of the sweater.

"It was taken the week after she agreed to help us. Your mum insisted on it. I'm not sure why. I suppose she always intended to tell you. In a way I suppose she did. After all, it was her diary that told you in the end." He held out the other photo. "This one is of your mother."

Her mother was in exactly the same pose.

"Like two peas in a pod. People were always saying that when they saw them together. They were often mistaken for twins, not identical obviously but you can see why. Your mum was the elder by two years but it doesn't show, does it?"

Liz nodded her head in agreement. The poses, the clothes they wore, even the way they had dressed their hair that day was identical.

"It was as if your mum wanted the two of them to look as alike as possible. It was her idea that they dress the same," Donald said as if reaching into her mind.

Liz nodded in agreement, unable to find words to explain how she felt. Finally she found her voice. "Dad, there's just one question that's been praying on my mind. Just one."

"What is it?"

"I think you'll find it difficult to answer but I need to know."

"Go on then," her father sat down at the table in the chair next to her.

"Did you...did you and Aunt May have sex? To get me, I mean."

Liz watched her father as he looked out of the window into the garden, his mind taking him back, recreating the past so it was alive and fresh in front of him. She let him go, waiting patiently until finally he returned and looked back at her.

"You have to understand it was a long time ago. Things were different then, Elizabeth. We didn't know much about artificial insemination in those days. Of course, being a doctor I understood the fundamentals but the practicalities of getting it from one place to another," he stopped and Liz caught the flush across his face and smiled at how young and vulnerable he suddenly looked.

How could a medical man get embarrassed about the mechanics of the human body? Still, she supposed there was a difference talking to your daughter about her conception and doing a consultation in his capacity as a doctor.

"So did you?" she asked, prompting him. helping him.

"Yes we did."

"And?"

He looked up at her sharply. "You don't want details, surely?"

Liz smiled. "No, not details, Dad. I just want to know if it was nice, or was it, you know, mechanical?"

Donald coughed and then said, "It was very pleasant. A little awkward at first but no, not mechanical. Not in the least bit mechanical. May and I were very fond of one another. Always were. I was very sorry to hear of her death."

"How did she die?"

"Motorbike accident in Greece. You were only young at the time," he laughed. "Those two. Your mother and May. Two little adventurers they were. You couldn't meet a more exciting pair of girls, though I think May was more flighty and dangerous, less keen on settling down. We were always getting postcards about her adventures." He shook his head smiling.

"Did you love May?"

"Not in the way you mean. I loved her for what she had done for us. I loved the parts of her that reminded me of your mum, but I adored your mum. She was simpler than May. More peaceful. May always seemed to be running from one place to another, one man to another. She had a big heart but a restless spirit. I can't say I envied the man who fell in love with May. She was like an exotic bird or a mermaid, difficult to catch. No Elizabeth, make no mistake, I loved your mother. Heart and soul." He paused and looked sad for a moment, then he looked up and Liz and smiled. "I suppose that's why this thing with Ruth has been so hard."

Liz smiled back at him and put her hand over her fathers. "Thanks, Dad. For the photos, for everything. And don't worry about mum. All she ever wanted was for us to be happy. She'd approve of Ruth," Liz laughed. "Especially when she bakes such fab cake. Can I have some more then or are you hoarding it for yourself for when I'm gone?"

Jackie waited in the lobby of the college. It had a smell only schools and colleges could have. A mixture of old cabbage, chalk and ink. She pulled the hem of her skirt down again. Was it too short? She wished she'd worn trousers now.

That morning Emma had grinned at her over the table.

"Just think, we might be sitting down to do our homework together in September."

"We'll see."

"Are you nervous, Mum?"

"A little. I'm just going to have a chat with them. Nothing may come of it."

"I think you're very brave."

"Why?"

Emma shrugged. "Dunno. I just do."

I think you're very brave. As she recalled them the words struck Jackie in the chest. They would be okay. They would support each other. Everything would be all right. Her meanderings were interrupted.

"Mrs Lawson? Come this way please."

As she stood up and followed the woman she realised she was wrong. She wasn't here just for a chat. Things had changed. She had changed. And she couldn't change back. Not now. Not ever. No matter how much she had kidded herself since she made the appointment, this was no time to try to go back. She tossed aside the ideas she had come with and entered the office with an open mind.

When Janet showed Nikki into Philip's office he stood behind his desk and gaped. Nikki! She had never been to his office before. He glanced down at his diary. 'Mrs Hunt' it said and he blanched with realisation.

"Nikki!" he said finally as Janet left, coming round the desk.

"Hello, Philip."

"Please, sit down." He indicated a carver armchair. "It's good to see you."

"I'm sure it isn't," she said as she sat down. "You know why I've come."

"Not entirely," he said moving back round to the other side of the desk.

"Come on, Philip. You're a bright person."

"I got your cards, if that's what you mean."

She placed her handbag in her lap but said nothing.

"What do you want?"

"You."

"Nikki we've been through this–"

"No Philip! No, no we haven't!"

Philip stood up and bounced his hands in a placatory manner. "Nikki, please."

She smiled. "What? Worried I might make a scene?"

"Nik, things aren't that easy–"

"I know about the letters Philip, about Sean Hunt, the whole story."

"Are you threatening me?"

"I knew something wasn't right," she said, ignoring him. "But I didn't know what at first."

"How did you know?"

"The letters, Philip. It didn't take a genius, just a little mulling over."

Philip sat back down in his chair, stunned. How had she found out? Had he told her one night when they were snuggled in bed and his guard was down? No. It wasn't possible. But he'd often left his notes and diary at her place. It wouldn't have been difficult for her to... "Did you snoop? Did you look at my things?"

Nikki laughed lightly. "What a ridiculous question."

"Why? Why would you?"

"Oh don't come all moral on me now, Philip. You are so used to using people and then moving on, just took out a little insurance in case you did the same to me."

"Surely this isn't just about us?"

"What else?"

"But how? Why? I mean...you weren't bothered...were you? I mean when I came to tell you that day you seemed so...so...so calm."

Nikki stood up abruptly. "Of course I was bothered," she said. "I was very bothered."

"Nikki, please, sit down."

"Why? Worried I might start shouting and get your boss in here?"

"He's not here."

She started walking round the office. "Small, isn't it?" she said with contempt, ignoring his lie. She turned to face him, her face set hard. "You lied to me. You lied to your bosses. You lied in court."

"But I—"

"And for what? So you could have what *you* wanted."

Philip realised it was pointless to argue.

"What do you want, Nikki?" His voice heavy with effort.

Nikki softened. "You, Philip, it's as simple as that, I want you."

Philip propped his elbows on the desk and lay his head in his hands. If he were honest he wanted her too, more than he liked to admit. She frightened him and excited him and moved him in a way Jackie never did, never had.

"Jackie has asked me for a divorce."

"But you haven't agreed."

He looked up and shook his head.

She let out a hard laugh. "I know you, Philip," she said. "You won't agree to a divorce. You'll bully her into staying with you."

"I don't know what to do."

She sat back down. "Why do you stay with her? I know you don't love her."

Philip shrugged. "Why are you doing this, Nikki? What's it all about eh?"

Nikki looked down at the carpet. It was an old Wiltshire, threadbare at the edges. The pattern blurred a little but she blinked hard and looked up at Philip. "I sent you cards and you didn't respond. I left messages and you didn't reply. You hurt me, Philip," her voice was soft. "You *really* hurt me."

Philip, seeing a chink in her armour, moved round the desk and knelt by her side. "I know. I know and I'm sorry."

"What's worse is you lied to me. You pretended you loved me and made me believe we had some sort of future. I never asked anything from you. You didn't have to do that, but you did."

"Nikki I never lied. Really I didn't. I did love you, I still do."

"Then why?"

"I don't know. When Jeremy mentioned they always had room for a good family man I suppose I panicked. My career is everything to me. You know that."

Nikki nodded.

"And my parents, they're the kind of people who believe marriage is for life. A more unhappy couple you're not likely to meet." He laughed. "I swear they're each waiting for the other to die." He paused, realising the truth in his joke. "I freaked I suppose. I was worried I'd done something stupid."

"Like faking evidence?"

"Don't you see?" he said. "That was the problem. I thought after I won the case everything would be sorted but then I started thinking that Hunt would come after me, for more money. If he did he would ruin me. So I wanted to look as if I'd be the last person who would do that. I was scared. I lost it. I wanted to appear squeaky clean and being married, a long term relationship, a father, the whole kit and caboodle, well, it seemed more…respectable somehow. There's a part of me that's still scared."

Philip stood up and started pacing the room. "You know, he still could. He could still come after me."

Nikki stood up. "There is another possibility," she looked at him and her eyes narrowed. "*I* could tell."

Philip turned, his eyes wide. "Why would you?"

"Because you used me, Philip, like you used those people on that case. Like all the men in my mother's life used her. Well, I won't be treated as a cast off, I won't."

"Please, Nikki, it wasn't like that."

"Then leave her, Philip. Prove it to me," she saw the pained expression on his face and it pulled at something deep inside her. "I thought you were different," her voice thick with emotion she said it again. "I thought you were different."

"You can't go, we need to discuss this," he said quietly.

"There's nothing to discuss." She turned to leave. "I thought when the chips were down you'd have the courage to do the right thing, but I was wrong. You're a coward, Philip, a weak pathetic coward."

"Hold on, hold on. Please," he called after her.

She stopped. "Don't worry, I won't tell. It was a cheap dig and I'm bigger than that," she walked to the door.

"Wait! Wait! Oh Nikki please," Philip's voice softened in despair. "Please don't do this to me."

Nikki's chest ached and her throat tightened. She swallowed hard before turning round. "Philip, I'm not doing anything to you. I loved you. Really loved you, and I came here to see if there was a chance for us. We had something very special, so special. But not anymore."

"Just give me a little more time."

Nikki shook her head. "Time's up, Philip. I'm no mug. I watched that game too much as a child. It's over. I've realised I'm not the cast off, you are. Goodbye." And she turned and fled before she could weaken. She was not her mother. She was *not* her mother.

Philip slumped behind his desk. Nikki was right, he was afraid to leave Jackie. It wasn't his career or his duty that kept him with her, it was fear. But fear of what? Being alone? No. And the bubbles of realisation rose as he sat there, bubbling up and nearly drowning him in realisation.

It was fear of his parents disapproval. The need for their approval was in his blood stream, an injection of serum at birth, fed through the placenta and the breast milk. That need had kept him paralysed. Made him unable to make choices freely.

Even decisions he had made to irritate, decisions he made to oppose them, were really only his way of showing they had no hold over him, no power over him, when in fact, he made those decisions *because* of that very power.

But that was in the past, he wouldn't let them paralyse him anymore. He couldn't let it. He couldn't live his life that way, not anymore. He had lost everything because of it. Everything that was important anyway.

He had lost Nikki, his love. She had just walked out of his office and he knew deep down that no matter how hard he tried, no matter what he did, he'd broken something between them. Part of him hoped he could fix it but even if she took him back it would never be the same again. Like a favourite vase glued together, they would always see the brown cracks where the glue held.

His marriage was over too. He knew that. He reflected on the significant relationships he had had with women during his life. His mother; Jackie; Nikki; Emma, and shook his head in despair. Perhaps he was destined to make bad connections with women.

He looked round his office. All he had now was this job. He took in the bookshelves, the prints on the wall, the neat pile of case notes, the tidy desk in front of him. This was it. This was all he had to keep him warm. His consolation.

But there was Emma. Perhaps Emma. His Emma. Perhaps it wasn't too late for him and his daughter, he could still be a part of her life. He still had a chance at one successful female relationship, and surely the most important in a man's life. If he could get that right it would be worth something, *he* would be worth something, everything he had strived for all his life would be worth something.

He knew with a certainty he had never felt before that whatever he did he would fail in his parents' eyes. It was just a matter of letting it go, of detoxing and letting the serum work it's way out of his body. It would take time, it wouldn't be easy, old habits die hard and all that, but he needed to do it, he needed to take steps to live his own life.

The first one was easy. Well, it was easy to know the first step, less comfortable thinking of it. He sighed, it was no good, he had to do it…Jackie would get her divorce.

Chapter 38

"I don't know what to say," Liz handed Jackie a mug of tea.

Jackie had been telling Liz about the conversations she'd had recently with Emma.

"Nothing to say."

"She's really growing up!"

"I know. Taught me a thing or two. Anyway, I've an appointment to start counselling next week. It's going to take time but it already feels as if a weight's been lifted."

"And Phil?"

"That's my last hurdle. At the moment he refuses to even discuss divorce. We just circle the house like a couple of gladiators."

"Maybe you need to see a solicitor."

"I'd rather not." She cupped the warm mug in her hands.

"Perhaps you could represent yourself!"

"Ah, well, no. I'm not taking law."

Liz raised her eyebrows. "What? I thought you loved it?"

Jackie saw Philip's contrite face as he made his confession. "I did, but people change. It's not what I thought it would be. I wanted to make a difference…"

"So what changed."

"Watching Philip I suppose."

"But you're not going to turn out like him."

Jackie drank from her mug. "No, but I'll have to mix with people like him, and I don't want to."

Liz shrugged. "Fair enough. What you doing?"

Jackie smiled. "Interior design."

"You're kidding!"

Jackie shook her head.

"But that's fantastic! You'll be great at it, your house is fabulous."

"I hope so. Trouble is, I'll be nearly forty before I qualify."

"Well, you're gonna be forty anyhow. Might as well be a forty-year-old interior designer."

"Hadn't looked at it like that."

Jackie moved her cup in small circles on the table. Liz drank quietly.

"Will you move?" Liz asked eventually.

"If, *when* we get divorced we'll have to."

"Where will you go."

Jackie shrugged. "Not sure. There's a good deal of equity in the property so my share should be enough to buy a small place."

"Your dream place?"

Jackie laughed. "That'll have to wait a few years yet. Besides, I'm not sure I want it any more. Not just yet anyway. Maybe I was just running away."

"You know you…" Liz stopped.

"What?"

Liz shook her head. "Doesn't matter."

"No, tell me."

"Well, I was going to say you and Emma could always stay here."

Jackie bit her lip.

"Look, it was just a suggestion, I didn't want –"

"No, it's okay, I understand. You don't need to explain."

Liz stood up. "D'you want some cake? My dad's girlfriend made it and she's a fantastic cook."

Jackie nodded.

"Carry on, I'm listening," said Liz as she moved across the room.

Jackie laughed. "You sound like Frasier off the telly," she said.

Liz giggled as she opened the cupboard door and took out side plates.

"I'm not sure I want to move in with you like that," Jackie said when the giggles had died down.

Liz put the plates on the table. "I didn't mean we'd share the same bed."

Jackie blushed.

"I meant we'd share the house."

"When I was drinking I wasn't able to eat stuff like that," Jackie indicated the huge chocolate gateau Liz brought to the table.

She watched her friend cut the cake.

"Have you got the room for us here?" she asked, her eyes fixed on the cake, unable to look at Liz.

"Sure. You could have the spare room and I could move the dark room into the attic then Emma can have the little back room. Same as she has at home. And you could advise me on the décor of this place. I'm great with the outdoors but interiors," she shrugged. "Not my area of expertise at all I'm afraid."

Liz scooped a lump of chocolate cream off the top of her slice and crammed it into her mouth. "That's really piggy."

"I know, but I can't help it."

"You'll have to run twice as long tomorrow."

Liz nodded and smiled. "Worth it though."

"I'm not sure about moving in Liz, I—"

"It's cool. Look, don't make up your mind now. Take your time, think about it."

"I'm still coming to terms with a lot of things. I think it'd be a mistake to move in with you when my head's so messed up."

Liz nodded and licked her lips clean of chocolate. "You're probably right. It was just a thought."

"I appreciate it."

"Well, the offer's there if you get stuck when you're looking about. It's an offer made from one friend to another. No ties, just friends."

Jackie nodded. Liz pushed the plate over to Jackie. "Here, have some cake, it's delicious."

That evening when Philip arrived home Jackie was ready. Whatever he said, however much he tried to badger, cajole or bully her, she would stand firm. She would get her divorce. Still her heart beat faster as Philip entered the kitchen. He looked pale and drawn.

"Hi," he said.

"You okay?" she asked.

He shook his head and threw his keys onto the counter. "Not really."

"Bad day at work?"

"Something like that. Look, I've been thinking—"

"Me too."

Their eyes met and for a brief moment her heart somersaulted. He was different. He didn't look so hard and threatening. Instead he looked young and vulnerable, like the boy she met years ago, before all this began. It made what she had to say all the harder to say.

"Philip," her voice came out light and she coughed to clear her throat. "Philip I *need* a divorce."

"Me to," he said to her surprise.

"So you agree?"

He rubbed his hands over his face as if he were washing. "Do I have a choice?"

Jackie pulled her mouth into a tight smile. "No, not really," she said misunderstanding his statement. There was an apology in her voice and for once she hoped he could hear it.

He dropped into a chair. "What a mess eh, Jay?"

She smiled at the old college name he used to use for her. She hadn't heard it in years.

She sat down next to him and took his hand. "We'll be okay, you know? All of us. You, me and Emma. This is for the best."

He looked at her and smiled. "You always were the brave one," he said. "I'll miss that."

Her heart warmed to the silly weak man. She had shared almost half her life with him, and today they had agreed not to anymore. It felt strange. Like the anchor had been lifted.

He stood up. "I'll go and pack a bag."

"Where will you go?"

"I'm not sure yet," he grinned. "But not my parents."

The old fear returned until she reminded herself she didn't need to worry what they thought of her anymore. She watched him retreat, feeling sad for the years they had wasted but thankful for the ones they still had.

Liz placed the double frame gently on top of her piano and stood back to admire it, the tears blurring her vision of the two photos side by side.

The two women did look similar, sat next to each other like that. Margaret and May. The only difference was the dimple. Liz looked at herself on the mirror above the fireplace and touched the dimple in her right cheek. It had never occurred to her to wonder where she got it from. Never. But now she knew.

She sniffed back the tears, unsure whether they were for the sadness she felt at never having the opportunity to tell her mother it didn't matter, or the happiness at the peace she felt seeing the two of them.

Looking at them she knew she had gained something precious, something deep and nameless, undefined but precious, like a small jewel in the bottom of the sea of her soul.

It was over. It was over. She knew where she had come from, knew where she belonged, and knowing made it all so much clearer. She could see where she was going. And she could let her mother, correction, her *mothers* go.

She hugged herself, letting the tears flow as she laughed.

Chapter 39

It was three months since Philip had left. They'd filed for divorce and the house had sold quickly. When the estate agent had valued the house he had told her they wouldn't have any trouble selling it. He described the interior as 'superb.'

It was Friday evening, her last night here and she walked round, touching the walls and doors of each room, saying goodbye.

She had spent years preening and cleaning this place. She'd clung to it with the illusion that here she had some control in her life. Under this roof and within these walls, behind these doors.

Now her steps echoed off the empty walls and shelves. There were now only a few essentials to pack up in the morning.

She entered Emma's bedroom. Her heart expanded as she stood watching her daughter sleeping. Her face the epitome of angelic peace. She leaned over and kissed her forehead, careful not to disturb her.

I won't be here tomorrow, she thought as she climbed down the stairs. *It won't be our home anymore.*

Finally she came to rest in the living room, half watching the flickering pictures on the TV. She heard the sound of Liz playing the piano. It was a soulful moody piece. She muted the TV so she could hear better. For the first time the sound filled her with peace.

She was ready. She'd tread water long enough, it was time to swim.

The End

Printed in the United Kingdom
by Lightning Source UK Ltd.
108012UKS00001B/205-261